THE PREDATOR OF BATIGNOLLES

Claude Izner

Claude Izner is the pen-name of two sisters, Liliane Korb and Laurence Lefèvre. Both booksellers on the banks of the Seine, they are experts on nineteenth-century Paris.

Lorenza Garcia

Lorenza Garcia translates from French and Spanish. She currently lives in London.

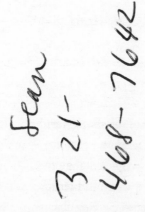

Jean
321-
468-7642

THE PREDATOR
OF
BATIGNOLLES

THE PREDATOR
OF
BATIGNOLLES

CLAUDE IZNER

Translated by Lorenza Garcia

GALLIC BOOKS
London

This book is supported by the French Ministry of Foreign Affairs as part of the Burgess programme run by the Department of the French Embassy in London. www.frenchbooknews.com

Liberté • Égalité • Fraternité
RÉPUBLIQUE FRANÇAISE

A Gallic Book

First published in France as *Le léopard des Batignolles* by Éditions 10/18

First published in Great Britain in 2010 by Gallic Books,
134 Lots Road, London, SW10 0RJ

A CIP record for this book is available from the British Library

ISBN 978-1-906040-25-3

Typeset in Fournier MT by SX Composing DTP, Rayleigh, Essex
Printed and bound by CPI Bookmarque, Croydon, CR0 4TD

2 4 6 8 10 9 7 5 3 1

To those without whom
Claude Izner would never have existed:
Ruhléa and Pinkus
Rosa and Joseph
Étia and Maurice

To Boris

To our bouquiniste friends on the banks of the Seine

When Paris closes its eyes at night
In the dark of the cemetery
Screams escape from the stones
Of the wall

> Jules Jouy
> (*Le Mur*, 1872)

So who ordered this terrible violence?

> Victor Hugo
> (*'Un cri'*, *L'Année terrible*, 1872)

CONTENTS

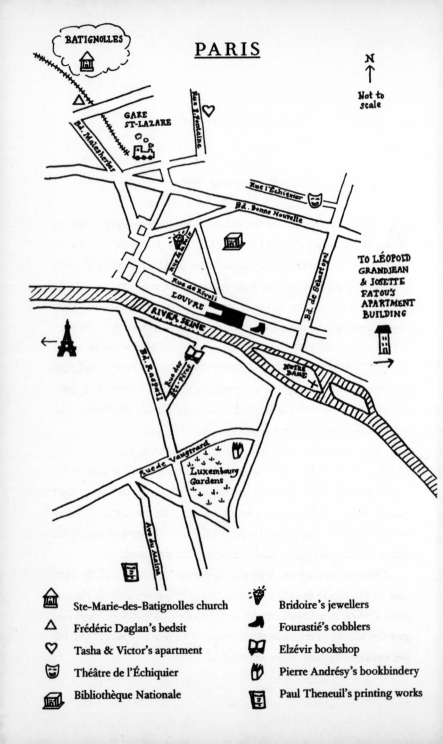

PROLOGUE

Paris, spring 1891

A WINDOW opened on the second floor and the light glancing off the panes caught the attention of a passer-by. He saw a woman leaning over a pot of geraniums, and next to it a little dog watching the comings and goings on Rue Lacépède, its muzzle pressed up against the latticed railing. The woman tipped a small watering can. *Splish splash!* Water dripped onto the pavement.

The corpse lies face down on the ground. A pinkish trickle seeps from the faded blue jacket, staining the gutter. Already stiff, the fingers rest on the butt of a bayoneted rifle. A soldier in a grey greatcoat seizes the rifle; the blade pierces the lifeless body. The soldier braces himself to pull it out.

The little dog barked; the image dissolved. The man quickened his pace, anxious to escape the past. But just as he reached Rue Gracieuse a horse yoked to a delivery cart stumbled and fell. The cart tipped on its side and began sliding down the hill, dragging the poor creature by its harness. The mare kicked, struggled and then gave up, defeated.

The linesmen swarm before the shattered barricades. They take aim at the Communards who flee, trying desperately to rip the red stripes, their death warrant, off their trousers. A volley of machine-gun fire ploughs into a trench where a bay horse is trapped. A terrible whinnying rings out above the thud of bullets.

A cry goes up: 'The Versailles Army!'

A headlong rush, caps, flasks, haversacks and belts scattered everywhere. The city has turned out its pockets.

The man leant back against the shop front of a dairy. Eyes closed, jaw clenched, stifling a sob. He must rid himself of these images once and for all! When would they stop tormenting him? Would the passing years never drown out the horror?

A few people had gathered around the cart. The driver, with the help of a local constable and a couple of passers-by, managed to get his horse back on its feet and with a crack of the whip he was off.

The man moved on, calmed now by the peaceful surroundings of Rue de l'Estrapade. He passed a blacksmith's reeking of singed hoof, then a confectioner's and a drycleaner's. A delivery girl came out of a bakery carrying a load of four-pound loaves. A costermonger wheeling her barrow cried out, 'Cabbages! Turnips! Bushels of potatoes! Who'll buy my lovely lettuces! Handpicked this morning at dawn!'

In her curlpapers and faded calico dress she looked like a princess fallen on hard times. She winked at the man as he stepped aside to let her pass, and bawled at the top of her voice, 'Cherry ripe! Cherry ripe! First crop of the season! Don't be the last to taste them!'

'Too dear,' retorted a woman coming the other way.

'That's because they're like gold dust and they still make cheaper earrings than rubies!'

The man found himself singing:

> *'I will for ever love the cherry season*
> *Those distant days have left in my heart*
> *A gaping wound!'*[1]

Ravaged façades of buildings, cobblestones blackened with gun-powder and strewn with belongings thrown from windows. In Place de l'Estrapade soldiers from the Versailles Army with their sabres and tricolour armbands form a firing squad. They aim their rifles at a Communard officer with double-braided silver bands on his cap.

'Fire!'

In Rue Saint-Jacques, the clatter of a passing cab freed the man from his nightmare. Some sparrows and pigeons were fighting over a pile of dung as a woman scooped it up with a shovel. A drunkard stumbled out of a bar-cum-cobbler's, run by a man from the Auvergne.

'What will those ministers of *in*justice cook up next to crush us common folk!' he roared through wine-soaked breath.

The man felt a sudden thirst and was about to enter the bar when a sign caught his eye:

SAXOLEINE
Certified, refined paraffin oil, deodorised, non-flammable . . .

A brunette with a plunging neckline was adjusting the flame of a lamp whose red shade stood out against a bluey-green background.

The poster was now a palimpsest. A long list appeared on the grey wall. Six columns with hundreds of names:

WOMEN PRISONERS
At Versailles . . .

Outside a wine shop, an old man is sprawled across the pavement. He is barefoot, his legs covered in sores. A policeman leans over and presses the neck of a bottle to the man's lips; laughter rings out. Inside, at the counter, Versailles Army officers and civilians loudly toast victory, their faces flushed with drink. In Rue des Écoles, firing squads are carrying out summary executions on a huge expanse of wasteland.[2] A wagon crawls along, a pile of corpses visible through its open door. Policemen in shiny-buttoned uniforms force the locals to take down a barricade. A woman cries over some bodies, their skulls smashed in. A soldier slaps her.

On Rue Racine, a firing squad trains its rifles on a boy accused of stuffing a handful of incriminating cartridges through the grating of a drain to help his father. The officer raises his arm.

'Wait!'

A beggar next to the boy is resisting efforts to push him forward.

'I took these shoes off a dead soldier, I swear!'

'Line them up!'

> *Line 'em up!*
> *We heard the captain shout*
> *Stuffing his mouth*
> *'N' filling his cup*
> *Line 'em up!*[3]

The man realised that he would have to give in: he hadn't the strength to bury the past.

4

The leaves on the horse chestnuts cast pools of shade over the alleyways in the Luxembourg Gardens. Boys in sailor suits rolled their hoops around the statue of a lion guarding the Observatory steps. The man collapsed onto a bench and watched the hoops turning under the light touch of the sticks. Twenty years on, he could still see the woman.

Clasping an infant to her bosom, her expression frozen like a death mask, she has just recognised her husband among the prisoners. She hurls herself towards him. A blow from a rifle butt sends her reeling; the baby falls to the ground.

A hoop rolled up to the man's shoe, wobbled and fell over.

The sightless eyes of the statues contemplate the bodies piled up on the lawns. Rows of men, their faces pale with fright, file out of the Senate and are led over to the central pond: Communards, civilians informed on by their neighbours, people with dirty hands or who just don't look quite right. The rifles dispense death. The first rows of men crumple and are immediately buried under those falling on top of them. The blood flows; the soldiers doing the butchering, the endless butchering, are knee-deep in blood. The mass graves are numberless: L'École Militaire, the Lobau barracks, Mazas, Parc Monceau, Buttes-Chaumont, Père-Lachaise. Upholsterers bear the bodies away. Paris reeks of rotting flesh.

Eight days was how long it went on for. Eight days. Every afternoon, at the foot of Pont Neuf, respectable folk gathered to witness the massacre. Twenty thousand souls put to death in Paris by court-martials and summary executions.

Eight days that refused to dissolve into the thousands of others the man sitting on the bench in the Luxembourg Gardens had experienced. Eight days that would haunt him until his dying breath.

The gunpowder, the blood, the hatred, the walls – people had been lined up against the nearest wall and shot.

Would he go insane? Or would he find his own walls, his own way of meting out justice?

A toy boat streaked across the central pond. Cries, laughter, bursts of music, a refrain:

> *Here comes the flower seller.*
> *Buy a spray of forget-me-nots*
> *To brighten up your day.*

Forget? He couldn't forget. He must act. It was the only way of freeing himself from this insufferable burden: an eye for an eye, a tooth for a tooth.

CHAPTER ONE

Two years later

Sunday 11 June 1893

THE train deposited a dozen punters in striped pullovers and straw boaters on the platform before letting out a long jet of steam. The passengers clogged the exit for a moment before setting off towards the riverbank, where families dressed in their Sunday best and a podgy man in a checked bowler hat were also headed.

The man made a beeline for Pont de Chatou without so much as a glance towards the shimmering water, which was dotted with boats in the unseasonably warm spring weather. A barge whistled. The man dabbed his forehead with a handkerchief and paused to light a cigar before shuffling off again.

Meanwhile an imposing-looking fellow sat sipping a glass of beer at a table outside Cabaret Fournaise in the middle of the island. His eyes were fixed on the potbellied figure in the checked bowler. He was momentarily distracted by the couples dancing beneath the poplars to a lively polka being played by three musicians on a nearby bandstand; tapping his foot to the music, he admired a narrow skiff as it darted out from behind the bend in the Seine. But his attention soon turned back to the portly chap, who was making the floorboards creak as he approached.

'Right on time! You certainly don't keep people waiting,' he said, stretching nonchalantly.

'This blasted heat! The sweat's dripping off me. Is there somewhere quieter where we can talk?'

'I've reserved a private room upstairs.'

They crossed the restaurant where waiters were busy bringing plates of fried smelts, sautéed potatoes and jugs of white wine to the tables. A flight of stairs took them up to a landing and they entered a room at the end. They sat down, face to face, and studied each other. The man in the bowler had puffy eyes and broken veins on his fleshy face, which was framed by a mop of curly hair and grizzled whiskers. He looked like a shaggy dog.

No wonder they call him the Spaniel, thought his companion, who had an aquiline nose and a jauntily turned up blond moustache.

He himself had a cat-like physique. His expression was half mocking, half disdainful, and he looked constantly on the verge of laughter. He exuded an innate charm, which made him very successful with women, but so far had failed to win over his sullen companion.

'Call the waiter, I'm in a hurry,' grumbled the Spaniel, crushing his cigar stub underfoot.

'Don't worry, Monsieur, they know we're here. I'm a regular. We'll get the royal treatment. While we're waiting, tell me how much I'll be getting.'

'Two hundred. It's an easy job.'

'What do I have to do?'

'Purloin a few cigar holders.'

'You're pulling my leg, Monsieur! Two hundred francs for some cigar holders?'

'They're made of amber. Will you do it, Daglan?'

'How many do you need?'

'About fifty – more if possible.'

'And where do I find this junk?'

'Bridoire's Jeweller's. Rue de la Paix, on the corner of Rue Daunou. If you pocket any trinkets, put them on ice – you can fence them later.'

The door opened and two waiters came in, one carrying a roast turkey, the other a bottle of Muscadet, glasses, plates and a bowl of *frites* on a tray. The waiters laid the table, carved the bird, served the wine and left.

'Enjoy, Monsieur.'

The Spaniel gave a whistle.

'Well, blow me, no wonder you're always broke if you spend your money like this, my lad,' he mumbled, piercing a drumstick with his fork.

'A smile at last! I've a confession: the turkey didn't cost me a penny. But then they don't come craftier than me!'

Indeed, in his criminal career, Frédéric Daglan had distinguished himself in many ways – enough to make the list of the ten brightest and best brigands. He had started out as a thief, substituting fake silver for real, then became apprenticed to a confidence trickster. He possessed keen powers of observation, was a talented scout and had a fertile imagination. He was also well versed in the penal system, and had become an expert in coded language, thus avoiding any mishaps should his messages be intercepted.

'So this turkey cost you nothing? How very amusing! Then tell me how you came by it,' said the Spaniel, stuffing a huge piece of roasted skin in his mouth.

'Yesterday, I was hanging around in the lobby of the Palais de Justice, waiting for a friend, and I saw His Honour Judge Lamastre, you know the fellow I mean – wields his gavel with the ease of a carpenter and sends people down for nothing! That's when I heard him mutter to a colleague: "Damned nuisance, I left my watch at home this morning. Can't bear not knowing the time during a hearing. And I'm on duty until late tonight: the jurors are deliberating in the high court." His words didn't fall on deaf ears! I've been hobnobbing with these law lords for years, and where they live is no secret to me. I didn't hang about. I bought a nice fat turkey, and rang our dear Judge Lamastre's doorbell.'

'You rogue!' bawled the Spaniel, taking a swig of wine.

'A servant let me in and I told him: "I've come to deliver this stuffed turkey, which His Honour Judge Lamastre purchased on his way to court. It's for lunch tomorrow. He told me that while I was at it I should fetch his chronometer, which he left at home this morning, and assured me I'd be paid for my trouble." See how polite I can be, Monsieur.'

'I see that you're a prize scoundrel.'

'The servant informed his unsuspecting mistress, Madame Lamastre, who took delivery of the turkey and handed me the watch together with a fifty-centime tip – those worthies are a stingy lot.'

'What did you do with the watch, you rascal?'

'I sold it sharpish, for forty francs. It was worth at least a thousand. Times are hard, Monsieur, and fences are unscrupulous in their dealings with the poor.'

'And the turkey?'

'Early the next day, I sent my mate to fetch it. There it was already roasting on the spit, its skin turning that golden brown which is a delight to anyone who's fond of their food. "Quick," said my friend, "hand over the turkey. His Honour Judge Lamastre has sent me to fetch it. The thief who stole his watch is under lock and key and the court demands to see the incriminating evidence." This explanation seemed credible to Madame Lamastre, who swallowed it whole. She ordered the bird to be removed from the spit, and given to my chum, who hurried off, not wanting to keep the judges waiting, you understand. And how is my bird?'

'Utterly delicious, you devil!' acknowledged the Spaniel, quivering with laughter.

He wiped his mouth and began cleaning his teeth with a toothpick.

'So, can I count on you?'

'When do you need your cigar holders?'

'A week today, here, same time.'

'That's not much time.'

'You'll have to manage as best you can. And if anything goes wrong, mum's the word, all right? We've never met.'

'Rest assured, when Frédéric Daglan's lips are sealed, the Devil himself couldn't prise them open. Go on, drink up and eat your fill. It'd be a shame to waste such a handsome bird, especially as I can't promise you another one next Sunday!'

The afternoon of the same day

The Église Sainte-Marie-des-Batignolles with its triangular pediment and Doric columns was reminiscent of a Greek temple. Beside it, an ornamental grotto, a waterfall and a tiny stream were laid out in an oasis of greenery which overlooked the railway tracks. Frédéric Daglan strolled around the miniature lake where a few ducks were splashing. Slung over his shoulder was a case with a faded coat of arms on its flap depicting a blue and gold leopard passant. He reflected on the situation: two hundred francs was a lot for stealing a few cigar holders, even if they were made of amber. What was that fat pig cooking up? He would have him tailed – he had to cover myself.

He stopped next to a park keeper's hut. An elderly veteran in a shabby uniform gave him a military salute.

'Good afternoon, Monsieur Daglan.'

'Good afternoon, Brigadier Clément. How's life treating you? Any pickings today?'

'A teat, a stick without its hoop, a knitting needle and a comic. Oh, Monsieur Daglan, the worst thing is not being able to sit down! They're giving me the chop, you know. They say I'm too old, even though I do my job properly. After fifty you're a burden on the state. I'll be gone by the end of August. The missus is worried sick, what with our boy scarcely earning his crust at the Gouin machine shop, and a growing girl at home! We'll just have to manage on the small pension they give me. By the way, the missus said to thank you for the cherries. They're very dear this year so she was pleased as punch. She plans to make jam out of them and a special jar of cherries in brandy for you.'

'Don't mention it – they cost me nothing.'

'Are you going to work, Monsieur Daglan?'

'Yes, I'm going to write out the evening menus. It's pretty straightforward. The taverners give the leftovers from lunch another name and, hey presto, tuna in *sauce verte* becomes tuna mayonnaise, tomatoes in butter sauce turn into stuffed tomatoes, and so on.'

Daglan slipped the old man a coin.

'Here's a little something for you, Père Clément. And don't worry, you won't need to hock any of your belongings while I'm around.'

'Oh no, Monsieur Daglan, no charity, please!'

'Charity, Père Clément? Do you want to hurt my feelings? The path of life is strewn with obstacles. Somebody helped me once – now it's my turn.'

Friday 16 June

A builder with face and hair covered in plaster dust was passing the stables owned by the Debrise Brothers, a stone's throw from Église Saint-Denis-de-la-Chapelle. He stopped outside a bar and washed his hands at a pump where carters filled pails for watering their horses. The air smelt of fresh cheese and milk. The builder pulled down his cap, crossed the roundabout near the coal yard and walked down Rue Jean-Cottin, with its hotchpotch of buildings.

The builder passed a boy bouncing a ball against a fence. The boy gave him a knowing look and began chanting:

> *'General Kléber,*
> *At the gates of Hell*
> *Met a Prussian*
> *Who wished him well.'*

The builder gave a faint nod, and entered the courtyard of a run-down building. Slowly, he climbed the stairs up several floors. On reaching the third floor, he took a pick from his pocket, slipped it into a keyhole without touching the escutcheon, found the latch and carefully lifted it.

The first room was cluttered, with a mirrored wardrobe, a table, a glass-fronted bookcase, four chairs and a stove.

The builder removed his shoes and began a meticulous search. The wardrobe contained only two jackets, a waistcoat, three pairs of trousers and two sets of bed linen. In the bedroom were an unmade bed, a pile of dirty laundry and a slop bucket. He lifted the mattress quickly. The tension in his face eased as his eye alighted on a brown briefcase in the middle of the bed base. He pulled a bundle of documents out of it and studied them closely. He froze in amazement.

'Good God! The dirty . . . !'

His throat tightened; he could scarcely breathe. He tried to stifle his mounting rage. Stay calm, he told himself.

Outside the boy squawked:

> *'Who left the people to rot?*
> *That was Riquiqui's lot.'*

The builder drew back the curtain. Two women stood chattering in the courtyard.

He put everything back in its place and, checking that he'd left no traces, picked up his shoes and went out. After clicking the latch behind him, he started back down the stairs.

At the bottom, Frédéric Daglan tied his shoelaces, his hands shaking.

Saturday 17 June

At lunchtime there was no one left in the shops on Rue de la Paix. A wave of clerks and female workers headed for the cheap eateries on the Boulevards. Dressmakers, salesmen, seamstresses and clerks jostled one another, pushing past the cashiers from Crédit Lyonnais who were enjoying a smoke in the doorways of the restaurants where they would feast on boiled beef and bacon stew. A pair of constables eyed up the apprentice dressmakers in their white blouses, black skirts and coloured ankle boots forced onto the road by the crowds. A laundress paused in a doorway, took a croissant and a slab of chocolate out of her bag and began eating, oblivious to the bawdy comments of a housepainter sitting astride his stepladder. Gradually, the neighbourhood fell silent. The only people left were a news vendor sitting in her kiosk, a bread roll on her lap; a concierge sweeping the pavement vigorously; and a lad in an apron listlessly cleaning a jeweller's shop window under the watchful eye of a constable.

A donkey and cart pulled up next to the constable. The driver, a youth of seventeen or eighteen, doffed his cap.

'Excuse me, Constable, could you direct me to Bridoire's Jeweller's, please?'

'It's right here,' said the copper, pointing at the shop window, which the lad in the apron had just finished cleaning.

'Bother, it's closed! I was supposed to deliver a crate here this morning. I won't have time this afternoon. What if I leave it in the doorway? Nobody would dare steal it with you around . . .'

The constable paused, scratched his head then nodded.

'All right, son. The shop assistants will be back at one thirty.'

Together they heaved the crate up against the shop door.

'It weighs a ton. What have you got in there, lead?' asked the policeman.

'It's marble. Much obliged to you!'

The cart moved off down Rue Gaillon, briskly overtaking two cabs and an omnibus, then turned into Rue de Choiseul.

Constable Sosthène Cotret discharged his mission with remarkable zeal considering he stood to gain nothing. In the meantime he allowed himself the pleasure of contemplating an amber smoking kit, which was displayed next to a gold-plated tumbler and a set of sapphire jewels. He pictured himself blowing smoke rings into Inspector Pachelin's face, and imagined his superior gazing enviously at Madame Julienne Cotret wafting through the police station in a sparkling tiara.

He was so rapt in his daydream that he didn't notice the same cart pulling up three quarters of an hour later. The young delivery man had to tap him on the shoulder, immediately apologising for his forwardness.

'I only delivered the wrong blooming crate, didn't I? My boss almost killed me! I've brought the right one this time. Would you mind helping me swap them over?'

They replaced the first crate with the second. Sosthène Cotret's joints groaned under the strain and he cursed his bad luck for being allotted this beat.

'Blimey, what a weight! Is this marble, too?'

'Yes. The difference is this one's red and the other one's black. Much obliged, Constable.'

Sosthène Cotret cursed as he rubbed his aching back, knowing that his blasted sciatica would soon make him pay for his obliging nature.

Monday 19 June

Perched on his stepladder behind the counter at the Elzévir bookshop, 18 Rue des Saints-Pères, Joseph Pignot, bookshop assistant, was reading aloud from *Le Passe-partout* for the benefit of his boss, Victor Legris, who was paying little attention to what he considered a trivial news items.

'. . . It was at one thirty that the shop assistants of Bridoire's Jeweller's noticed the break-in. Curiously, only smoking accessories had been stolen. Why had the thieves ignored the diamond bracelets, precious pearls, watches and valuable silver and gold pieces? Equally puzzling is the fact that policeman Sosthène Cotret, who was on duty in Rue Daunou at the time, saw nothing – despite claiming that he didn't take his eyes off the shop window. The authorities should supply him with a pair of spectacles!

When the second crate was opened it was found to contain nothing but sand.

According to Inspector Pachelin, the burglar must have hidden in the first crate, which had a removable side. He then cut a disc-shaped hole in the door of the jeweller's just wide enough for him to enter the shop. Having grabbed the loot, he climbed back into the crate, replaced the wooden disc and covered his traces with putty and a paint containing drying agent. All he had to do then was wait until his accomplice came back to swap the crates.

'Clever, isn't it, Boss? Still, it seems like a lot of trouble to go to for a few cigar holders and pipes!'

Glancing up from his newspaper, Joseph was dismayed to see Victor absorbed in reading the order list.

'You're not listening.'

'You're wrong there, Joseph. I'm hanging on your every word. This crime reminds me of Hugo de Groot's[4] daring escape.'

'Who?'

'Hugo de Groot – a seventeenth-century Dutch lawyer who was imprisoned for life in Loevestein Castle. Escape seemed impossible. He was allowed books, which he devoured in such quantities that they had to be ferried in and out in a trunk. Two years into his incarceration, Hugo decided to try his luck. He climbed into the trunk and managed to escape. You see how reading brings freedom, Joseph.'

'Yes . . . but I don't see what that has to do with cigar holders?'

'Nothing . . . Aren't you supposed to be delivering a copy of Pierre Maël's[5] *Honour and Country* to the Comtesse de Salignac?'

'I've already been there, and it wasn't any fun! I see you have great faith in me! You're getting a bit tyrannical, Boss!'

Joseph, furious, snatched up a pair of scissors and cut out the article, muttering to himself. 'The boss should learn to hold his tongue. If this goes on much longer, I'll be off to greener pastures.'

'Believe me, Joseph, you'd soon tire of the countryside; nothing can compare to the thrill of the city. I'm sorry if I upset you – I didn't intend to.'

'You're forgiven, Boss,' Joseph decreed loftily.

'Would you like to see the gift Mademoiselle Iris and I have chosen for Monsieur Mori's birthday?'

'When is it?'

'The twenty-second.'

'How old will he be?'

'Fifty-four. You're invited to the little gathering.'

'I shan't be going, and you know why. What are you giving him?'

'A rare volume on Japan.'

'Are you trying to make your adoptive father homesick? How long is it since he left, twenty or thirty years? He should take his daughter on a pilgrimage. They're very strong on loyalty over there!'

'A little more respect for Mademoiselle Iris, please, Joseph. She hasn't been unfaithful to you.'

'I'm only pointing out that your half-sister's European side has made her frivolous.' Joseph added, bitterly, 'And anyway, what's keeping me here?'

'Oh, for heaven's sake! All you do is whine and moan and feel sorry for yourself! Show a bit of spirit, for goodness' sake! Don't give up at the first hurdle! I'm sure she loves you and is full of remorse; she never stops saying so, you great dolt!'

Victor composed himself then paused before adding, 'Jojo, I hope that you two haven't . . . er, well, you know, the birds and the bees and the butterflies . . .'

'No, Boss, we vowed not to give in to our animal instincts before marriage and, if you want the truth, I regret it,' replied Joseph.

He looked at Victor with a strange expression then burst out angrily, 'If it had been you, if Mademoiselle Tasha had behaved like that, you would have had fifty fits, with your suspicious nature!'

'Me? Suspicious?'

Shocked and horrified, Victor threw his arms up to heaven, ready to swear that he'd cured himself of his bad habit, when the doorbell tinkled.

Blanche de Cambrésis swept in. The lace trim on her dark-red pleated dress snagged on a pile of Émile Zola's *Doctor Pascal*, recently published by Charpentier and Fasquelle, bringing it crashing to the floor. Victor gathered up the books while his visitor remarked on how cramped the shop was.

'We remove the chairs, replace the desk with a pedestal table and still the battle-axe isn't satisfied,' muttered Joseph, who was hiding behind a wall of quarto volumes.

'Is it any good?' asked Blanche de Cambrésis, whose haughty expression made her look like a nanny-goat.

'Tripe, Madame, utter tripe. How may I help you?' Victor enquired in a conciliatory voice.

Unable to bear it any longer, Joseph made a dash for the back of the shop where he vented his anger.

'Just listen to him fawning. He probably expects me to grovel at his sister's feet, though he wasn't exactly keen on our engagement in the beginning, any more than Monsieur Mori. But now the tables are turned, they can't wait for me to marry her and put a stop to all the gossip. Even Maman has turned against me. It's not fair!' he muttered, dusting off the coats-of-arms on the backs of a set of hardbacks.

The touch of leather in his hands calmed his rage. Images of the not so distant past flashed painfully through his mind. How fleeting his joy had been back in February when his bosses had not only celebrated his engagement to Iris but given him a rise. Since then he'd been earning one thousand six hundred francs a year. This allowed him to put aside a substantial sum as he and Iris would be taking over Monsieur Legris's old flat above the bookshop. Joseph had been keen to move in as soon as possible, but had said nothing to his future wife, who appeared not to share his need for independence, and was still very attached to her father.

And then Mademoiselle Tasha, whom he so admired, had taken it into her head to paint Iris's portrait! How was he to know it would be the cause of such strife? Accordingly, he'd no more objected to his fiancée posing for her than he'd tried to dissuade her from taking twice-weekly watercolour lessons with Mademoiselle Tasha's mother, Madame Djina Kherson. The latter had recently emigrated from Russia via Berlin and thanks to Monsieur Legris was now living in Rue des Dunes, near Buttes-Chaumont.

March had been taken up with preliminary drawings. Iris could talk of nothing else, to the point where Monsieur Mori had nicknamed her 'Mona Lisa'. And then one day a painter friend of Mademoiselle Tasha's, the conceited Maurice Laumier whom Monsieur Legris had never liked, had seen one of her sketches on an easel. He had praised her artistic progress and the model's beauty. Who was she? Mademoiselle Tasha replied that she was Victor Legris's half-sister. Maurice Laumier had used the age-old method of the lightning strike – his main weapon surprise, his lure throwing himself on his quarry's mercy. He had approached her hat in hand.

'Mademoiselle, I don't usually accost young ladies in the street, but when I saw you coming out of my fellow artist Tasha Kherson's house I couldn't stop myself. You see, I've been commissioned to paint an exotic portrait of the Virgin Mary to exhibit at this year's Salon, and when I saw those extraordinary eyes, that flawless complexion, your adorable face, I . . .'

Later on, in floods of tears, Iris had given her father, brother and fiancé a blow-by-blow account of the repulsive tale. She'd portrayed herself as a poor innocent girl, ambushed outside Tasha and Victor's home by a man whose name she already knew. Why should she have mistrusted this attractive charmer in search of a model with Asian features?

At this point in the story, Joseph had had little difficulty imagining the young girl succumbing to the virility of the handsome dauber; he could understand why she would prefer this Don Juan to a hunchback like him; he could understand how from then on she'd woven her web of lies in order to be able to carry on her twice-weekly meetings with that libertine from Rue Girardon. Yes, he understood – he was a writer, after all – but he could not forgive!

The 'poor ingénue' had then explained to Djina Kherson that she must give up her watercolour classes and had begged her not to tell anybody. She wanted to surprise her fiancé. She'd had no difficulty believing her own lies: she would buy Maurice Laumier's portrait as well as Tasha's and make a gift of them to Joseph as a mark of her undying love!

Joseph did not want to know what had really taken place in the notorious womaniser's studio. According to Iris, after four or five sessions the painter had stolen a kiss, and two or three weeks later he'd taken liberties that had earned him a slap. Finally, towards the middle of May, when she had confused her dates and turned up at Laumier's studio on the wrong day, he had appeared at the door in shirt-tails and declared his love for her. At that very moment, the door separating the studio and the bedroom had opened to reveal a totally naked woman. The shrew had bombarded Iris with insults, which she was too polite to repeat, unless she washed out her mouth with soap and water afterwards.

She had confessed everything to Joseph and begged his forgiveness. She'd been so filled with remorse that even Euphrosine Pignot, outraged by her son's heartlessness, had leapt to her defence, growling, 'Men! Scoundrels the lot of them!'

Joseph had been unbending. He announced that he was postponing their wedding date, set for the end of July, indefinitely. For the past six weeks, Iris, in a state of despair, had shut herself away on the first floor; Kenji was giving his assistant the cold shoulder and Victor was playing go-between. As for the guilty party, when questioned by Mademoiselle Tasha he had cynically summed up events in a mocking voice.

'What do you expect, my dear? She's a very pretty girl; what man wouldn't want to have his way with her? A shame she showed up unexpectedly and Mimi laid into her!'

Blanche de Cambrésis pursed her lips and took her leave of Victor Legris after purchasing a novel she had delightedly unearthed by Arsène Houssaye. Joseph waited until she had left before emerging from his hiding place at the very moment that Kenji Mori descended the stairs. The two men pretended not to notice one another.

'I have an appointment with Dr Reynaud,' Kenji announced glumly.

He surreptitiously touched the bust of Molière on the mantelpiece above the hearth for luck, and fired a question at Victor.

'Tell me honestly, Victor, do you think I'm shrinking?'

'We're all subject to the laws of gravity. What's the matter with you?'

'It's my back.'

Oblivious to Joseph's presence, they began discussing their health before moving on to 'poor Iris's' state of mind. All that was missing was the tea and muffins!

'Aren't you lunching here?' Victor asked. 'Euphrosine has made celery and turnip croquettes.'

'No thank you, really,' said Kenji. 'I'll see you this evening – wish me luck.'

'Women! They're all alike,' grumbled Joseph. 'Look at Monsieur Mori, wasting away because that cancan dancer Fifi Bas-Rhin went off to St Petersburg with her Russky archduke!'

'Don't you believe it, Jojo. I suspect he prefers his meat to the vegetarian regime imposed by my sister and has gone off to Foyot's to enjoy escalope Milanese or tournedos in pepper sauce.'

Victor's envious expression betrayed a strong urge to do the same as his adoptive father. However, at the thought of Madame Pignot's wrath, he abandoned the idea.

Frédéric Daglan walked with his hands in his pockets and a case slung over his shoulder along the fortifications separating Paris from its suburbs. The outlying boulevards bordered by huts and wooden shacks spread out across the parched grass at the foot of the fortifications.[6] The sky above Saint-Ouen was black with the smoke billowing over from the factories. Frédéric Daglan walked through the tollgate at Clignancourt. He always began his rounds at Anchise Giacometti's bistro. Anchise was a fellow countryman who had given him a helping hand the day he had arrived at Gare de Lyon, penniless, jobless and with no prospects.

Frédéric was forty-three. He had warm memories of his father, Enrico Leopardi – a Garibaldian killed at the battle of Aspromonte in 1862. His widowed mother had emigrated to Marseilles, confident of a better future. She had sweated fourteen hours a day at an India rubber and gutta-percha factory on Avenue du Prado and had gone without in order to send Federico to school. The boy's schoolteacher, Monsieur Daglan, was a good man, and had taught him reading, writing and arithmetic.

When his mother died of a heart attack, Federico Leopardi bought a train ticket to Paris, where he became Frédéric Daglan. He was just fifteen.

He was a rebel and a loner, full of care for the exploited and downtrodden, for the nobodies of the world. His job as a calligrapher served as a cover for his so-called criminal activities. He worked alone, undercover, occasionally soliciting the help of Theo, the nephew of Brigadier Clément, the park keeper. He never stole more than he needed to help his friends and to enjoy life and love. His philosophy was simple:

'Faced with the sad fact that life is a vale of tears, I have chosen to prey on the rich rather than lose my self-respect begging at their table. Society is a jungle where the strong devour the weak and the moral of the story is that we all end up six feet under. That's what I call liberty, equality and fraternity. I do nobody any harm, I simply cream off a tiny surplus. Besides, rich or poor, we can't take it with us, not even what might fit through the eye of a needle.'

Only he was still very much alive, and in it up to his neck. The papers in the brown briefcase had left him in no doubt: he must go undercover and sort things out.

Le Piccolo run by Anchise Giacometti stood on the edge of the working area. It resembled a village inn with its blue-painted bar, checked tablecloths and rustic sideboard. Anchise Giacometti, a silent patriarch with a flowing moustache, presided over the bar while his wife, a tiny Calabrian woman as dark as an olive, ran the kitchen. At lunchtime, the restaurant filled up with market gardeners and employees from the toll office.

Frédéric Daglan greeted Anchise and sat down in the corner at an unlaid table. The landlord brought him a stack of oblong cards together with the lunch menu. Frédéric opened his calligraphy case, took out his bottles of ink, his pens and nibs and went to work. He carefully wrote out the names of the dishes on each card, separating them with an arabesque. He used fine script for the desserts and bold characters for the beef and cabbage stew. Anchise poured him out a tumbler of wine and went back to polishing his glasses.

Frédéric gulped it down in one.

'Anchise, do you know somewhere I can hide out?'

'Mother Chickweed's, Porte d'Allemagne.[7] Just say Anchise sent you.'

CHAPTER TWO

Six o'clock in the morning, Wednesday 21 June

LÉOPOLD Grandjean lived with his wife and two sons on the fourth floor of a building in Rue des Boulets, near Place de la Nation. His rent was three hundred and ten francs a year, which included the door and window tax and the cost of the chimney sweep. In return, his three-room lodgings were equipped with running water and gas lighting. He had always loved reading. History, geography, science and literature – everything interested him. He could quote whole passages from Jean-Jacques Rousseau. Two lines from *The Social Contract* had influenced him in particular:

Man is born free, but everywhere he is in chains.
The fruits of the earth belong to everyone and the earth to no one.

On Sundays, he would take a stroll with his family along the fortifications and spend the day walking and setting the world to rights. Life was good.

His enamelling business was thriving. It was by no means a life of luxury and he occasionally had difficulty making ends meet, but everything about him suggested a relaxed and bohemian attitude towards life. Léopold had been an apprentice engraver then a porcelain painter. He adopted the attitudes of an artist and didn't give a damn what his neighbours thought. His factory – a shed with a glass roof – stood at the end of Passage Gonnet in the shade of a lime tree whose dense foliage in summer was a haven for birds. Beyond it was a patch of wasteland where ragged children whooped and ran wild. The premises were divided into the factory proper and the sales room. Its shelves were filled with the most commonly enamelled objects of the day: sweet dishes, powder compacts, bowls, brooches, and pommels for canes and umbrellas. Once spring arrived, Léopold would get to his workshop at dawn in order to work on the more difficult orders. This time he had to produce a picture based on an icon; the task he'd set himself was complicated, but he felt confident that he would succeed. He began by making a quick, bold sketch.

'Perfect. Now let's fill in the detail.'

He added a finishing touch to his design then went over to a lathe, which had a copper plate covered in a first coat of clear enamel resting on it. He transferred the plate to a low table crowded with pots, paintbrushes, spatulas, and jars of gold and silver leaf. He cherished such moments of solitude as a respite from mass production and book-keeping; they were his secret moments of creativity. At thirty-nine, he still looked like a young man. Broad-shouldered and of medium build, he gave an impression of calm determination. Rarely did anything disturb his equanimity.

At this early hour, the workshop was bathed in an atmosphere of peace; even the chirping sparrows were scarcely audible. Léopold applied his colours, placing blobs of paste onto the lighter areas of the design then blending them gradually in the cloisonné sections. This preliminary task allowed his mind to wander freely.

If business went well, he'd buy a plot of land in Montreuil and grow peach trees; they'd give a good return. His two sons would take over – they were better off there than in a factory – and his wife would finally have the kitchen garden she'd always wanted.

A milk cart rattled down the quiet street, followed by the clatter of dustbins being hauled across the courtyard and wooden shutters banging. There was a sudden murmur, as though these noises had woken the sleeping neighbourhood. Léopold set down his brush. In half an hour his workers would arrive; it was time to snatch a cup of coffee. He whistled as he donned his jacket and battered hat, and stuck a cigarette in his mouth.

The Chez Kiki café stood on the corner of Rue Chevreul and Rue du Faubourg-Saint-Antoine surrounded by grocers, charcuteries and wine merchants. A steady flow of garrulous, sharp-tongued, sharp-eyed housewives streamed in and out of these shops lit by oil lamps. On his way to the bar, Léopold greeted Josette, the dark-skinned flower girl, back from Les Halles where she had stocked up her cart. He was feeling in his pockets for a match when a man sprang from nowhere and offered him a light. As Léopold thanked him, his smile suddenly faded. The man whispered something in his ear then stepped away, lowering his arm. Léopold fell backwards. He could see a flock of sparrows flying overhead, the façades of the buildings, the sky dappled with clouds . . .

His vision became blurred and his stomach throbbed. The last thing he heard before sinking into oblivion was a song:

> *But the cherry season is short*
> *When two go together to pick*
> *Red pendants for their ears . . .*
> *Cherries of love all dressed alike*
> *Hanging like drops of blood beneath the leaves.*

Afternoon of the same day

'Hell's bells! What do you want: a juicy chop, or would you rather have thin broth?' yelled a man dressed in breeches, stockings and a plumed hat.

The chambermaid felt her cheeks turn red. Tears blurred her vision. She began to curtsey and almost dropped her tray, causing a cardboard chicken and some wax pears to roll around precariously.

'I-I don't understand,' she stammered.

'And yet it is quite simple, my dear,' the gentleman retorted. 'If you want the juicy chop – in other words, success – you'll have to serve Henry IV, alias muggins here, with a bit more panache. Wiggle the bits that matter, front and back! Then turn to the audience and say:

> *'Although he's good and kind and brave*
> *Our sovereign's nonetheless a knave.*

'I'm not asking for the moon! Stop snivelling . . . what's your name again?'

'Andréa.'

'That's a pretty name. Now, blow your nose, Andréa. We'll win them over. Break for fifteen minutes.'

Edmond Leglantier, actor and director of *Heart Pierced by an Arrow*, a historical play in four acts, leapt down off the stage and went to join the actors playing Maria de Medici and Ravaillac sitting in the third row.

'So, what do you think, children? Will the audience be impressed?'

'The claque will applaud rapturously every time the actors come on, and I'm certain the play will be a success,' Ravaillac assured him.

'Let's hope the gods can hear you . . . What rotten luck! How were we to know that two other plays about the same subject would be put on this summer? They're already advertising *The Flower Seller of The Innocents*[8] at the Châtelet and *The Doll's House*[9] at Porte-Saint-Martin! And you're in the starring role!'

'Me?'

'Not you, you fool – Ravaillac! Including our one, that makes three. And there I was hoping to pull out all the stops for the re-opening of Théâtre de l'Échiquier.'

Edmond Leglantier cast a dispirited eye over the Italianate auditorium whose refurbishment had plunged him up to his eyes in debt. He was staking everything on this production. If it was a flop, his creditors would be baying for his blood . . . Unless of course the swindle he was planning at the club paid off.

The stage manager stuck his head over the balcony.

'Pssst! Monsieur Leglantier! Philibert Dumont is looking for you everywhere. I told him you were at home.'

'What a nuisance the man is! I'll have to keep my eyes peeled. Thanks anyway.'

'Who is Dumont?' asked Maria de Medici.

'The author of the play and a terrible bore. On that note, I'm going to have a quick smoke and then we'll rehearse Act III. Sharpen your sword, Ravaillac!'

As soon as Henry IV had left the auditorium, Andréa asked her two fellow actors, 'What's got into him? I'm not used to being spoken to like that!'

'Well, you'd better get used to it. Monsieur Leglantier's very tense these days,' said Ravaillac. 'He's sunk every last penny into this theatre. It's his pride and joy.'

'But the theatre hasn't even opened yet. Where does he get his money?'

'A rich uncle or some shady business deals? How should I know? Apparently he's sold a painting.'

'I know where he gets it,' said the buxom Maria de Medici. 'At the gaming table. He goes at it with the same passion as good King Henry when he was seducing young maidens. Edmond personifies the two masks of classical theatre, laughing one minute, crying the next. If he's splitting his sides, it means he's winning at baccarat; if he's grimacing, he's been cleaned out the night before. Fortunately he laughs more often than he cries!'

Ravaillac was surprised.

'I don't know where he finds the time. He spends hours at the theatre ordering the wardrobe mistresses about, spying on the stagehands, pestering the actors and explaining *Hamlet, Le Cid* or *Andromaque* to the extras who couldn't give a fig!'

'Oh, he finds the time all right, don't you worry! He's as strong as an ox, despite being fifty. It's common knowledge that he has several mistresses. The official one is Adélaïde Paillet. She gets two nights a week and, when he's fulfilled his obligations there, his passion for cards takes him to the club on the Boulevard. He goes on gambling, promising himself he'll stop as soon as he makes a big win. He's been on a winning streak the past few nights, which means his purse is full and we'll get paid.'

'Does he never stop?' asked Andréa.

'He goes to bed at dawn and gets up at noon.'

'You seem to know an awful lot about him, Eugénie,' remarked Ravaillac. 'Anybody would think you were privy to the maestro's secrets . . . Pillow talk, perhaps?'

'Isn't Maria de Medici Henry IV's other half, clever-clogs?'

A voice boomed, 'Company on stage!' and they scurried back to the boards where King Henry sat on high in an open carriage while some stagehands struggled to put up a backdrop representing Rue de la Ferronnerie, with its letter-writers' and washerwomen's shops.

'Hey! Wake up, Ravaillac! Where's your wig? You're supposed to be a redhead. What on earth possessed me to hire such a ham! For heaven's sake, you're meant to cut my throat, not sit around jabbering with these ladies!'

The manager's office was on the second floor, above the foyer. As soon as the rehearsal had finished, Edmond Leglantier hurried upstairs to change. He peeled off his false beard, smothered his face in cold cream, cleaned off the greasepaint and coloured his salt-and-pepper moustache with some make-up filched from Eugénie. He crooned as he buttoned his shirt:

> '*No more gaming at the table*
> *Ding dong! The horse is in the stable.*
> *A fine, handsome role awaits me*
> *A Don Diego or an Othello!*

'I can smell it. That fickle mistress fame will be mine! I'll spare no expense, gilt chairs and electric lighting in the auditorium if you please! Who would dare question my luck? I shan't be playing baccarat tonight, I'll be playing the players, and it will be the performance of a lifetime!'

He took a bundle of shares from a drawer, and studied one of them. An elegantly crossed pipe and cigar holder framed in wreaths of smoke a text, which he read out pompously:

> '*Public Company*
> *AMBREX*
> *Statutes registered with Maître Piard, Notary of Paris,*
> *14 February 1893*
> *ISSUED CAPITAL 1,000,000 francs*
> *Divided into 2,000 shares of 500 francs each*
> *HEAD OFFICE: PARIS*
> *The holder is beneficiary of the share*
> *Paris, 30 April 1893*
> *Director   Director*

'Perfect,' he concluded, with a smile. 'The artist has surpassed himself.'

He kissed the shares in the manner of a bashful lover.

'You are ravishing, my beauties, decked out in all your finery. You catch more flies with honey than with vinegar! Nothing reassures an investor more than seeing with his own eyes, in finely engraved copperplate, the gold mine that promises to make his nest egg grow. The gold mine in this case being these smoking accessories, which look every bit as authentic as a picture in a magazine – and people will believe anything they see in print.'

He counted out twenty-five share certificates, stored the remainder in a safe from which he took an equal number of cigar holders, and placed the whole lot in a briefcase. Then, standing before a cheval glass, he knotted his tie and declaimed in a quavering voice worthy of a member of the Comédie-Française, 'Never will a better use be found for paper than converting it into hard cash or potential dividends from shares in variform enterprises.'

The adjective so pleased him that he rolled the '*r*'s in an exaggerated fashion, and continued, '. . . Variform enterprises such as the intensive farming of knobbly trees in an as yet unexplored region of our colonies or the transformation of fossilised resin into pipes! Prepare for your entrance, Leglantier my friend, the performance is about to begin!'

The wide pavements of Boulevard de Bonne-Nouvelle were thronging with people running errands or idling at tables outside cafés. Edmond Leglantier checked that the sandwich men lugging the advertisements for Théâtre de l'Échiquier, which was tucked away down a quiet street, were doing their job properly.

He saw one of them parading back and forth in front of a building housing a general store. Another one was pacing up and down the esplanade outside the Théâtre du Gymnase, proud to be the focus of attention of the onlookers lolling on the benches. Satisfied, Leglantier continued on his way towards Boulevard Poissonnière.

It was when he reached Boulevard Montmartre that he noticed the fair-haired fellow in the light-coloured suit. He ducked into a urinal, his mind racing like quicksilver, and tried to gather his thoughts by softly chanting:

> *'And slyly when the world is sleeping yet*
> *He smooths out collars for the Easter daisies*
> *And fashions golden buttercups to set*
> *In woodland mazes.'*[10]

He had seen the man before. First when he was leaving the theatre and then at the bar in Muller's brasserie, not far from the table where the fat man had handed over the cigar holders and share certificates. He'd suspected nothing at the time, but now . . .

If he follows me, I'll know for sure, he thought.

He walked out of the urinal and made straight for a barber's shop where the window served as a convenient mirror. The man in the light-coloured suit had disappeared into the crowd.

A frantic wave of anglomania was transforming the neighbourhood into a little corner of London. Every shop was British, from opticians to hatters, not forgetting the tailors and bootmakers who all boasted the words 'modern' or 'select' in their signs. In contrast, the street vendors who pestered passers-by were unmistakably French.

'Cool off with a refreshing coconut ice, ladies and gentlemen!' shouted a trader, clanging his bell and stooping under the weight of his tinplate barrel.

'In the Russian style, ladies, in the Russian style,' shrieked the flower seller, pushing her cartload of variegated blooms, the violets the star of the show.

Edmond Leglantier bought a red carnation, which he put in his buttonhole, brushing aside a man peddling risqué photographs entitled Pauline's Bath. Sluggish from the sweltering heat of late afternoon, he paused to consider whether to catch the Madeleine–Bastille omnibus or take a glass of quinquina at one of the tables outside the taverns.

He felt the weight of his briefcase and decided to continue on foot. He needed a clear head for the matter in hand.

He was greeted at the entrance to the club by a woman of gargantuan proportions nicknamed 'La belle Circassienne' although she came from Romorantin. She served the triple function of moneylender, fortune teller and purveyor of young flesh. As was the custom, Edmond Leglantier gave her a one-franc piece in exchange for a meaningful wink and the name of a young soprano singer in need of a benefactor.

'Her name's Rosalba, a dear plump little thing,' the ogress whispered.

Edmond Leglantier declined with a smile.

The Méridien was an open club and thus allowed entry to both members and non-members alike. Its clientele consisted of artists, men and women of letters, socialites and captains of industry. They went there to lunch, to dine, to write their correspondence, but above all to gamble.

The main room, with its monumental fireplace, its walls covered in enamel plates – would-be reproductions of Bernard Palissy – and its gilded tables, was lit by five-branched chandeliers. Standing to attention near the hearth, a melancholy-looking fellow responsible for handing out the chips greeted Edmond Leglantier, who replied absent-mindedly, 'Hello, Monsieur Max.' He surveyed the crowd gathered in one of the side rooms. It was the hour of the green fairy. The absinthe drinkers poured their magic potion drop by drop into a glass, filtering their poison through a sugar cube held in a slotted spoon. Card games were well under way. Excited by the activity around them, punters jostled eagerly for position around the banker. For some people, gambling was a true panacea. They expected the cards to provide enough money to live on. They played safe, weighing up the probabilities and placing bets only when they felt comfortable. They earned their living from gambling. But many others succumbed to the demon that could make or break them in a single hand, although their faces betrayed none of their dreadful anxiety. Only outside did they let their disappointment show.

This perennial drama was drowned out by snatches of trivial chat or profound observations. A neglected poet vented his spleen.

'Novels and plays are churned out as if by machine. Today's literary manufacturers cater to all tastes! I despise such publishers!'

'What can I say, my friend, money is more important than art.'

'Guess what he had the cheek to say to the author!' bawled a gossip columnist. '"Monsieur, I've read your manuscript; choose your weapon." Have you seen his new play? It doesn't stand up at all; it's completely overblown and then it just fizzles out! Ah! At last! Leglantier!'

A general murmur greeted the arrival of the man whom fellow club patrons considered as something of a mentor. A score of men in black tailcoats, most of them sporting monocles, immediately gathered round the manager of l'Échiquier. A heterogeneous bunch, they included military men, aristocrats and members of the middle classes, like the gossip columnist and the thwarted poet. Edmond Leglantier was good at smoothing away tensions. His inside knowledge of the latest Paris gossip, the favours he received from a few well-known actresses and the subtle way he had of denigrating his peers made him a leading light who was much in demand. And yet the moment his back was turned, his admirers attacked him viciously.

'My dear fellow, we were just waiting for you in order to begin,' exclaimed a retired colonel.

'Apologies for the delay. I was so caught up in the renovations at the theatre that I lost all sense of time.'

'And yet there's a rumour going round that work has been suspended due to lack of funds.'

'"Slander, Monsieur, I've seen honest men all but destroyed by it",[11] my dear Colonel de Réauville. Lady Luck will soon be smiling on me and I shall reap the full benefits!'

'By what miracle?'

Edmond Leglantier spread out his twenty-five share certificates on the green baize.

'Thanks to these beauties. It's a pity I'm short of funds otherwise I'd have bought more. They're about to soar – I'd swear to it.'

'Ambrex? Never heard of it,' remarked the gossip columnist.

'Ah, that's because the company isn't listed on the stock market yet, but next month . . . Expect a *coup de théâtre* – rest assured this investment will revive my finances. Your health, gentlemen,' he concluded, waving one of the shares in the air.

Colonel de Réauville muttered, 'Ambrex, Ambrex, dashed funny name!'

'Come on, Leglantier, stop beating about the bush. Tell us the whole story. What is this Ambrex?' demanded an art dealer from Rue Laffitte.

'There's no mystery. Look,' said Edmond Leglantier, holding up a cigar holder. 'What do you suppose this is made of?'

'Amber.'

'Wrong. It's a perfect imitation, an invention that will revolutionise the jewellery industry.'

'Come on, Leglantier, we've all seen imitation amber before, it's just yellow glass!' exclaimed Colonel de Réauville.

'This isn't glass.'

'Gum lacquer?'

'No.'

'Tortoiseshell?'

'No, no! I assure you it's an original formula. Believe me, I'd never have put money on this company if I wasn't convinced of its success.'

He slipped the cigar holder into his pocket, pretended to hesitate then reopened his briefcase.

'Here, a gift for the future audience of *Heart Pierced by an Arrow*. Help yourselves, and be sure to bring your wives, daughters and mistresses to Théâtre de l'Échiquier!'

Every man examined the cigar holders, going into raptures about their quality. The transparency, the colour, even the tiny insects trapped in the resin looked uncannily like Baltic amber.

'I can't tell the difference,' muttered the gossip columnist.

'The patent has just been registered,' added Edmond Leglantier.

'Are you in partnership with the inventor?'

'He's an acquaintance from my youth, who invited me in on the deal.'

'Really . . . Well, I for one am interested,' replied the art dealer.

'We're *all* interested,' seconded a tall fellow with the handlebar moustache, close-cropped hair and florid complexion of a hussar.

'My dear Coudray, this is a limited offer only. My "acquaintance" wants to start off slowly. As Racine wrote in *Les Plaideurs*, Act I, Scene 1: "He who will travel far . . ."'

'All right, *chi va piano va sano*, we know the expression.

Count me in anyway,' Coudray went on. 'I want fifty of these shares.'

'And I'll have seventy!' said a man with a monocle.

'I want fifty, too.'

'Count me in! I'll buy thirty.'

'Don't forget me! Forty!'

Edmond Leglantier began to chuckle.

'Calm down, gentlemen, calm down; we're not on the trading floor now. I'll do my best, but I can't promise anything. I'll have to make sure there are enough to go round . . .'

He opened a jotter and began taking down the orders.

'Two hundred and forty shares . . . Gentlemen, it's your lucky day. I think I'm in a position to give you what you want. As long as the shares remain unlisted, I'm the intermediary, but we'll need to act quickly. Meet me back here at seven o'clock this evening . . . Oh, and no promissory notes, cash only.'

Edmond Leglantier left. His performance had been such a resounding success that he allowed himself to pat La Circassienne's behind on his way back out onto the Boulevard.

'Fiddle dee dee! The simpletons! It's in the bag. Let's see, two hundred and forty times five hundred is a hundred and twenty thousand . . . sixty thousand for me! And if I manage to wheedle at least another hundred thousand francs out of that old codger the Duc de Frioul tonight, I'll be in clover!'

A bare-headed young laundress smiled at him.

He doffed his hat and called out, 'Mademoiselle, you are utterly delightful!'

He straightened up. The fair-haired man in the light-coloured suit was leaning against a lamppost. He kept looking at his watch as though waiting for a romantic tryst. Had he been spying on him ever since he arrived at the club?

Ecce homo,[12] thought Edmond Leglantier.

It occurred to him to approach the stranger, but he decided against it. He resisted a momentary urge to flee, and instead sat down at a table outside a café. He conjured up the face of the man who had hired him. Edmond Leglantier had sensed that beneath the easy-going exterior he was someone of formidable character and devilish intelligence: setting up a fraud of such complexity required total control of the situation. Was he having Leglantier tailed to make sure he didn't try to swindle him? Edmond Leglantier shuddered. With a man like that he'd be well advised to play straight.

His shadow paced up and down, looking as though he were carrying the weight of the world on his shoulders.

'They'd boo him off stage,' Edmond Leglantier said to himself. 'Well, that's enough of that!'

Having ordered nothing, he walked back home, making sure he kept to the side streets. He forced himself not to turn round.

'Remember Lot's wife!'

When he reached the entrance to his building, he peered carefully about him, but his shadow was nowhere in sight.

CHAPTER THREE

Tuesday 4 July

FRÉDÉRIC Daglan was peeling potatoes. The weather was mild and he felt safe in the middle of the overgrown garden with its riot of viburnum, bindweed and elderberry bushes threatening to invade the vegetable patch. Mother Chickweed lived at the foot of the fortifications, which had been built in order to protect Paris but had failed dismally to do so.[13]

Two weeks earlier, when Frédéric Daglan had come to her, she had asked no questions. Anchise had sent him and that was recommendation enough; he could stay here and sleep in the shed, preparing the meals when she was out.

Mother Chickweed was about forty years old and fiercely independent. She had left her drunkard husband and found a way of making a living all year round.

She trudged the streets with her basket of wild grass flecked with white flowers, crying out, 'Chickweed for your songbirds!'

The concierges, housewives and people working from home looked out for her every day. For the songbirds would soon stop chirping and tweeting if they didn't have their chickweed. These tiny creatures hanging from the window jambs in cages were a symbol of happiness for the poor. They would always find a sou to buy chickweed even when times were hard.

By late spring, the herb was getting scarce, its season over, but Mother Chickweed continued to provide plantain spears and fresh millet for the local songbirds.

Frédéric Daglan gathered up the potato peelings in some old newspaper and was about to take them over to the rabbits when an article at the bottom of the page caught his eye. His face tensed. He checked the date on the newspaper: 22 June 1893.

MURDER ON RUE CHEVREUL

A man was stabbed to death yesterday at seven o'clock in the morning, on Rue Chevreul. The victim was an enamellist by the name of Léopold Grandjean. The police are questioning a witness . . .

'Damn it!' he cursed under his breath.

Later that evening

Paul Theneuil had been waiting outside the premises in the rain for a good quarter of an hour. For him, punctuality was a cardinal virtue, and he loathed wasting his time. He had received the telegram that morning, just after opening time, and had taken several minutes to digest its content. Standing next to the window of his office, he had looked down on the bustling print works below, fingering the blue paper before tearing it up. He hated feeling forced to obey what seemed more like a command than a request. What a nerve – pestering him now after they'd agreed to sever all contact once the transaction was completed!

Paul Theneuil was not a man to lose himself in conjecture;

he left nothing to chance, and once he made a decision he stuck to it. Other than Monsieur Leuze, his book-keeper, none of his staff would ever dare question his orders. Paul Theneuil knew that this time he had a tough opponent on his hands, but he was a past master at playing with loaded dice, and he was not going to let anybody harass him.

He had left his print works in Petit-Montrouge in the late afternoon in order to arrive at this fellow's place by seven o'clock, leaving himself plenty of time to pop in and warn Marthe. The thing was not to change his habits under any circumstances. He'd walked up Passage des Thermopyles and into the haberdasher's. It was empty. He could hear Marthe stirring her pots in the adjoining kitchen.

'Is that you, Paul?'

'I'm just going to meet a client who has ordered some posters. Mmm, that smells delicious! What are you cooking?'

'Jugged hare.'

Paul Theneuil had taken a swig of Sancerre, changed his jacket and grabbed an umbrella.

'Put a plate aside for me, dear.'

His 'dear' had blown him a kiss and gone on adding white wine to her roux.

The heavens had decided to open just as Paul Theneuil stepped onto an omnibus. He was a stocky, coarse-looking man of about sixty. His broad face gave the impression of being covered in stubble even when it was clean-shaven. His thin, straight hair was greying at the temples and he wore a pince-nez on his red, bulbous nose. The typesetters and apprentices called him 'Ugly mug' behind his back.

The rain had eased off. The courtyard and the street beyond were empty. Paul Theneuil realised that the man had not specified whether to meet him indoors or out. After that downpour he was most likely inside. All the better, it would make his job easier. He reached for the latch. The door opened onto a stack of empty boxes. Light filtered dimly through the grimy windows. He glanced around the room, taking in its contents: a desk covered in papers, two chairs, shelves lined with files and a workbench running along one wall.

'Hello! Is anybody there?'

He heard the sound of breathing.

Something moved to his left.

Paul Theneuil swung round.

Wednesday 5 July

As he left Professor Mortier's house, Joseph aimed a kick at a dustbin. He was livid. They'd sent him halfway across Paris to deliver a dictionary of Ancient Greek with only sixty centimes in his pocket! Before Iris's betrayal, he would have been allowed to take a cab, but nowadays Monsieur Mori treated him as though he had fallen from grace. He walked up to the first in a row of omnibuses. A puckish-looking conductor was sitting on the platform puffing on a cigarette while he stared at his shoes.

'Have I time to buy a newspaper?' Joseph enquired.

The man spat without letting go of his fag end.

'We're leaving in two minutes, lad.'

In his hurry, Joseph bumped into an old man buying a copy of *Le Figaro* from the news vendor.

'You oaf!'

Joseph muttered an apology and, his *Passe-partout* under his arm, ran back to the omnibus, which was just moving off. His only thought was to find a seat, open his newspaper and make the journey in comfort. He knew the route off by heart: the boulevards and then, as they neared the centre, the more fashionable streets.

'Hot, isn't it?' a man remarked.

'Dreadful time of year.'

'The newspapers forecast rain.'

'Well, you can't always believe what you read . . .'

Some bored-looking firemen on duty were leaning out of the mezzanine at the Bibliothèque Nationale, watching the traffic below. Through half-open windows, public servants could be seen busily idling. One, however, was sharpening a pencil.

The clippety-clop of the horses' hooves echoed as they passed under the archway leading to Cour du Carrousel. Two men alighted.

Leaden clouds presaged a dull day. A passing dray poked its nose in above the platform. The conductor cried out, 'Two-legged animals only, my beauty! Room for two more downstairs, numbers seven and eight!'

Ding a ling a ling.

With a deafening clatter, the yellow omnibus turned the corner into a wide avenue. At every stop, people clamoured and waved their numbered tickets at the driver. The 'full' sign was put up. The conductor, who'd seen it all before, said in a jaded voice, 'With omnibuses as with books – you never know what you'll find inside.'

Then he pulled the cord to alert the driver, who reined in his horses to allow another faster omnibus to overtake.

'It's going to bucket down!' the driver called out.

'It'll make the grass grow!' the conductor cried back. 'Louvre, Châtelet, Odéon, room for one more upstairs. Number six!'

On the pavement, a score of disappointed faces looked up at the sky and decided it was perhaps a good thing there was no room for them on the upper deck. At last number six came forward.

Ding a ling a ling.

'Get your *Figaro, Intransigeant, Petit Journal*!'

A news vendor made a few speedy sales.

Joseph opened his *Passe-partout*, handily just as number six, an enormous woman laden with shopping baskets, stepped on board. Nobody offered her their seat.

'It's no good, Madame,' the conductor observed. 'You'll have to go upstairs. Here, I'll give you a shove. Heave-ho!'

Joseph shrank into his corner, feeling deliciously guilty, and skimmed the headlines.

GUY DE LA BROSSE'S BODY FOUND

The remains of Guy de la Brosse, founder of our Natural History Museum, have been discovered in an abandoned cellar – formerly the museum's zoological gallery . . .

'Tickets please. What the blazes is going on here?'

The Plaisance–Hôtel de Ville omnibus was struggling up Boulevard Saint-Germain, blocked by a noisy crowd. Stuck at the back of the vehicle, Joseph was thinking that he must go back to writing his novel, *Thule's Golden Chalice*, when his attention was suddenly drawn to page two:

ENAMELLIST MURDERED

There are still no clues in the case of the murder victim, Léopold Grandjean, stabbed by an unknown assailant in Rue Chevreul on 21 June. The sole witness is unable to describe the killer, having only seen him . . .

The large woman with the shopping baskets had come back downstairs and was complaining loudly about young people today. Joseph stood up reluctantly, and with a polite gesture offered her his seat.

'Madame, allow me . . .'

He pushed his way over to the platform and listened idly to a couple of servant girls chatting.

'Why have we slowed down?' the plumper of the two asked the other.

'I haven't a clue. I expect it's those good-for-nothing students demonstrating again. It's all very well railing against society, but who does all the work? Us, that's who!' exclaimed her companion, a pretty brunette, who winked brazenly at Joseph.

'Are they still warring at your house, then?' she asked her friend.

'I'll say. Madame's husband has a mistress who wants him to leave her and understandably Madame's afraid she'll be out on her ear.'

The demonstrators' angry shouts began to crescendo.

'Sparks will fly,' the plump one said.

'And at my place, too,' retorted the brunette. 'What with Monsieur's saucy remarks and his straying hands . . .'

A sudden jolt ended the young women's intimate exchange. A group of students had stopped the team of three horses, and, despite the stream of invective from the driver, was now leading them into Rue de l'Échaudé. The passengers downstairs panicked and tried to leave but were blocked by a flood of people descending from the upper deck.

'What's all the fuss about?' the brunette shouted.

'It's that cold fish Senator René Bérenger.[14] He's got them all up in arms by denouncing their costumes at the "Quat'zarts Ball".[15] Licentious he said they were,' a lanky fellow announced placidly from behind his newspaper.

'What's licentious?'

'Pornographic, Mademoiselle. The Guardian of Public Virtue would have done better to cover his eyes. Nothing annoys the electorate more than encroachments on its freedom to go about in a state of undress,' he added, giving Joseph a knowing wink.

Joseph blushed and made his way to the edge of the platform. Next to a kiosk in flames, a tram had been derailed and turned into a barricade. The boulevard was a battlefield. On one side demonstrators were sacking shops and shouting, 'Down with Bérenger! To hell with Bérenger!' and, on the other, the police were rolling up their capes ready to use as batons.

With the conductor's help, the driver fought off the assailants and regained control of his horses. The omnibus took off with a loud clatter down Rue de l'Ancienne-Comédie, only to be surrounded once more when it reached the Faculty of Medicine.

'Off you get, you sightseers!' yelled a scruffy-looking individual.

The alarmed passengers scattered, regrouping around the statue of Paul Broca. The driver managed to unharness his horses and led them off at a trot to Carrefour de l'Odéon. Flattened against a Wallace fountain, Joseph looked on as the omnibus was pushed onto its side. Flames instantly began devouring the inside to loud cheers. A police charge dispersed the arsonists.

Without knowing quite how he had got there, Joseph found himself hurrying along the pavement of Rue Dupuytren, muttering abuse at the blasted students, the forces of order, his bosses and the world in general. Rue Monsieur-le-Prince was still peaceful. He leant against a lamp-post to collect himself.

'Is it revolution?' he asked a carter delivering vegetables in crates.

'Could be. Someone died yesterday. The mounted guards of the 4th Central Brigade killed a shop worker having a drink outside Brasserie d'Harcourt. There's going to be trouble all right. Gee-up, off we go!' he cried, clambering back onto his cart.

Joseph made his way along the street to the bookbinder Pierre Andrésy's shop. Monsieur Mori had asked him to stop off there and pick up a Persian manuscript.

'Talk about a constitutional! I deserve a bonus!' he grumbled.

He was very surprised to find the door locked; the shop was usually open at this time of the morning. He stepped away from the door and peered through the narrow shop window with its samples of morocco, vellum and shagreen, then pressed his face up to the window of the storerooms next door. He could dimly make out the percussion presses and an assortment of other tools, but there was no sign of Pierre Andrésy.

'This really is the limit!' he muttered to himself, irate at being forced to come back later.

Was there no end to the humiliations he must suffer? He felt like the victim of some monstrous plot. Sulking, he walked back up Rue Monsieur-le-Prince, turned into Rue de Vaugirard and entered the Luxembourg Gardens.

Who would have believed that such violent clashes were taking place only a stone's throw from these peaceful avenues. The month of July was sweltering that year, and ladies everywhere carried silk and gauze parasols with mother-of-pearl knob handles, resembling tiny iridescent suns twirling beneath a blue sky.

By the Medici fountain, Joseph passed two young women in foulard dresses out for a stroll. The prettier of the two was slender, olive-skinned and wore a large red hat with ribbon spilling down the back. She was the spitting image of Iris! He gazed at her figure. A silent grief overwhelmed him. All was lost. He wished he were dead! He smiled bitterly, like a character in a melodrama. Slumped on a bench, he watched the ballet of the goldfish in the water. He singled out one with a purple spot between its gills, and called it Ajax.

'I'll never marry, Ajax. I'll have mistresses, but I won't

become attached to any of them; they'll suffer. Oh, roll your eyes all you like – you're not the marrying kind either! It's just not worth it. What's that? Be magnanimous? Forgive and forget? That's what she wants! Never, do you hear! I'll never join the ranks of the cuckolds. If you read more you'd know that *woman is fickle, men must beware*.[16] This affair has already caused me to neglect my second novel and leave Frida von Glockenspiel in the lurch . . .[17] I refuse to give up literature! Eat, drink and be merry, for tomorrow we die,' he concluded in a mournful voice as Ajax descended to explore the depths of the pond.

He rose to his feet, dejected, and continued his soliloquy, hoping to blot out the pain of his broken heart.

'And to think that palm reader told me I was blessed by Venus. What twaddle! Anyway, I prefer it this way. I value my independence.'

His heart was pounding and his eyes were moist with tears. He dried them furiously. Between him and his resolve stood the shadow of a young woman with almond eyes who filled him with a passionate longing.

A woman cyclist in a hazel-coloured homemade outfit of shorts gathered just below the knee and a waisted bodice that highlighted her plump figure rode into Quai Malaquais. She slowed to a halt outside 18, Rue des Saints-Pères. She was preparing to dismount when she noticed a row of faces peering out at her from the Elzévir bookshop. There was a slight kerfuffle before the cyclist was dragged inside.

'How can you be so reckless, Fräulein Becker?' cried Victor.

'Have you suddenly become just like all those male misogynists, Monsieur Legris? A bicycle means freedom for a woman. It is a legitimate way of escaping the supervision of her family. It also gives her an opportunity to modify her dress, which is why men like you frown on women cyclists. You're afraid we'll wear the trousers. Will you please let go of my bicycle!'

'You've got it all wrong, Mademoiselle Becker,' Victor assured her, grasping her bicycle with both hands and wheeling it to the back of the shop. 'It's nothing to do with that.'

'What is it to do with then? Monsieur Mori?'

Kenji Mori took refuge next to the fireplace.

'The body of a man killed during the clashes in the Latin Quarter yesterday has just been taken to Hôpital de la Charité,' he replied, placing a hand on the bust of Molière.

'I was there, I walked slap bang into a squad of municipal guards coming out of Rue Jacob,' bleated Euphrosine Pignot. 'I said to myself: "The Uhlans are coming. It's the Siege all over again!"'

She pointed accusingly at Kenji.

'And to think you sent my boy on an errand today of all days! He'll be massacred.'

'We were unaware of how serious things were – this was supposed to be a peaceful procession. Don't worry, Joseph can take care of himself,' mumbled Kenji.

'Cold-hearted, that's what you are,' muttered Euphrosine. 'I saw the students in a semicircle outside the hospital gates holding their canes end to end. The sergeant raised his white glove and gave the order to charge. I didn't hang about – I ran straight here,' she told Helga Becker, who had taken off her Tyrolean hat and was busy straightening her braids.

'*Ach, ja, das ist wirklich,*[18] Madame Pignot, soldiers are a threat to women's virtue. Incidentally, Monsieur Legris, are you happy with your new Swift Cycle?'

'I hardly think this is the right time . . .'

Victor hurried to open the door to a man in an opera hat, whom he greeted with great reverence, like an honoured guest.

'Please, come in, Monsieur France. What news?'

'The protestors, about a hundred and fifty of them, were perched on the hospital railings. The police from the sixth arrondissement made them get down and the mounted guards of the 4th Brigade gave the charge. Can you hear? They're clearing the streets right now.'

The sound of thundering hooves grew louder.

'I'd advise you to bolt the door,' said Anatole France.

Outside, people were scattering in all directions; some flattened themselves against the walls, others fled towards the river Seine pursued by mounted guards waving sabres. The riders' costumes formed a red streak merging with the black and bay horses. Victor, strangely detached, wished he had a chronophotographic camera to capture these events in motion.[19]

Silence descended once more, punctuated by an occasional distant sound. Rue des Saints-Pères was strewn with canes, hats and shoes, evidence of the violent nature of the clashes.

'This situation bears some similarities to July 1789, when the people of Paris learnt of Necker's dismissal – the French Revolution, what a marvellous subject. Who knows, I may write a novel about it one day,'[20] said Anatole France. 'Kenji, dear fellow, what's become of the chairs?'

'Revolution!' cried Euphrosine. 'Holy Mother of God! And my boy's out there all alone! He'll be torn to shreds. Jesus, Mary and Joseph, bring him back to me alive!'

No sooner had Joseph reached Rue de Vaugirard than the noise from Boulevard Saint-Germain became audible again. He was enjoying the gentle breeze, when suddenly he screwed up his eyes at what looked like plumes of filthy smoke curling above the rooftops at the other end of Rue Monsieur-le-Prince. It was clear from where he was standing a few blocks away that this was no small fire. He raced towards the blaze, turning his face away from the bursts of heat. A faded four-storey building stood above two shops. Enveloped by flames, the colours on the shop signs had turned acid yellow. Joseph stopped dead in his tracks. The bookbinder's premises were by now a roaring inferno, which had begun to spread to the storehouse next door. A frail hand squeezed his arm and a hoarse voice made him jump.

'I was having a kip while my mates were at the bistro having lunch and I had a dream. Yes, Monsieur, I dreamt I could smell burning and it woke me up. I'd be a goner otherwise!'

The man staggered off to join the other tenants on the pavement opposite. They stood, motionless, surveying the scene of devastation in silence, grey confetti raining down on their heads.

Joseph went over to an old man in a workman's smock.

'How did the fire start?'

'Dunno. I was having a snack at the cheese seller's with my workers when we heard a bang and suddenly the whole lot went up in flames. Lucky we weren't inside,' he said, pointing to the storehouse.

'What about Monsieur Andrésy? Have you seen him?'

The old man shook his head.

Joseph searched in vain for the bookbinder among the people who'd escaped the blaze, but he was nowhere to be seen.

'This is terrible! What if he's trapped inside?'

The man shrugged helplessly.

Joseph suddenly felt sick and leant against the wall.

'He's dead,' he wailed.

He wiped his face and hands with a handkerchief.

'Here's the fire brigade at last!' a woman cried.

The firemen with their extending ladders, hook ladders, ropes and pumps formed a team of muscle and machine to fight the blaze. A fireman grabbed a slack hose and his sub-officer signalled to the man in charge of working the steam pump. The hose jerked into life, its spirals slowly unwinding on the pavement, water spurting at intervals from its nozzle.

It took more than two hours to bring the blaze under control. A blackened frame was all that remained of the bookbinder's shop and apartment.

Head down, Joseph took advantage of the general confusion to step over the charred threshold. The books had been reduced to a soggy mass of cinders. He picked up a scrap of leather, which fell apart in his hands. He found three burnt tubes about four inches in length and, without thinking, put them in his pocket, then he went up to the owner of the storehouse.

'Are you sure you heard an explosion?'

'Well, I suppose it could have been those blasted students. What a disaster! Now we're out of a job. What the blazes will we do?'

'It could have been a gas explosion,' ventured a woman with a beaky nose.

'Have you seen Monsieur Andrésy?'

'The poor fellow was trapped inside,' the woman replied. 'My charcuterie is just opposite. I can see everything from my window. He was leaning over his press when the fire started. It's terrible, and with all that paper in there . . .'

The Elzévir bookshop had ceased to be a temporary refuge. The customers filed out, and Anatole France followed, escorted by Kenji. Only Fräulein Becker resisted venturing out on her bicycle until the rioters were fully under control. She said she would go to the top of the Ferris Tension Wheel – the pièce de résistance at the Chicago World's Fair[21] – sooner than expose herself and her precious machine to the dangers of the arsonists and the forces of order.

Much to Victor's annoyance, Madame Ballu, the concierge at number 18, burst in, eager to exchange impressions with her friend Euphrosine. The three women, like the three Fates, were standing at the counter prattling away when suddenly they cried out in unison at the sight of Joseph in the doorway, his face flushed, his cap askew. Before he could say a word, his mother had flung her arms round him, thanking all the saints for having brought her son back in one piece.

'My poor boy, you're all out of breath! Did the brigands chase you? I told you, didn't I, Monsieur Legris, they're nothing but a pack of wild animals! Look at the poor lad! He's dripping with sweat!'

'Maman!'

'Calm down, Madame Pignot, he's not going to dissolve in a puddle,' retorted Victor, prising his clerk from his mother's grasp.

'B-boss, it . . . it's terrible! Monsieur Andrésy . . . The book-binder . . . He's dead! Burnt alive!'

'Oh, God help us, those monsters are setting fire to people now!' howled Madame Ballu.

Victor tried to usher Joseph to the back of the shop, but the three excited women blocked their way.

'Let the boy speak!' thundered Victor.

'Some say it was the students, some the anarchists, others think it was an accident, but for the moment they're groping in the dark, clueless, flummoxed,' exclaimed Joseph, who had recovered the use of his tongue.

'Flummoxed?' asked Helga Becker.

'In the *schwarz*,' barked Victor.

'There was a fire, a huge fire. The place was burnt to the ground!' concluded Joseph.

'I'll go there straight away. You stay and look after the shop, and not a word to Monsieur Mori about this,' warned Victor, pulling on his jacket and reaching for his hat and cane.

'What shall I do if Mademoiselle Iris asks where you've gone?' murmured Euphrosine, glancing at Joseph.

'Remain as quiet as the doe in the hunter's sights,' Victor

commanded, with an inward nod of approval to Alphonse de Lamartine for this fitting aphorism.

Madame Pignot wrinkled her mouth, flattered by the comparison. Joseph stood motionless, his gaze fixed on the beautiful half-Asian young woman in a red and white striped chiffon dress and silk ruff fastened with a black ribbon.

'What are you worried that I might ask, Madame Pignot?' enquired Iris, her eyes sparkling.

As he was trying to hail a cab, Victor recalled the strange creature who had caused such a sensation at the Folies-Bergère the previous winter. That will-o'-the-wisp in gossamer veils, flapping like a butterfly in the projectors' coloured beams, reminded him of his own life. His routine was occasionally interrupted by complex choreographies *à la* Loïe Fuller;[22] he cavorted with the unknown, tussled with danger, only to fall back, exhausted, into the clutches of an ennui that had been the bane of his life. Only Tasha had the power to draw him out of these depressions and give his life meaning.

The traffic was inching forward. There wasn't a cab in sight. He decided to walk. Having finally left the hubbub on Boulevard Saint-Germain, he reached Rue Monsieur-le-Prince, where he came across a sign:

ROAD CLOSED

He walked round it and arrived at what had once been the book-binder's shop. The firemen's hoses had transformed the charred rubble into a boggy mess. A crack, like a grinning mouth, had spread across the wall of the adjoining building. The remains of books and half-burnt pages lay strewn across the pavement where somebody had left a pile of chairs and a trunk.

'Any victims?' he asked a policeman on watch.

'Fortunately, the men at the storehouse were having lunch at Fulbert's when the fire broke out!'

'What about the bookbinder?'

'He wasn't so lucky – burnt alive.'

'He was a friend of mine.'

'According to the firemen what's left of him is not a pretty sight.'

Victor shuddered inwardly; burning your finger with a match was bad enough . . . imagine the agony of being consumed by fire! He could only hope that Pierre Andrésy had been overcome by fumes first.

'Does anybody know how it started?'

'The firemen think a gas lamp probably blew out, and the poor wretch lit a pipe or a cigarette and boom! The inspector and the coroner will accompany the body to the morgue, but with all the to-do in the neighbourhood it'll take time.'

'I assume there'll be an investigation?'

'We're expecting the detectives to arrive at any moment.'

While they were talking, Victor surreptitiously stepped over the rope cordoning off the area around the shop. The policeman held him back by his sleeve.

'You can't go in there, Monsieur. You might destroy vital evidence.'

'I'm terribly upset. I just wanted to make sure that . . .'

'Give me your card and if we salvage any of his personal effects we'll let you know.'

Victor walked away slowly. Pierre Andrésy's death had set him thinking about his own existence, which he had been deliberately avoiding. More than half his life had gone by and what had he done with it? The hours spent hunting for rare books, trawling through catalogues, outbidding other dealers at auctions appeared as meaningless to him as his numerous conquests of women – pleasurable interludes that only satisfied a sexual need. By the time he reached Rue des Saints-Pères, he had come to the conclusion that his love for Tasha was what compelled him to engage in battle with this chaos of cruelty, greed and beauty.

Man believes he is able to commune with the divine powers by building places of worship, he thought. Can he not achieve that communion by considering a blade of grass or a bird on the wing, by marvelling at a work of art, or listening to the wind or contemplating the stars at night . . .

Upon entering the bookshop, Victor was horrified to discover that the three Fates had been replaced by two of the battle-axes. Blanche de Cambrésis, her sharp chin wagging in the direction of the Maltese lapdog Raphaëlle de Gouveline was clasping to her bosom, was as oblivious to his entrance as she was to her companion greeting him with a nod. She was too busy venting her virulent opinions.

'These excesses are an utter disgrace! The authorities must show these degenerate students no mercy. My husband is quite right. Our Catholic youth is being manipulated by hidden forces that threaten to destroy the very fabric of society. The flood of immigrants from the East is encouraging the spread of socialism! What is this country coming to! . . . What is it, dear? Do you have a crick in your neck?'

Raphaëlle de Gouveline cleared her throat. The lapdog yapped, and she set it down on the floor next to a schipperke, which growled and bared its teeth.

'Come now, Blanche dear, you're letting yourself be influenced by a lot of nonsense. Christian charity teaches us to be tolerant, isn't that so, Monsieur Legris? What a naughty man you are keeping us waiting like this!'

Blanche de Cambrésis quickly changed the subject when she saw Victor.

'Did you know that divorce is on the increase worldwide? In Japan one in every three marriages ends in it. Good afternoon, Monsieur Legris. I'm back. This time I'm looking for *The Blue Ibis* by Jean Aicard.'

Victor doffed his hat, taking care to hide his displeasure: he found Blanche de Cambrésis's aggressive voice as insufferable as her diatribes.

'Good afternoon, ladies. Joseph will take care of you.'

'I'm still waiting for him to come back from the stockroom. A charming reception, I'm sure!'

Victor curbed his irritation.

'I shall return in five minutes. I must speak to Monsieur Mori.'

He left them, and hurried upstairs to the first floor.

Blanche de Cambrésis straightened her pince-nez.

'What manners! Although it should come as no surprise from a man living in sin with a Russian émigrée who exhibits her unspeakable paintings at Boussod et Valadon! Decent women aspire to live within the holy sacraments of marriage, to make a home and bring up children!'

'Not all of them, my dear, not all of them. Polly Thomson, the oldest living British subject, has just celebrated her one hundred and seventh birthday. She never married, she says, because men enslave women. She preferred having only herself to feed.'

'Well, all I can say is this: I hope that she's still got enough teeth to eat stale bread!' exclaimed Blanche de Cambrésis.

Kenji was studying a Kitagawa Utamaro print, which he had purchased in London and had just hung above his Louis XIII chest.

'What do you think of *Woman Powdering Her Neck*, Victor? Isn't she life-like? Why the long face? Is something the matter?'

'There's been a terrible tragedy. Pierre Andrésy has died in a fire at his shop.'

Kenji turned deathly pale. He felt a pang in his chest, as if he'd been run through with a sabre.

'Kenji, are you all right? I have to go downstairs, there are some customers waiting.'

Kenji nodded distractedly.

'Yes. Go . . . Death is vaster than a mountain yet more insignificant than a grain of sand,' he said, as Victor left the room.

He sat limply on the corner of the futon, his glasses resting on his forehead, and stared into space.

'There is a purpose in every event. People die; a purpose is fulfilled.'

He pictured himself and his beloved Daphné strolling along the paths in the Chelsea Physic Garden, near the Royal Hospital. He could almost taste her scent on his lips. Daphné was buried in Highgate Cemetery. Fifteen years already! He had felt lost without her – a prisoner to hostile forces that threatened to engulf him! And then he had begun to understand that death may claim people's bodies, but their souls live on.

'The dead are thinking of us when we think of them.'

He felt a sudden overwhelming need of affection. The image of Djina Kherson imposed itself on him. He had only met Tasha's mother twice, but she was a woman of undeniable grace. Her heart-shaped mouth and auburn hair reminded him of Dante Gabriel Rossetti's magnificent portrait, *Astarte Syriaca*, which he found arousing. She radiated maturity, and possessed an almost male energy, which attracted, disconcerted and captivated him. Kenji was a conqueror by nature: when he wanted something he took it. His solitude whispered, 'Try, you never know.' But he knew, he knew that Djina Kherson would probably never mean anything to him.

Tasha pushed away the plate of courgettes à la crème. She had no desire to eat in this heat. She decided to add the finishing touches to the painting she was working on. Since returning from Berlin with her mother, she spent two days a week giving watercolour classes, and the rest of her time was taken up with illustrating a translation of Homer. Her own work was suffering as a result. And yet she was happy to be able to help Djina out. She missed the two other people dearest to her heart: her sister Ruhléa, who was living in Cracow with her husband, a Czech doctor called Milos Tábor, and her father Pinkus. He tried to sound positive in his letters from New York, but they betrayed his feeling of rootlessness.

During her time in Berlin, Tasha had realised how strong her attachment to Victor was, and although she was in no hurry to get married, she had agreed to move in with him. Their home consisted of a bedroom, a kitchen, a bathroom and a darkroom. On the other side of the courtyard, the space she used as a studio doubled when necessary as a sitting-cum-dining room.

The bond between her and the man she loved had deepened since she had decided to create a series of paintings based on his photographs.

Victor's studies of children at work had led to him photographing a troupe of young acrobats. From there his interest had turned towards the world of fairgrounds, to which he felt an irresistible attraction. The freaks, strongmen, lion tamers, fire-eaters, clowns, showmen and jugglers were the magical made real, and he loved working in that milieu – especially as Tasha shared his fascination. She had drawn inspiration from his prints of a wooden carousel. One of her paintings depicted a pair of soldiers capering about with two buxom women, who were dizzy from spinning, their skirts lifting as they turned. Another portrayed a solitary lad gripping the reins of his nag as he streaked past the finishing line to win the Chantilly Derby cup.

She was satisfied she had followed Odilon Redon's advice on abstract backgrounds, and she thought the relaxed posture of one of the women leaning back to kiss a soldier worked well. Her fluid brushstrokes resembled those of Berthe Morisot, differing in the precision of her contours.

Victor loved this collaborative work, which he referred to as 'their baby'. Djina was trying to encourage her daughter to marry and have children; she would soon be twenty-six. Tasha didn't object to the thought of marriage, but she couldn't imagine having a baby for several years; she was determined to be free to continue what she'd started. Victor never mentioned it any more. Did he really want to be a father? She stretched her arms, her body filled with a delicious lethargy. Madame Victor Legris! She was already associated with his photography; he'd be over the moon if she agreed to take his name as well. He was doing his best to curb his possessiveness. Of course he didn't always succeed, like on that Thursday the previous March.

They had gone to view an exhibition by the painter Antonio de la Gandara[23] at the Durand-Ruel gallery.[24] She had spent ages looking at the pastels and drawings, in particular the portraits of Comte de Montesquiou and Prince Wolkonsky. An oil painting entitled *Woman in Green* had fascinated her. Impressed by his masterful brushstrokes and the texture of his fabrics, she had wanted to congratulate the artist, an attractive Spanish aristocrat. He had thanked her for the compliment, and with a knowing wink had suggested she sit for him. With forced good humour, Victor had swiftly pointed out that his companion preferred painting portraits to posing for them. He had then pretended to become absorbed in a drawing of a bat, but the glowering looks he kept shooting at Gandara made it perfectly clear what was on his mind.

'Thank God you're here! I was beginning to get worried.'

Victor had just walked in. He embraced her, and she snuggled up against him.

'What's wrong?'

'There's been rioting in the Latin Quarter and . . .'

He told her briefly about the bookbinder's death.

'How horrible!'

She held him tight. Those unforgettable images of the pogrom . . . Rue Voronov splattered with blood, the flickering flames, the man stretched out in front of the house, the soldiers on horseback waving their sabres . . .

'Was it an accident?'

'Apparently . . . They're not sure . . .'

The image of a hand tossing a scrap of burning paper into Pierre Andrésy's shop flashed into his mind. He blotted it out.

Tasha flinched, as though she'd been reading his thoughts; would this tragedy turn into an excuse for a new case? She began to say something then stopped and brushed her lips against his cheek.

'I do love you, you know,' she whispered. 'I feel so afraid sometimes. I can't imagine life without you.'

'Don't worry, my darling. I shall endeavour to endure your difficult nature with stoicism.'

He began to unbutton her blouse as she pulled his shirt out of his trousers.

CHAPTER FOUR

Friday 7 July

'You really have excelled yourself, Monsieur Daglan. The way you've fashioned the *p* in pigs' trotters à la Sainte-Menehould! They look good enough to eat off the page! As for the spelling, I'll take your word for it.'

The plump woman's double chin quivered as she examined the finished menu based on a rough draft. She tried to pay the artist, but he refused with a smile.

'A glass of beer will do, Madame Milent. Just carry on being my eyes and ears.'

'That goes without saying, Monsieur Daglan. The more I see of your upstrokes and downstrokes the more I'm convinced you'll make the ministry one day. I'm ashamed of my spidery scrawl.'

'Come, Madame Milent, you're the queen of cordon bleu. It's the quality of your cooking that matters, not your handwriting.'

Frédéric Daglan finished off his beer and put away his things. By mid-morning, the main room at Madame Milent's establishment in Rue de la Chapelle became the exclusive domain of carters transporting heavy loads, and cab drivers from a nearby rank. The back room, which was screened off by a thin partition and had a secret connecting door to the courtyard of the adjoining police station, would shortly be occupied by assistant chief of police Raoul Pérot, his colleagues, and a few literary friends.

Frédéric Daglan wiped his mouth with the back of his hand and said goodbye to the landlady. After he'd gone, she remained thoughtful.

'What a handsome fellow, so charming, so elegant! Ah! If only I were twenty years younger and forty pounds lighter . . .'

The sun shone weakly on the peeling façades of the buildings and the sky was dappled with fleecy clouds as far as Plaine Saint-Denis.

Like shaving cream, thought Frédéric Daglan.

It was still quiet at that time of the morning after the workshops had opened. He felt euphoric during this delightful lull when the street was the preserve of delivery men and tramps. It was as if he had cast off the shackles of everyday mediocrity that gripped the city. He was master of his own destiny and, even though he'd had the odd taste of prison, no bars had ever really threatened his independence; his inner rejection of any form of authority delivered him from slavery.

'The man who can clip my wings hasn't been born yet,' he muttered, walking towards the tiny public garden swarming with children, a perfect spot from which to watch without being seen.

He sat down on a bench and opened the morning paper. There it was, on page two:

He skimmed the article. The police were making no headway. The only clue was a visiting card with an unintelligible message on it about amber, musk, incense and leopard spots. The attack had happened so fast that the only witness was unable to describe the killer.

Frédéric Daglan suddenly felt sick.

'Of all the filthy tricks!'

A ball landed at his feet. As he sent it flying back, the pages of his newspaper scattered around him, rustling like dead leaves. He walked away. In Rue de la Chapelle, the advertising hoardings on the blank end-walls of the buildings caught his eye. His gaze wandered from a giant mustard pot to a magnificent red Lucifer holding a pair of bellows and spraying a jet of sulphur:

VICAT INSECTICIDE POWDER

The louse! The dirty louse! How dare he! He would crush him.

Joseph paused, picked up a copy of *Boule de Suif* and placed it between *On the Water* and *A Life* then walked out onto the pavement and stepped back to judge the overall effect. Monsieur Legris would be pleased. The window display was a tribute to the works of Guy de Maupassant, who had died the previous day.

With no customers in the shop and all the deliveries done, Joseph felt free to relax. His favourite pastime was updating his scrapbooks, which were stuffed with strange articles taken from various newspapers. He leant on the counter and began going through the pile of newspapers in front of him, pausing only every now and then to take a bite of his apple.

He picked up the copy of *Le Passe-partout* that he'd been reading on the day of the Bérenger protests, and began cutting out a news item.

ENAMELLIST MURDERED

There are still no clues in the case of the murder victim, Léopold Grandjean, stabbed by an unknown assailant in Rue Chevreul on 21 June. The sole witness is unable to describe the killer, having seen him only from behind. The police discovered a mysterious note on the victim's body, the content of which we have decided to print for the benefit of our discerning readers: 'Like amber, musk, benzoin and incense, May has made of ours a solitary pursuit. Can an Ethiopian change the colour of his skin any more than a leopard his spots?'

Our reporter Isidore Gouvier thinks the references are probably literary. The police . . .

The stair creaked. Joseph's heart started pounding. Although Iris had been avoiding the shop since their break-up, he both longed for her to appear and dreaded it. He soon recognised Monsieur Mori's heavy gait and hastily crammed his scrapbook and cuttings into the back of a drawer.

'A mill without grain turns its sails in vain,' remarked Kenji – pretending not to have noticed his assistant, whom he only spoke to now when absolutely necessary.

He sat at his desk, intent on finishing drafting a note.

'What's the boss droning on about mills for?' Joseph muttered. 'Oh! I get it! It's a warning. He's saying I should get a move on or else . . . Well, he can stuff his metaphors, and what's more . . .'

'Still carping?' whispered Victor, emerging from the stockroom.

'You crept up on me, that's not fair!'

Kenji raised his head; if he had overheard he didn't let it show.

'Come and have a look, Victor. I've written a short description of the manuscript I left with Pierre Andrésy. I mean to give it to whoever is in charge of the case. If there's any chance some of the books have been saved . . .'

Touty Namèh *or* The Parrot's Stories: *a collection of fifty-two short stories by Zya Eddin Nachcehehy. An octavo volume with a red vellum cover embossed with a bouquet of gilt flowers. The book contains 298 pages illustrated with 229 miniatures and was previously in the possession of Mohammed Hassan Chah Djihan and Omra Itimad Khan respectively.*

'I'm afraid you may have to kiss it goodbye,' said Victor.

'I'm finding that hard to accept. It's such a rare volume and I'd all but sold it to Colonel de Réauville for one thousand five hundred francs. I'll have to give him back his deposit.'

Hunched over the order book, Joseph made a face, and muttered under his breath, 'Isn't that just typical of the boss, always counting out his grains of rice? If one went missing he'd probably commit hara-kiri.'

'Keep your malicious thoughts to yourself, Joseph, or go and join the ranks of Blanche de Cambrésis and her band of detractors,' Victor warned.

Unperturbed, Kenji had begun sorting out the index cards for his next catalogue. The door bell tinkled and a man in a dark frock coat stood staring at them quizzically.

'Is this the Mori–Legris bookshop? My name's Inspector Lefranc. I've come to take Monsieur Mori and Monsieur Legris down to police headquarters to identify certain items recovered from the body of a bookbinder by the name of Andrésy, first name Pierre,' he said, without pausing for breath.

Victor and Kenji donned their hats and followed the man, leaving Joseph behind.

'I see, so I count for nothing! Even though Monsieur Andrésy and I discussed everything. He wasn't prejudiced. We confided in one another, I liked him. But I'm just a lowly employee. Good for watching the shop while they strut about like a couple of peacocks! Well, the bosses had better watch out or the worker will down tools!'

Inspector Aristide Lecacheur's office was stark. He detested the beige patterned wallpaper with its drab brown rectangles repeated ad infinitum. The only decoration was a portrait of Abbé Prévost hanging next to a mottled mirror.

Victor and Kenji sat down on a pair of cane chairs. Their host, a tall man, towered over them. Despite the hot weather he was sporting a flannel waistcoat.

'I hoped I'd seen the back of you, Monsieur Legris,' he

grumbled. 'You're like the cursed hand my nanny used to tell me about: you throw it in the gutter and it comes back in the night to pull your toes.'

'It's your destiny,' declared Kenji.

'I'm no less tired of you, Monsieur Mori. However, enough of my misgivings! I shall see it through to the bitter end.'

'I assume this speech is only a polite preamble?'

'Quite right, Monsieur Legris, let's get on with it,' boomed the inspector, pointing to an assortment of fragments.

Kenji seemed relatively composed as he examined the objects spread out on the inspector's desk, but Victor noticed one of his eyelids twitching slightly.

Inspector Lecacheur watched him.

'Well?'

'I can't say with certainty.'

'How about you, Monsieur Legris?'

'I, too, am at a loss. I very rarely went to his shop. As for his clothes . . .'

'Where is the body?' Kenji asked.

'At the morgue.'

'Who is taking care of the funeral?'

'His family, I suppose. We're placing a notice in the newspapers.'

'If nobody comes forward, may I see to the arrangements?'

'Yes, once the investigation is over.'

'What investigation?'

'We've yet to determine the cause of the fire. We'll know more in a few days.'

'Were any of the books saved?'

'The firemen arrived too late on account of those blasted students who had the nerve to try and attack police headquarters!'

'It's rumoured we're to have a new chief of police,' said Victor.

'That's right. Monsieur Lepine.[25] He'll soon restore order.'

As Victor turned a half-melted fob watch over and over in his hands, the inspector stared at him so intently that it was all Kenji could do to stop himself from saying: 'Beware the cobra that fixes you with its gaze.'

'Yes, to the bitter end . . . Whenever a murder or serious accident occurs in Paris, who turns up like a bad penny? You, Monsieur Legris. It's becoming tiresome. How do you explain that so many of the people you associate with come to a bad end? Is it simply bad luck on your part or can you see into the future?'

'No doubt I have a sixth sense.'

Inspector Lecacheur walked over to him, scarcely able to contain his exasperation.

'Another of your evasive remarks! I won't let you wriggle out of this one – I demand an explanation!'

Kenji intervened politely.

'Pierre Andrésy was my friend, Inspector. Monsieur Legris knew him on a strictly professional basis. Their paths crossed purely by chance.'

'A timely coincidence, eh? And just now you were talking to me about destiny!'

Aristide Lechacheur rummaged in a drawer and pulled out a cigar and a box of matches. He drew lustily on the cigar, exhaling a puff of bluish smoke.

'All right, I've been a little blunt, but you must confess,' he conceded gruffly, 'that if something's bothering me I speak my mind, especially with a fellow like him. Strange sort of bookseller who can't even manage to find me a limited edition of *Manon Lescaut*! Did your friend use flammable substances in his work?'

'Not as far as I know.'

'Did he have gas or oil lamps?'

'I think I saw oil lamps in his shop.'

The inspector leafed through a file and continued his questioning without looking up.

'Are you aware of any enemies he might have had?'

'Good heavens, no! He was liked by everyone . . . Do you suppose it might have been arson?'

'I'm not here to suppose, but to investigate. And I don't need any help from you, so I suggest you let me get on with my job and you two get on with yours, which is selling books. You're free to go now. If I need you again I'll let you know. Have I made myself quite clear, Monsieur Legris?'

'Clear as day, Inspector. Incidentally, am I right in thinking that you've given up cachous?'

'When I heard you two were coming, I decided I needed a smoke to calm my nerves.'

Kenji walked slowly across Pont Neuf with a stooping gait. Victor's heart went out to him. He fell into step beside him.

'You were fond of Pierre Andrésy, weren't you?'

'Yes. How absurd and pathetic,' he murmured.

'I beg your pardon?'

'Ashes. They're all that remain of a man, of his dreams and aspirations.'

Victor resisted the urge to place his hand on Kenji's arm; displays of affection played no part in their relationship. He leant over the parapet and watched a steamboat ferrying its passengers along the river Seine, from Charenton to Point du Jour. Inspector Lecacheur's insinuations had aroused his curiosity. What if it hadn't been an accident? What if . . . ? Another case? It wouldn't be easy. His thoughts returned to Tasha. He'd curbed his fondness for mysteries out of love for her, and it frustrated him. He lit a cigarette and remained pensive, mechanically clicking his lighter on and off. No! No more cases; a promise was a promise.

'Inspector Lecacheur asked me if I knew of any enemies he might have had. That's absurd! It can't have been arson. Everybody held him in the highest esteem!' said Kenji.

'I suppose he's just doing his job. He has to explore every avenue. But you're right. In Monsieur Andrésy's case it does seem absurd. Did he have any relatives?'

'A distant cousin in the country.'

'Would you care for a cordial, Kenji?'

'No. I'm concerned about Iris; she's taken to going out in the afternoons – I've no idea where. And she's not eating properly. She's going to make herself ill. I knew it: lovers in disarray will a wedding delay. I don't feel I'm being a very good father, but what can I do? She won't listen to me. Couldn't you . . . ?'

'I've given Joseph a talking to, but he won't budge. I think he feels as if he's an ugly duckling. If Iris agreed to make the first move, it would restore his injured lover's pride.'

'Eat up, little ones, eat up! Gobble it all down and grow nice and plump then we can eat you!'

Mother Chickweed raised her voice above the cackle in the poultry yard.

'Monsieur Frédéric, your coffee's ready. I'm leaving now.'

Frédéric Daglan woke with a start. For a split second he imagined that he was back in Batignolles at 108, Rue des Dames, where he rented a bedsitting room. The sight of his light-coloured suit hanging from a dismantled sideboard brought him back to reality. He threw off the coverlet, pulled on his trousers, shirt and shoes and left the shed. On a makeshift table beneath a shady arbour he found a pot of coffee, a bowl and a round loaf. He sat down and cut himself a slice of bread. He'd waited long enough, now it was time to act. First he'd call at Anchise's place and borrow his case of liquor samples. Then he'd be ready to find the witness.

'I've been hoodwinked, but it's not too late – I can still fight back.'

He went to wash his face at the pump.

On Sundays, those who were able to leave the city streets would go up to the ramparts with their families. From there, they liked to think they could see green fields and misty forests. In the distance they could just make out the river Seine with its barges sailing towards the sea. There were merry-go-rounds, sweet sellers, and open-air cafés serving mussels and cheap wine. In springtime when the grass was still green there was even a sprinkling of daisies. Shop girls and maidservants enjoyed a few hours' rest from their drudgery. All they saw of the city was the backs of shops and stifling kitchens, but up here they could cherish their shallow dreams of marrying a butcher's boy or a grocer's assistant, of escaping from under the thumb of their employers, of being free at last!

Frédéric Daglan enjoyed roaming over that man-made hill and mingling with society's outcasts, whom he saw as his brothers in humanity. A little girl wearing a folded newspaper as a sun hat was leading a procession of goats. A donkey, its spine bent out of shape, its coat marked from the harness, basked in the sun. A man hurtled down the slope to the delight of a little boy on his back. Below, mounds of refuse spewed out by the city lay piled up in the ditches.

It was muggy. Frédéric took off his jacket. When he looked closely at what was going on around him, it seemed as unreal as the memory of a dream. And yet while you were still dreaming the most illogical situations seemed perfectly normal.

His jacket slung over his shoulder, he reached the outlying boulevards. The city's early-morning symphony had begun: horses yoked to dustcarts hammered on the cobbles with their hooves, the din of carts and lorries drowned out the harsh voices of the hawkers. A woman wearing an old coat and a grubby night cap came out of a tin-roofed hovel and emptied a slop pail into the gutter, the handle of her bucket falling back with a clang as a cockerel's shrill crows rang out.

'Spare a coin for a miserable beggar, Monsieur. My insides are crying out for food. I'm on my uppers and supper's a stranger to me now. For the last two years one meal a day is all I get.'

Frédéric Daglan slipped a ragged man with a bright-red nose a coin. He skirted round the blackish puddles and reached Porte de Clignancourt. The streets were dirty and the breeze brought with it a dusty smell. He felt a sudden thud of panic. What would he do when he found the witness?

The demon drink will kill you
But without it you'll die just the same

was written above the bar.

Frédéric Daglan stood in the doorway of Chez Kiki on the corner of Rue du Faubourg-Saint-Antoine and Rue Chevreul. Outside, a few spindle trees shielded a row of tables. Inside, a small area was separated from the main room by a glass partition. In the middle of the larger room stood a stove and, at the back, the bar. On weekday evenings, at about five o'clock, local shopkeepers would arrive and take over the tables, benches and chairs. They jealously saved places for their partners who would turn up like clockwork to play manille, black jack, dominoes and backgammon. The smaller room was reserved for casual customers. On the left of the main room sat the card players and on the right those wishing to talk or read the newspaper. Everybody had their appointed place on a bench or a chair and no one ever changed seats. The waiter was conversant with every customer's needs and it made his job easier.

The owner of the establishment, a stout woman of about

thirty-five who wore her blonde hair in a bun with a fringe, was sitting by the till knitting. At that time of the morning, apart from a young soldier composing a letter, the café was empty.

'Are you the owner?'

The plump woman stopped her knitting, calmly looked Frédéric Daglan up and down and, liking what she saw, replied with a half-smile, 'Yes, I'm Madame Mathias. What can I do for you?'

Frédéric Daglan smiled back. She had a friendly, straight-forward manner that boded well. Daglan was a smooth talker. He could put on a refined, even aristocratic air or pass himself off as a man of the people.

'An amusing motto,' he commented, pointing to the sign.

'That came from my grandfather. He fought in the Crimean War. It's a Russian proverb, which says what it means.'

'I know, drink kills us slowly but who cares since we're not in a hurry.'

'You don't say! Are you from around here?'

'Not really, I'm just passing through. I'm a travelling salesman – I sell spirits. I can offer you very competitive prices.'

'I'm all stocked up.'

'That's a shame. I must have been born under an unlucky star. I always seem to arrive too late.'

'Well, let's have a look. I may be able to help.'

Frédéric Daglan opened the lid of his case, which was lined with miniature bottles.

'Top quality, Madame.'

'I believe you, but my customers have tough insides – they go for the green fairy or cheap red wine. I won't sell any fine cognacs or armagnacs in here, my good fellow. You'd do better to try the bars on the Boulevards.'

'Never mind. I'll have a coffee and then I'll take your advice.'

'So you called in by chance, did you?' she asked, subtly pulling down the front of her blouse.

'Yes, just trying my luck, I've been to the taverns in Faubourg Saint-Antoine *pedibus cum jambis*, but nothing doing. Tell me, am I mistaken or does the name of your café, Chez Kiki, sound familiar?'

'Well, there was the incident.'

'What incident?'

'When that nice Monsieur Grandjean, the enamellist from Rue des Boulets, was murdered. It was in all the papers. He came here every morning for his coffee. He used to tease Fernand, he's our waiter: "A white coffee please, Fernand. In the cup not in the saucer!"'

'Were you there?'

Madame Mathias cracked her knuckles and poured two glasses of white wine.

'Yes, my good fellow, I was the first to arrive on the scene. There was blood everywhere, before they cleaned it up of course. Upon my word! I still get dreadfully upset when I talk about it. Feel,' she said, seizing his hand and placing it over her heart.

'It is beating very fast,' agreed Frédéric Daglan, his hand lingering on her ample bosom, which heaved like a rolling sea at his touch.

Madame Mathias gave a sigh and Frédéric Daglan took his hand away.

'Oh, you naughty man,' she simpered, 'you've got me all flustered. I can't remember what I was saying.'

'Do go on, you're an excellent storyteller,' he murmured, leaning closer to her.

'Oh yes, I'll never forget those staring eyes. I screamed every bit as loud as Josette Fatou. She's the one who alerted the whole neighbourhood – she saw the whole thing. I went out and calmed her down; she was hysterical, and with good reason. I told Fernand: "Go and fetch the police." Ah! We have so little – we should have some fun when we can, eh, my good fellow?'

'Josette? Who's Josette?'

'A little dark-skinned flower girl who lives in Rue des Boulets.'

'Did she see the murderer?'

'Who knows? She swears she didn't, but understandably she's scared. Just imagine if he came back to shut her up. Have another glass of Sancerre – on the house.'

'It's very kind of you, Madame, but I really must be going,' he said wearily.

'Let me twist your arm. There are no customers at this time of day. Stay to lunch. I'll make you a potato omelette. You'll never taste better.'

Seeing that he was wavering, she added, 'My cooking is like music; it soothes the stomach. And who knows,' she said, lightly brushing his sample case with her fingers, 'I may even change my mind.'

She chuckled and looked at him archly. 'The sad truth is that I've been a widow a long time, and at my age a woman gets lonely . . .'

Micheline Ballu pulled on her cotton stockings.

'It's going to rain,' she muttered. 'My corns are giving me gyp – that's a sure sign.'

She went over to the window, flopped into her armchair and surveyed the coming dawn.

'Well, a spot of rain would save me having to wash the courtyard. Cleaning really takes it out of you in this heat! Anyway, it rains every other Bastille Day without fail.'

She would begin by emptying the dustbins then wait for the postman. After that she'd heat up some coffee and finish reading her serial. The years had flown by since her poor husband Onésime had died, and her rheumatism was so bad now that she dreaded the day she'd no longer be able to carry out the tasks required of her. The landlord had already made it plain that he was doing her an enormous favour by allowing her to manage his building all on her own. With only one living relative – her cousin Alphonse, who was in the army and always on the move – what would become of her if her services were no longer needed? Thank heavens for that nice Monsieur Legris – such a kind and considerate gentleman. He'd promised her the free use of a maid's room he owned on the top floor of the building so that she wouldn't be forced to leave her beloved neighbourhood.

She put on her old slippers. Since poor Onésime had died, she'd grown stout and her face, once graceful, had become bloated and jowly. She drew some consolation from the knowledge that her friend Euphrosine was on the same slippery slope. It created a bond between them, like an old couple, sharing confidences, falling out with each other, making up, each alert to the slightest hint of a reproach from the other.

Micheline Ballu hauled herself up out of her chair.

'There are no two ways about it, life's a rotten joke and the last laugh is on us! Our bodies grow dilapidated but inside we still feel fifteen.'

Rue Visconti ran along between Rue de Seine and Rue Bonaparte. The house where Madame Pignot and her son lived was located in the narrowest part of the street. A studded door led into a cobbled courtyard where stables once used as coach houses had since been transformed into sheds.

One of these, adjoining the old lodge of a seventeenth-century nobleman's house, was Joseph's study, his refuge, crammed with books, magazines, newspapers and military paraphernalia from the Franco-Prussian War. This ivory tower gave on to the two-bedroomed ground-floor apartment and kitchen he shared with his mother, Euphrosine, former costermonger now housekeeper to her son's bosses, Monsieur Mori and Monsieur Legris.

Just inside the entrance to the apartment stood a small stone privy, which Euphrosine called either her house of ease or her *buen retiro* – an expression in vogue among the upper classes. This relic from the Age of Enlightenment was her pride and joy, despite not having a flushing mechanism. The wooden seat with its acanthus-leaf design and the chipped pink marble bowl offered a degree of comfort that was only found in middle-class homes. The biggest drawbacks were the smell and the flies, which in stormy weather would spill over into the bedrooms. Euphrosine tackled these twin pests with copious amounts of water and ammonia, a product that irritated the mucous membranes. For Joseph this chamber, which even the king entered on foot, was a godsend: he could lock himself in there for ages and dream up new plots for his serialised novels away from his mother's prying eyes.

'Run along, pet! I'm going to give your father's museum a good scrubbing before it gets too hot. It's the early bird who catches the worm.'

'And why not the owl?' protested Joseph, packing up his things and leaving the room.

Armed with a duster, shovel and broom, Euphrosine began her relentless assault on his sanctuary.

'Jesus, Mary and Joseph! Ah! The cross I have to bear! I am the most unfortunate of souls!'

She glanced up at the crucifix wedged between two piles of journals, and rubbed her back before kneeling awkwardly.

'Lord, have mercy on me for I have sinned. I know very well that a fault confessed is half redressed, but however will I explain to my boy that me and his dad lived outside the sacraments of marriage? I'm afraid it might drive him to despair if he finds out that in the eyes of the law I'm still Mademoiselle Courlac. He's such a sensitive soul!'

She rose to her feet and half-heartedly dusted a sideboard then appealed despondently to the crucifix.

'And while I think of it, try to make him a bit more tolerant, and force him to be less harsh on Mademoiselle Iris. Let them get married and give me some grandchildren, even if they do look Chinese. *Amen,* thy will be done.'

Feeling more cheerful, she began whistling the first few bars of *Les Cuirassiers de Reichshoffen*[26] as she set about cleaning with gusto.

Joseph was meditating on the edge of the toilet seat. His novel had been languishing in the doldrums since his love life had turned sour. He was finding it extremely difficult to think up what might happen next in *Thule's Golden Chalice*!

'Concentrate. Frida von Glockenspiel is in the cellar. Her mastiff is scrabbling furiously at the floor. Where do the human shinbones that the mutt digs up come from?' he pondered.

His gaze fell on the wodge of newspaper cut into squares that was hanging from a hook to the right of the toilet. He tore one off and read under his breath:

'Nobody knew that the man strolling beneath the arcades on Rue de Rivoli had once been a renowned writer. Alas, fame is all too fleeting! An author's words are written on the wind.[27]

To be continued in the next issue[28]

'There's no danger of that happening to me. They'll still be talking about my *Chalice* in 1950!'

He pulled off another square. In the middle of the advertisements section, a notice framed in black jumped out at him.

Cousin Léopardus
invites friends and customers of Monsieur Pierre
Andrésy, bookbinder of Rue Monsieur-le-Prince,
Paris, to attend his funeral at La Chapelle Cemetery
on 25 May.

'For the blossom in May beckons us from the fields.'

Stunned, Joseph reread the text. Impossible! The fire had only happened last Wednesday!

He searched frantically for the name of the newspaper as he tore the squares off the hook. He crammed the whole lot into his pockets and raced back to his study.

Euphrosine had mounted a successful operation and the dust had been routed. A sprig of anemones brightened up the rows of books and magazines next to the gleaming spiked helmets and shell cartridges ready to pass muster. The cretonne curtain was drawn across the window.

Joseph made a quick assessment of the damage: an urgent assignment would require returning the room to its former chaos, which was key to his creativity.

'I hope you haven't used any of *my* newspapers for toilet paper!' he yelled.

'May God strike me down if I ever dare touch your things, pet! Madame Ballu lets me have *Le Figaro* once she's done reading her serial. You should be grateful to have them at hand instead of grumbling. And don't give me that tragic look! Just like an old bachelor with his quirky habits! Monsieur's breakfast is served.'

'Do you know the dates for these *Figaro*s?'

'How should I know? I only cut them up for toilet paper. You'll have to ask Madame Ballu!'

Joseph, his mouth twisted in a bitter smile, couldn't help himself and declared, 'I wish I was an orphan!'

This was the last straw. Euphrosine's face turned bright red.

'And to think I work my fingers to the bone day in day out, washing his clothes, cooking him nice meals, slaving away and all for what? Just so that I can pick up the pieces!'

'What pieces?'

'The pieces of your broken marriage! Oh, I'll have a clear conscience when I leave this world. I bled myself dry to bring up this great oaf. I made sacrifices. I never took up with another man. And this is what I get for giving up life's pleasures. Monsieur refuses to make me a grandmother!'

Euphrosine Pignot beat her chest vehemently.

'I can forget about bouncing babies on my knee, even if they are half Japanese half Charentais!'

She went away grumbling to herself, 'Oh, the ungrateful brat! This is the thanks I get for giving him a nice new toilet! Honestly!'

Resigned, Joseph placed the scraps of newspaper on his desk and slipped the death notice into his jotter.

'I tell you, Madame Primolin, these students! The government's closed the local trade union office. Talk about a hullabaloo!'

'My husband is very concerned. I expect we'll be going to stay with our cousins in Ville-d'Avray,' replied an elderly lady with a sigh, before beginning her climb to the fourth floor.

'That's right, fly away, little birds, it'll make less work for me,' muttered Madame Ballu, bumping into Joseph with the dustbin she was pushing.

'Watch where you're going, lad!'

'Sorry. I came to ask about the copies of *Le Figaro* you gave my mother. Do you know the date they came out?'

'It's written on them.'

'They've been torn up so it's impossible to tell.'

'Well, it's nice to know my gifts are appreciated! I gave her a huge pile. The tenant on the third floor lets me have them. I love the serials. The one I'm reading now is terribly sad. It's about an old writer who . . . That reminds me, how's your serial going?'

'I'm about to finish it. About those newspapers, do you have any idea of the date?'

'The beginning of the month.'

'Which month?'

'This month of course, July!'

Joseph hurried off to open the bookshop, leaving the concierge standing there ranting at the dustbin about the general decline in manners.

The guardian angel of shop assistants was watching over Jojo: Monsieur Mori had gone out and Monsieur Legris was sailing up and down on his bicycle between Debauve & Gallais, purveyors of fine toiletries, and the bookshop.

'Boss, I've something most peculiar to show you.'

He handed the notice to Victor, who examined it critically.

'The typesetter was probably in his cups. I say, it seems Salomé de Flavignol has had a revelation. Now that Guy de Maupassant is dead she wants to read his complete works. Kenji has made up a parcel for delivery this morning.'

'Is that all you can say?' Joseph was fuming. His boss, who fancied himself a super-sleuth, was pooh-poohing his discoveries.

'It makes no sense, Joseph! Pierre Andrésy died on 5 July so the date of the funeral couldn't possibly be 25 May. I don't suppose they'd hold his corpse for burial until next spring. You really shouldn't believe everything you read in the newspapers.'

Narrowing his eyes, Joseph snatched up his cap and the parcel of books.

'Well, if that's the way it is, I'm off. It's stifling in here!'

Jojo stormed out. Victor leant on the counter, resting his chin on his clenched fists. A shadow danced before him, beckoning. No! He wouldn't give in to his old demon. He'd promised Tasha: no more cases.

'*Abandon all hope, ye who enter here,*' Jojo murmured, quoting Dante.

He had got shot of the parcel at Mademoiselle Flavignol's house and, acting on a whim, had dipped into his own purse for the cab fare to Porte de la Chapelle.

After wandering about for quarter of an hour looking for the phantom cemetery, he asked directions from an old tramp who was sharing a piece of cheese rind with his dog.

'Cross the ramparts and go up Rue de la Chapelle then turn

off when you reach Chemin des Poissonniers. You'll find your city of the dead at Saint-Ouen!'

Joseph wandered through a maze of rusty sooty railway tracks, lost his way, then reached Rue du Pré-Maudit,[29] which he left as fast as he could. He walked back past buildings covered in obscene graffiti, seedy hotels and vacant lots over-grown with wild oats, where circus strongmen were rehearsing. Behind the Ceinture line station stood the grim bulk of a railway arch. He passed some alarming figures: ragged girls on their way to buy groceries; pimps wearing espadrilles, a cigarette hanging out of their mouths; a group of vagrants, shivering after a night spent under the stars, heading for the slopes of the old ramparts.

Beyond this Wall of China, he found himself surrounded by a patchwork of factories and kitchen gardens. The gardens were so verdant and filled with flowers that, had it not been for the tall factory chimneys marking out the road, he would have believed himself transported to the countryside. Butterflies danced above the cabbages and buttercups, and a few cows stood in a meadow.

A funeral procession jolted down the avenues of the cemetery, the hangings on the hearse covered in a film of grey dust. The coffin was lowered, the family dispersed, the gravediggers filled in the hole.

Joseph decided that rather than search for a hypothetical grave, he would ask the keeper. The man consulted a register: there was no Pierre Andrésy buried there.

Joseph turned on his heel, muttering to himself.

'This needs investigating, there's definitely something fishy going on here. That was no typo. I'm going to pop in to *Le Figaro*, if only to annoy the boss.'

Caught up in his reflections, he walked past a small drinking fountain where a man who looked a little too smartly dressed for the neighbourhood had stopped to quench his thirst. A few small children holding jugs waited their turn.

Frédéric Daglan wiped his moustache, and walked over to a bistro where he sat down at an outside table and ordered a coffee. He pulled three newspapers from his pocket and began reading one of them. As he perused the second, he nearly sent his cup flying. Between a domestic incident and a drowning was a report about the disappearance of a printer named Paul Theneuil. His book-keeper had found a mysterious message in his business correspondence that mentioned a leopard.

A panting dog stopped to lap at the water running along the gutter. The whole world was thirsty.

Victor skimmed a pebble across the lake, disturbing the smooth surface of the water and scattering the ducks, which quacked furiously. He didn't pause to admire the reproduction of the Temple of the Sybil at Tivoli perched on the summit of an artificial cliff, but walked on towards the exit from Buttes-Chaumont. Joseph had had the nerve to return to the shop late in the afternoon with a smirk on his face. That lad was becoming a nuisance, and the prospect of having him as a brother-in-law was exasperating. Although nothing seemed less sure than that union. In two minds as to whether he should bring about its definitive end or restore his sister's happiness, Victor turned into Rue des Dunes.

The studio and living quarters he'd helped Djina Kherson rent were situated on the first floor of a plush apartment building. When he rang the bell Tasha's mother came to the door; she'd dispensed with a maid in order to save money. It was a point of honour with her to do her own housework, which in a cramped three-room apartment was quickly accomplished in any case. As for the studio, a functional room containing a few chairs and easels, it was accessible from the hallway.

Victor was surprised to find not only Tasha but also Iris and Kenji sitting around a samovar in the living room. Djina, who looked scarcely older than her daughter, was wearing a gathered skirt and a blouse decorated with Russian embroidery.

Despite his show of polite disinterest, Kenji did not fool Victor, who could see the unsettling effect their hostess had on him. For her part, Djina paid him scant attention. She filled Victor's glass.

'I only have black tea,' she said.

Then she resumed her conversation with Tasha and Iris.

'I'm glad he's keeping busy. He needs to be active or he loses his will to live.'

She had a soft voice, with only a hint of an accent.

'Who are you talking about?' asked Victor.

'Pinkus. He's sent us a letter – he's going to pay you back,' replied Tasha.

'There's no hurry.'

'It's a matter of pride,' said Djina.

She picked up the letter and translated a passage:

'. . . In the end life here in America is not so very different from in Vilna: the poor die of poverty and the rich get richer, but I'm not complaining. I live in a two-roomed apartment on the Lower East Side. No more sewing on a machine fourteen hours a day in a garret in the Bronx. I've fallen on my feet . . .'

'He's gone into business with an Irishman who owns a gaming parlour. Imagine!' exclaimed Tasha.

'Do you mean he takes bets?' asked Kenji, with a sidelong glance at Djina.

'He would never stoop so low,' she replied curtly.

'They're planning to invest in a new type of camera that uses twenty-four photographic images to give the illusion of movement. It's on display at the Chicago World's Fair,' Tasha explained.

Djina consulted the letter, trying to decipher the word. 'An electric ta-chys-cope.[30] Do you know what that is, Monsieur Legris?'

'It must be a perfected version of the praxinoscope.'[31]

Djina went on:

'. . . the models we'll be offering the public are marvellous pieces of machinery and I'm sure they'll bring in a good revenue . . .

'Your father, the revolutionary, managing a bar!'

'That's unfair, Mother. What's wrong with him earning his living? It's not as if he's exploiting anyone. He hasn't renounced his ideals.'

'I'd love to see some of those moving pictures,' said Iris.

Delighted that she'd finally expressed an interest in something, Victor suggested, 'I'll take you to Théâtre Robert-Houdin. Are you intending to take up your watercolour classes again?'

'We've just agreed on a day,' said Djina. 'Come with me, my dears. The new paints I ordered arrived this morning.'

As they left the room, Kenji drew his chair alongside Victor's.

'An Oriental manuscript was sold at auction last week to the Bibliothèque Nationale. A friend from the Booksellers Circle told me. It almost certainly isn't ours, but . . .'

'You suspect Pierre Andrésy of having sold *Touty Namèh* before he died?'

'Of course not! It never even occurred to me.'

'Exactly when was it auctioned?'

'That's what I'm going to find out.'

What's come over these two? First Joseph, now Kenji. It must be catching! thought Victor as the women filed back in.

He remembered his vow to Tasha and felt suddenly annoyed; he'd promised to keep his word, yet he felt painfully like a bird which had had its wings clipped. Why couldn't she accept his need for freedom? He was mortified to think that he behaved the same way with her, but the difference was that he was motivated not by jealousy but by fear for her safety.

He glanced up. This time there was no mistaking it: Kenji looked positively bewitched at the sight of Djina.

If he fell in love with her, the family portrait would be complete.

CHAPTER FIVE

Thursday 13 July

THE steel structure framed patches of night sky, and hundreds of flickering lights pierced the darkness. In the middle of Les Halles, to the right of Église Saint-Eustache, the flower market was in full swing. Josette Fatou greeted Marinette, a porter with a pockmarked face. Marinette was over sixty but still able to carry her enormous baskets of berries. The daughter of a tightrope walker, she had started out as an acrobat and a bearded lady.

'Hurry, my little bird of the islands, the flower auction's starting,' she called out to Josette. 'What a face! Is anything the matter?'

'No, everything's fine,' Josette replied, forcing a smile.

'Hmm, not so sure about that,' muttered Marinette, as she watched the girl weave her way between a pile of white lilacs and a mound of violets.

'Sunshine in a bouquet, Mesdames, brought to you direct from the Côte d'Azur!'

One side was known as Nice and the other Paris, the latter stocked by gardeners coming from Ménilmontant, Montreuil, Vaugirard, Vanves and Charonne with their carefully packaged boxes.

Josette relaxed. Her inner turmoil subsided. At least there she was on home ground. Since the previous day, she had had the impression that some hidden force had sapped all her strength. Despite her exhaustion, she could not give up because no work meant no food. Once she had paid the weekly five-franc fee for the pushcart she used to wheel around her perfumed crop, and the four centimes for her street-trader's licence, there was not much left in her purse. Every day, she looked for the best spot at the best time of day, watching out for and trying to attract customers. Selling at La Madeleine, where customers came to buy the more exotic blooms, was not the same as selling at La Nation, where workers hurrying to the factories had far too many cares to take an interest in such trifles.

The best bargains were to be found in Paris: roses, camellias, gardenias and snowballs sold like hotcakes. The thick southern accent mingled with the coarse language of the working classes from the *faubourgs*. Amid gesticulations and guttural cries, they haggled over bunches of mimosa or daffodils, jasmine or carnations. Josette Fatou made her purchases as if in a trance. The murder that had taken place before her very eyes three weeks ago had made her feel very isolated from the world, and nothing could erase that scene from her mind.

Grey dawn rose above the still-sleeping city. Gaunt-looking women searched among the slimy remains for rotten vegetables to make into soup. A haulier with a red belt swigged a bottle of wine. Next to a coach entrance, Mother Bidoche stirred her beef and bean stew, and ladled out helpings to fill the hungry bellies gathered around her brazier.

'Get that down your throats – it'll warm your insides – I can't abide seeing famished folk.'

Josette returned to her cart. She stepped over a porter asleep on a sack and began arranging her flowers. The constant bustle and deafening row did not succeed in distracting her from her fears: she felt haunted by the man who had followed her the previous day. Of course, she had not realised at the time that he was watching her – he was just another early-morning passer-by, whose cap pulled down over his face had caught her eye for a split second.

Was he hiding somewhere in this crowd?

She trudged through the streets, shoulders hunched, her back stiff from the bumpy cobblestones, taking care not to let her cart slip or get knocked. She was an anonymous foot soldier among the six-thousand-strong army of street vendors, their customers made up of the privileged few who would think nothing of spending a hundred francs on flowers at the market, and the vast majority for whom five, ten, twenty francs of their daily budget represented an enormous sum.

At Place de la Bastille she overheard a conversation between two tramps.

'Have you eaten?'

'Yes, down at the mission, pea soup. Like bullets they were, with respect, fire 'em from a gun and you could kill a man.'

Her throat tightened with fear. A terrible thought had formed in her mind. Monsieur Grandjean's killer! He's coming for me. He won't stop until he gets me!

In Rue du Faubourg-Saint-Antoine, a boy sobbing inconsolably over a broken bottle brought back visions of her own childhood. All she could remember was her mother and all the men hovering around her. They never stayed in the house for very long, but she was made to wait outside until they left, crouched in the stairwell, surrounded by silence, her eyes shut tight to ward off her fears. The local children shouted cruel names at her and the gossips called her *piccaninny*, and she resented her mother deeply for that. She quickened her pace, trying desperately to drive out these painful thoughts . . . Her mother, on her sickbed, her strength gone, abandoned by everyone, had revealed to her the truth about the gruelling work on the sugar plantations in Guadeloupe, the boat trip over to France, her employer coming to her room every night, her subsequent pregnancy and dismissal. She had had to survive on the pittance he had given her, as one would toss scraps to a dog. Josette had been born and her dream of returning to the sun-kissed isle had dissolved in the desolate squalor.

Josette shook her head. Who did she hate most of all, her mother or the father she'd never known? Her dark skin or men? Men, without a doubt.

Friday 14 July

Victor and Tasha were taking a stroll beside the river Seine. To the west, the sky was tinged with purple. A soft breeze had finally brought some respite from the heat. They watched the water lapping at the riverbank as a barge sailed by. Victor appeared to remember something.

'Heavens, I almost forgot!'

He handed Tasha a little package. She tore off the wrapping paper. Inside was a small sketchbook with a worn cover, and a small box, which she opened. She looked up at him in amazement.

'It's wonderful, darling! Thank you!'

She was admiring a gold ring with a blue stone setting.

'It's an aquamarine. Do you like it?'

He watched her intently, his hands clasped behind his back. He looked like a little boy trying to sit up straight at the dinner table.

'I love it! What's the occasion?'

'Well, I know we met on 22 June, but I wanted to celebrate our anniversary a little later this year. When I first saw you four years ago in the Anglo-American bar at the Eiffel Tower, you had your hair in a bun under your hat decorated with daisies and you were sitting between Isidore Gouvier and Fifi Bas-Rhin, and . . . I fell head over heels in love with you.'

'That was when she was still Eudoxie Allard, before the demon cancan possessed her. And Antoine Clusel was there too, remember.'

'I only had eyes for you.'

'You bought me a vanilla ice-cream and invented some excuse to accompany me back to Rue Notre-Dame-de-Lorette in a cab.'

'You got out and left me in the middle of a traffic jam.'

'You followed me.'

'You knew I would!'

'I dearly hoped you would.'

'I thought: she is meant for me – she is so different from the women I know.'

'What makes me so different?'

'It's hard to explain . . . You're self-contained, often inaccessible, wrapped up in your own world – from which I feel excluded at times . . .'

There was a catch in his voice.

'I've never felt this way about anybody else. You're so unpredictable, I feel as though I'm on a tightrope when I'm with you, and yet I suppose that is what satisfies my need for change. If I asked you what makes me different from other men, would you be able to tell me?'

'Yes,' she replied, 'I think so.'

They continued walking in the direction of Pont de Solférino.

'So, you had my old sketchbook all along! I've been looking for that everywhere.'

'It's a precious object. I'm returning it to you to commemorate the beginning of our life together.'

She turned the pages and examined a sketch of a woman sprawled over a bench.

'Eugénie Patinot,' she breathed, 'your first case. Victor, promise me you'll never . . .'

'You must have liked me, too. Look, you sketched my face. Tasha . . .'

She could tell that he was dying to ask her to marry him. She headed him off.

'I'm already yours!'

'I know. Don't worry I'm not planning to pop the question.'

'Are you upset?'

'No, but I won't give up. If necessary, I'll even swear before a notary never to try to stop you pursuing your career.'

'Now you know what it is I love about you, darling. I've found in you a soulmate who communicates his energy, warmth and enthusiasm to me. You ask so much of life. It stimulates me.'

They sealed their silent agreement with a passionate embrace: there would be no more criminal investigations and no more talk of marriage.

'I'll take you out to dinner. Let's go to the Eiffel Tower,' he suggested.

'But, Victor, you know you can't stand going up there.'

'In that case let's go to La Concorde. The Venetian festival will be starting soon . . .'

'Or we could just stay here. Look! What's going on over there?'

A row of people were leaning over the guardrail of the bridge watching a dog groomer at work on Quai des Tuileries below, next to a cockleshell boat with a tiny cabin. An assistant held the customer, a black poodle, across his knees while the dog groomer began clipping off the black fur, leaving four pompoms on its legs, a girdle round its chest, breeches on its haunches. Once the effect of a pantomime lion had been achieved, the assistant loosened the piece of cord around the animal's muzzle. The last customer of the day, looking sheepish, shook itself before being led away by a servant. The crowd of amused onlookers dispersed

'To think there's some folk that can waste ten francs on a stupid mutt while others have nothing to eat!' hissed a toothless hag.

In response to this remark, the dog shearer's assistant lit a spirit stove and began frying a panful of sausages. The delicious smell reached Tasha's nostrils.

'Do you think they'd sell us some?'

'But that's their supper . . .'

'They've got more than enough for four! Go and ask!'

Victor hesitated then gave in. The fellow doing the frying listened to his request, reflected for a moment then called out, 'Jean-Marie! There's a pair of hungry punters here with an eye on our dinner!'

The dog groomer emerged from his boat and after a brief exchange with Victor agreed to let them have two sausages, half a baguette and a jug of wine. He also lent them a couple of glasses.

Tasha declared that she far preferred their impromptu picnic to a table on the first floor of the Eiffel Tower. As they stood eating near the river Seine, they heard a murmur like a tidal bore and a wave of revellers invaded Quai des Tuileries. Jean-Marie showered the revellers with insults as they began tossing bangers at the sides of his boat. Victor became alarmed. The firecrackers going off all around reawakened his fears of an anarchist outrage. And where was Tasha? He suddenly couldn't see her! For a moment he thought she'd been swept away by the revellers. He stood on tiptoe and peered over the bobbing heads. He was already panicking when he felt himself being carried away. Just when he'd decided to give up trying to plug his ears and hold on to his wine glass at the same time, Tasha popped up and proposed a toast.

'Here's to us!'

The revellers finally moved on, leaving the way clear back

up the bank. They returned the jug and glasses to their owner. Tasha began pushing a small cardboard tube around with her foot.

'Are you playing hopscotch?' Victor said.

She picked up the tube and began drawing a book with two arched eyebrows and a bushy moustache, and a paintbrush in a skirt and boots.

V and T, till death us do part, she wrote.

'Is that supposed to be me? Those whiskers are worthy of a Gaul!'

'It's a caricature meant to show how unbearable I find that unspoken law which forces men to hide their upper lip.'

'It's supposed to affirm male virility in the face of female virtue.'

'Is it really! . . . Shall we go?'

'Don't you want to see the fireworks?'

'I'd rather you gave me a mouth-watering dessert at home. Come on.'

Night eclipsed the sun, which had easily pushed temperatures above thirty degrees in the shade. The smells emanating from the jubilant crowd combined with the aroma of fried food and the fragrant smell of peppermint rock. In the streets decked with tricoloured paper lanterns, shopkeepers, clerks and workers twirled to the rhythms of the accordion and the brass bands; couples danced with gay abandon. Chez Kiki was teeming. Madame Mathias looked on dotingly at the man helping Fernand.

Frédéric Daglan leant over the counter.

'Three beers and two white wines!' he cried, winking at the landlady.

Racing over to the smaller of the two rooms, tray aloft, he bumped into a dark-skinned girl. He moved out of her way then turned to look at her.

Josette Fatou stood motionless. Was he the man who had been following her for the past two days? Beads of sweat stood out on her upper lip in the heat. She felt that dreadful sense of danger again. What did he want from her? Who was he? She'd never seen him at Kiki's before. What should she do? Suddenly overcome by a fit of trembling and giddiness, she made her way over to the bar.

'What is it, Josette dear? Are you unwell?'

'No, no, it's just the noise, the crowds . . .'

'Good for business, isn't it? Here, have some lemonade – it'll perk you up.'

'Have you hired a new waiter?'

Had she sounded too urgent? Seemed overly surprised?

'I should be so lucky,' replied Madame Mathias, chuckling. 'He's a good friend of mine. Go and sit outside; it's cooler under the trees.'

Saturday morning, 15 July

A cart carrying stone blocks to repair a building had blocked narrow Rue Visconti. Joseph went out to complain to the two stonemasons who were unloading the cart outside number 24, former abode of Jean Racine and Mademoiselle Clairon.

'How long do we have to put up with this din?'

The builders, who were Italians, carried on working and singing a Neapolitan song at the tops of their voices.

'Don't waste your breath – they can't understand a word you say,' advised Père Huchet, the owner of a stall selling sparkling wine at ten centimes a glass.

Fuming, Joseph went back indoors and grabbed some bread from the kitchen to plug his ears with the soft part before returning to his study. He thanked his mother for having bought the fresh loaf before going to prepare lunch at Rue des Saints-Pères, where he didn't have to begin work until midday. Chewing on the end of his fountain pen, the only gift from Iris to which he was still attached, he cursed the bad luck dogging his literary creation, and tried to gather his thoughts.

'"Frida von Glockenspiel heard a creak and swung round brandishing a rolling pin like a club. Footsteps echoed at the back of the keep. Éleuthère bared his teeth. Who was approaching? . . ." *That is the question*,' he murmured with a sigh.

He pushed away the notebook entitled *Thules's Golden Chalice* and opened his scrapbook of news items, which he relied on for inspiration. The last two cuttings he'd added had come unstuck. He smoothed them out with his forefinger.

'"There are still no clues in the case of the murder victim, Léopold Grandjean, stabbed on 21 June . . . 'Like amber, musk, benzoin and incense, May has made of ours a solitary pursuit,'"' Joseph read out under his breath. '""Can an Ethiopian change the colour of his skin any more than a leopard his spots?'"'

He went on to read the death notice.

'"Cousin Léopardus invites friends and customers of Monsieur Pierre Andrésy, bookbinder of Rue Monsieur-le-Prince, Paris, to attend his funeral at La Chapelle cemetery on 25 May. 'For the blossom in May beckons us from the fields.'"'

He repeated, puzzled, 'The blossom in May . . . Cousin Léopardus . . . Can an Ethiopian change his skin any more than a leopard his spots? Why the insistence on animals in these two seemingly unrelated texts? And May is also mentioned twice. A leopard in May. Something to do with the zodiac? May . . . that's Taurus the bull and Gemini and the twins. A March hare or an April fool? I've no idea what this means, but I'm going to find out.'

Number 26 was an overly ornate building made of old grey stone on the corner of Rue Drouot and Rue de Provence in the heart of the boulevard district. In a niche above the entrance, a bronze statuette of Figaro from *The Barber of Seville* was exposed to the improprieties of the pigeons. Joseph nodded at him, and, to make himself feel braver, boosted his courage by recalling that he was a detective *di qualita*. He walked through the newsroom of the illustrious newspaper to where a dejected-looking secretary sat. Despite his slight hunch, Joseph was an attractive young man and brought out a protective instinct in the opposite sex. He put on his most forlorn look – tousled hair, doleful eyes – and sighed loudly.

'Mademoiselle, you've no idea how wretched I feel . . . Outside people laugh and sing while I . . . While I'm mourning the passing of my beloved uncle, who was like a father to me.

This I might be able to bear, but to think that some crank could find no better way of amusing himself than by giving you false information . . . !'

He whipped out the notice. The young girl, looking up, hurriedly straightened the satin-brimmed hat that covered her curls.

'I just write out the text, count the words and direct the customers to the cashier. Once they've paid their one franc fifty centimes per line containing thirty-four words and shown me their receipt, I send their message on to the printer. I'm not expected to do any more than that, Monsieur.'

But if you're nice to me there's no knowing what I might do for you, her expression suggested.

'Even so, Mademoiselle, giving notice of a funeral on 25 May for a fellow who breathed his last gasp on 5 July is no small blunder.'

'Oh, I've seen worse. How about: "Generous reward for the finder of Trompette, a Brahmapoutra chicken recently gone missing in the vicinity of Sainte-Geneviève mountain." In comparison to yours . . .'

'You have to admit, it's curious.'

'I'm not paid to be curious. All they ask of me is to publish. The number of nutcases who come through here, it's amazing!'

'I sympathise, Mademoiselle, and I admire your dedication. But if you could just check the date when this bizarre notice was placed, I'd be eternally grateful.'

She shrugged and began rummaging through a couple of desk drawers.

'How does it begin?'

'Cousin Léopardus requests . . .'

'L, L, L . . . Here it is. Somebody placed the notice on 4 July but don't ask me who. Is there anything else?'

'Do you really have no recollection of who placed it?'

The young girl moistened her lips then examined her nails.

'Straight off I'd say no, though sometimes I only need a little something, a sorbet or a drink to refresh my memory. I get off for lunch at one, so if you fancy . . .'

She blushed and, too nervous to look the irresistible fair-haired young man in the eye, began stamping a pile of forms.

Joseph beat a cowardly retreat.

'Poor girl, she tried and failed . . . A pretty thing, too. But I'm not as fickle as some people I know. I'll never pay for a favour in kind . . . 4 July, the day before the fire! I don't get it. Monsieur Anatole France is right: "We are only troubled by what we do not understand." I must resolve to look into this affair with Monsieur Legris's help. Even though his brain cells are painfully slow to get going, once they're fully firing there's no stopping him. When he's on form that is . . .'

Wrapped up in his thoughts, he reached Notre-Dame-de-Lorette. He was filled with sadness as he recalled the stroll he had taken there with a friend who had died under tragic circumstances.

'Denise de Louarn[32] . . . Valentine . . . Let's be honest, women find me attractive. Mademoiselle Tasha would doubtless have succumbed to my charms had it not been for Monsieur Victor. She used to call me her *moujik*. That's a point, Mademoiselle Tasha lives near here. With any luck at this time of day I'll find the lovebird still in his nest!'

Scarcely had he reached Rue Fontaine, when a clap of thunder boomed above his head. Rain poured down over the city. Joseph took shelter under the awning of a grocer's and waited impatiently for the torrent to subside. 'Hell's bells!' he shouted as a passing cab splashed him with muddy water. People scurried past, slipping on the wet cobbles; umbrellas collided. A mewling came from below. A ball of wet fur was rubbing itself against the hem of his trouser leg.

'Hey, stop that flea bag, clear off!'

A fawn mask with two little yellow eyes staring up at him plaintively broke down his resistance. He picked up the kitten and held it in his arms; he could feel its heart beating through his frock coat. One stroke was enough to set off a loud purring, and a rough tongue licked his wrist.

'Where did you come from, puss? Is he yours?' he asked a small girl standing next to him in the open doorway of the shop.

She had a terrible squint and began tapping on one of the shop-front mouldings.

> *'Onion soup's for boys*
> *Sorrel soup's for girls!*
> *Boys like toys*
> *Girls like pearls!'*

she chanted, much to the annoyance of her mother, who was busy serving a customer.

'Come back inside at once, you wicked child! You'll catch your death,' she called out.

'A great help,' groaned Joseph. 'Who does this clingy creature belong to? Hey, moth-eaten moggy, hop it!'

The kitten had snuggled up in his arms and was purring at full volume. Its muzzle and paws were white. As for its tail, it had a big kink in it and ended in a scrawny tuft that looked like it had been plucked.

'You're stuck with that alley cat, mister!' the little girl pronounced before disappearing into the shop.

After a night and a morning spent commemorating in bed the storming of the Bastille and the fête de la Fédération, Tasha had just said goodbye to Victor and pulled on a cotton smock when there was a knock at the door.

'Joseph! You're soaked.'

'To the skin! Is Monsieur Victor here?'

'You've just missed him. Oh! Isn't he gorgeous!'

'I picked him up in your street. I think he's hungry.'

He put the kitten down on the floor. It arched its back and took refuge under Tasha's skirts, purring like an engine.

'Have you seen his tail? It looks like a brush,' Joseph said.

'A proper artist's cat! He's superb with his little mask and stripy coat and white mittens . . . I'll go and fetch him some milk.'

While she was busy in the kitchen, Joseph, accompanied by his protégé, went to nose about in the entrance cluttered with canvas stretchers and books. His eye fell on a cardboard tube with charred edges lying on a pedestal table among the other bits and bobs. Tasha gave little brush-tail a saucer of milk, which he lapped up greedily.

'He's so funny-looking. I think I'll keep him.'

'You've taken a weight off my mind, Mademoiselle Tasha. Maman would have given me what for if I'd dared bring him home. What will Monsieur Legris say?'

'Well, Joseph, you know the expression: what a woman wants . . .'

Joseph had picked up the tube and was studying the drawings on it.

'We could have gone without streetlights for a month with the amount of Bengal lights they set off last night! Well, little brush-tail, is your tummy full? Would you be prepared to share my humble lodgings?' Tasha asked.

The kitten stopped preening itself and let out a loud *miaow*.

'Joseph, he said yes!'

'Maybe he speaks Russian and Japanese, too. You'll never be short of a penny with that clown around.'

Tasha scratched the kitten's belly then examined it more closely.

'Mm, I think he's got company . . . And what's more *he* is a *she*.'

'How can you tell?'

'There's a distinct lack of . . . How do you say that in French?'

'Er . . .'

'Male accoutrements. Little brush-tail, I hereby name you Kochka,' she announced.

'Kochka?'

'It means cat in Russian.'

'Well, Mademoiselle Tasha, Mademoiselle Kochka, I must

go. Maman will be here soon with your shopping and her army of mops . . .'

And, if I hurry, I can dally a wee bit at home before getting back to the grindstone in Rue des Saints-Pères, he thought as he said goodbye.

On his way home on the omnibus, Joseph had the niggling feeling that he had missed something important. However, rather like the phantom itching which no amount of scratching could relieve, the elusive thought kept escaping his grasp. It was only when he was shut away in his study, close to the crate he used for a desk, that an image materialised in his mind of a cardboard tube covered in caricatures identical to the ones lying between his pen and his novelist's notebook. This discovery sent an electric shock through his brain.

'Those tubes I found in the wreckage at Pierre Andrésy's shop! . . . Bengal lights? Roman candles? Blimey! What do you think, Papa?' he asked the photograph of the jolly-faced bookseller leaning up against a wall in Quai Voltaire. 'Might the blaze have been started by fireworks? You wouldn't know, eh?'

Joseph felt as if he were looking at the facts through murky water.

'But it doesn't make sense! Why would anybody let off fireworks ten days before Bastille Day? Unless it was deliberate . . . Good heavens! I've found a clue, I'm sure! I must let the boss know straight away.'

*

Intoxicated by speed, Victor was cycling along Boulevard Saint-Germain. His rubber-tyred chrome bicycle, fitted with a dynamo and a horn, filled him with pride. Perched on his sprung saddle, he dodged the traffic hold-ups. Farewell to interminable journeys and to sore feet!

The cobblestones raced beneath his wheels. At the corner of Rue Jacob stood the good ship Elzévir, where he was to take over the watch so that Kenji and Iris could spend the afternoon together. He allowed himself a calculated skid before mounting the pavement and rolling to a halt in front of number 18.

Of course Joseph was nowhere to be seen. Recently, he'd developed a casualness and laxity towards his work, which Victor found particularly irksome.

'I'll have to have a word.'

Having parked his precious bicycle at the back of the shop, he went upstairs to eat a plate of warm ratatouille washed down with a glass of white wine. When the door bell tinkled and a voice called out: 'Is anybody there?' he raced downstairs, intent on giving his assistant a piece of his mind. But Joseph wouldn't let him get a word in edgeways. He launched into a wild story about a death notice in *Le Figaro*, a leopard, the month of May and some empty tubes smelling of gunpowder.

The arrival of a customer stopped him in full flow. Scarcely had the young dandy, who had come to buy a copy of *Georges Brummel*[33] *and Dandyism*, left the premises than Victor said to his assistant, sardonically, 'May I point out that you're half an hour late.'

'I know, Boss, *mea culpa*. All I can tell you for sure is that such a long list of coincidences set my mind working. I found out that the notice wasn't a typo or the fault of a drunken typesetter. It was placed on 4 July, the day before the fire. As for who wrote it, I couldn't get a name.'

'So, correct me if I'm wrong, this twaddle is supposed to prove that Pierre Andrésy's death was a murder disguised as an accident?'

'There's another thing, Boss. On 21 June, an enamellist was murdered, stabbed to death. The police found a visiting card on his body. I bet you can't guess what it said!'

Victor placed his hand on the bust of Molière and prayed to heaven to give him patience. Joseph flicked through his jotter and read out, '"Like amber, musk, benzoin and incense, May has made of ours a solitary pursuit. Can an Ethiopian change the colour of his skin any more than a leopard his spots?" I checked in Paul-Émile Littré's Dictionary of the French Language. The first line is Baudelaire and the second the prophet Jeremiah. And the last line of the death notice, "For the blossom in May beckons us from the fields", is Victor Hugo.'

The silence that followed reminded Victor of when he fell into the Serpentine aged six. For a split second during which the world above was replaced by the stifling murky water, he'd been more terrified by his sudden deafness than by his fear of drowning.

'Boss? Boss?'

'Yes, Joseph, I'm listening.'

'Do you remember the beginning of the notice? "Cousin Léopardus . . ."'

Victor sat down at Kenji's desk and began tracing spirals on a blotter. What if he had drowned in the Serpentine that Sunday in 1866? What if everything he had experienced since that day had been a dream? The vision of Tasha's warm, sunny face appeared, and he felt reassured that he was alive.

'You're making it up, Joseph.'

'I didn't make up the empty cardboard tubes! I was wondering what they were, and so when I saw Mademoiselle Tasha's one with the sketches . . .'

'How the devil did you know Tasha had practised her talents on a Bengal light?'

'I stopped off this morning at Rue Fontaine, only you'd just left. Mademoiselle Tasha asked me in because I was soaked through and because I brought her . . . I brought you a small gift.'

He neglected to tell him what it was, worried that his boss might not appreciate the idea of living with a four-legged feline.

'So?'

'It struck me that the cardboard tubes I found at Monsieur Andrésy's shop were fireworks, and may have started the fire. I told you about it, only as usual you weren't listening!'

'Let's start again, Joseph. A few Bengal lights went off inside Pierre Andrésy's shop. And you've deduced from this that the sparks they gave off might have set oil ablaze?'

'They aren't Bengal lights, they're Roman candles, Boss, and Roman candles contain a mixture of gunpowder, saltpetre, sulphur, coal and any number of other combustible substances. I found three, maybe there were more. Ten or twenty of them could do a lot of damage.'

'Inspector Lecacheur hinted at arson, and . . .'

'He's on the right track, Boss, don't be pipped at the post by that . . .'

'Let me think,' replied Victor.

His intense concentration made him look as if he were frowning. He muttered, 'The wording on the death notice anticipating Pierre Andrésy's demise is similar to the wording on the visiting card left on the enamellist's corpse . . . Two murders, one murderer? We must study the pros and cons. Except that I did promise Tasha . . .' he concluded dreamily.

'Are we going to investigate, Boss?'

Joseph, his eyes shining, quivered impatiently as he watched for Victor's reaction. He looked like a dog waiting for a treat. Leaning over the desk with his mop of dishevelled hair, his expression was saying: Don't bore me with your silly crises of conscience – do I get the treat or not?

'We'll investigate, Joseph, but discreetly.'

'Yes, yes, yes, Boss! Nobody will get wind of what we're up to, especially not Mademoiselle Tasha. I certainly don't intend to let any women stand in my way!'

'We have two leads: Pierre Andrésy and the enamellist, what was his name again?'

'Léopold Grandjean.'

'His address?'

'He was knifed on Rue Chevreul. No doubt he lived around there. In any case an enamelling workshop should be easy to find.'

'Are you free tomorrow – it's Sunday?'

Joseph was about to say yes when he remembered he had promised to take his mother to the Folies-Dramatiques. A representative from Les Halles had given them free tickets to a matinee performance of *Cliquette* – a comedy in three acts.[34] They would have lunch beforehand at Gégène, in Les Halles. Euphrosine was so excited about their day out that he hadn't the heart to disappoint her.

'No. Worse luck!'

'That's too bad. We'll just have to put it off until Monday,' replied Victor.

For his part, he was sure of being able to get away from Tasha for an hour or two in order to go and nose about at Rue Monsieur-le-Prince.

'No point in worrying Monsieur Mori, mum's the word.'

'Count on me, Boss,' Joseph promised, delighted to be the sole accomplice of the famous Victor Legris.

CHAPTER SIX

Monday 17 July

ADOLPHE Esquirol's name suited him to a tee. With his prominent front teeth, rodent-like snout, red whiskers and pointed ears, he was the spitting image of a giant squirrel dressed in bell-bottomed trousers and a short jacket. Esquirol liked to think of his bookshop on Rue de la Sourdière as a tiny corner of Asia, which is why he wasn't at all surprised to see a Japanese gentleman walk through the door.

'Good day, Monsieur. I'm a fellow book dealer,' Kenji announced, presenting his card. 'I've been informed that at the beginning of this month the Biblothèque Nationale acquired at the Rue Drouot auction house a lot that belonged to you containing several Oriental manuscripts. May I enquire as to their origin?'

Adolphe Esquirol evaded the question, pushing out his lower lip and spreading his arms as if to say 'How the devil should I know?'

'Forgive my persistence. I simply wish to make sure that none of the works was entitled *Touty Namèh* or *The Parrot's Stories*. The auctioneer gave me an exhaustive inventory of the lot, which included a Persian manuscript with a missing first chapter and numerous miniature illustrations.'

The squirrel's brains began working; despite his slanting

eyes and his visiting card this fellow, whom he recognised from Rue Drouot, might be a police informer. And Adolphe Esquirol was loath to have his registers inspected.

'One accumulates so many documents of uncertain value over the years, and then one fine day one simply decides to get rid of the whole lot.'

'As a colleague I understand your reluctance to reveal your sources. Perhaps you could just tell me whether this unidentified text was sold to you and if so by whom.'

Adolphe Esquirol weighed up his options and decided to prevaricate. After all, this samurai in an opera hat seemed a nice enough fellow – why not give him something to keep him happy?

'The transaction took place in late June at a café near l'Opéra. I have no doubt as to the impeccable credentials of the seller.'

'What did he look like?'

'Somewhat plump, about fifty, with a florid complexion and salt-and-pepper hair.'

'Is that all?'

'When he stood up, he only reached my shoulder, and I'm not even five foot six.' Adolphe Esquirol frowned and blinked to show that the interview was over.

Kenji doffed his hat. Since nothing was biting upstream he would try downstream, venturing into the heart of the labyrinth that was the Bibliothèque Nationale.

Kenji walked through the enormous doorway on Rue Richelieu, opposite Place Louvois. A hallway took him into a courtyard and on the right a short flight of steps led to a corridor. He stopped to leave his cane in the cloakroom. Thanks to his membership card, he had no difficulty gaining access to the reading room, a vast square hall ending in a semicircle where the librarians' desk was situated. Kenji moved pleasurably through the hushed atmosphere of this temple of knowledge with its cast-iron pillars supporting a Moorish-style vaulted ceiling, its plush carpets, and the murmur of researchers who handled the books carefully and only interrupted their reading to dip their pens in their inkwells. He began by consulting the catalogues, but was quickly daunted by the scale of the task. He decided to ask one of the librarians.

'Is it a recent acquisition?' whispered a slight man with a stoop and a receding forehead. 'If so, I suggest you go to the acquisitions office.'

Kenji walked back the way he'd come, collected his cane and arrived at the north courtyard. He came to a succession of high-ceilinged rooms, their walls lined with thousands of books. A clerk was painstakingly separating the uncut pages of a dictionary with the aid of a finely sharpened blade, which he hurriedly set down, only too happy to escape this monotonous task.

'May I be of assistance by any chance?' he enquired in a high-pitched voice.

Kenji jumped. Two enormous eyes, as round and shiny as marbles, were peering at him through thick spectacles.

The clerk tugged at his left ear lobe as he studied the opportune visitor, and at once resolved to spin out the situation for as long as possible.

'My dear Monsieur, do you realise that you are standing on the shores of a veritable ocean of paper the level of which is continually rising and which no amount of evaporation can reduce?' he declared in a nasal voice, as he emerged from his lair.

'Yes, yes. The text I'm looking for is missing the first—'

'Two rivers whose waters never meet feed this ocean. One flows from the legal deposit, the other from public sales. Deposit and purchase, purchase and deposit, that's what it boils down to!'

'I'm sure you're right. I—'

'Consider the noble task it falls to us to perform. This flood of printed matter must be collated, assembled, guillotined, bound, stamped and numbered. Do you ever stop to think about it?'

'Every evening before I go to sleep,' retorted Kenji. 'However, I—'

'As soon as these volumes arrive, they're put away in special cabinets. It's hard enough already to find one's way around in here with all these additional weekly and monthly publications. And yet, Monsieur, they are a mere trifle compared to the number of periodicals that have seen the light of day at the end of this century. Three thousand a year, Monsieur, three thousand and counting! Worse still are all the French and foreign newspapers – sparing you those with the biggest circulation, such publications as *The Swiss Argus*, *The Western Bugler*, *The Charolles Gazetteer*, *The Picardie Press*, *The Southern Herald*. What do you make of it all, I ask you?'

'Nothing whatsoever. I'm leaving,' Kenji replied.

The clerk caught up with him in a panic, sorry to see his excuse to be idle slip away.

'Don't take it badly, Monsieur. If God gave us eyes to see with, it is so that we can use them as best we can. What can I do for you?'

'I wish to consult a Persian manuscript the title pages of which are missing. It was recently acquired by the library.'

'In that case, there's no point in me taking you to the stacks where the most valuable books are kept, eighty thousand all told – a phenomenal enough number, but when I tell you that the entire library is home to two million . . .'

'A fat lot of good that does me,' groaned Kenji.

'When you say "recently acquired" it leads me to conclude that your book is being rebound, for which we have at our disposal a budget of a mere thirty thousand francs. Naturally this limits our ability to purchase because . . .'

Kenji felt himself falter. Was there no escaping this fellow's endless patter?

'Is your manuscript at the binder's?'

'You just told me you thought it was!'

'Quite so, Monsieur. However,' the clerk resumed, 'you mentioned a Persian manuscript and anything relating to the Parsees attracts Hagop Yanikian like a bear to honey.'

Kenji was beginning to think that the man had lost his reason, when he added in a hushed voice, 'Hagop Yanikian is an employee of Armenian extraction whose job it is to deliver books for rebinding to the acquisitions office. Only, whenever he comes across a Persian text, he spirits it away so that his cousin can copy out any passages that might interest him.'

'What on earth are you talking about?'

'It's quite simple, Monsieur. If you return to the reading room, you can't miss this famous cousin, Aram Kasangian. He sits at the end of the big table to the right of the main desk. He's spent the last fifteen years wearing himself out compiling a Persian–French dictionary. He's a permanent fixture here. I wouldn't be surprised if he had your manuscript.'

His head spinning, Kenji left, after half-heartedly thanking the clerk, who looked up triumphantly at the clock. Hurrah! Only five minutes until closing time.

Outside, the heat was oppressive. Kenji stopped at a drinking fountain and quenched his thirst with the aid of a tin cup attached to a chain. It was almost six o'clock. Suddenly faint, he flopped onto a bench in Place Louvois.

'You miserable swine! What kind of performance do you call that? Are you going to make an effort or do I have to force you! You deserve a kick up the backside, you jackass! Do you want us to be booed off stage on opening night?'

Edmond Leglantier flung his plumed hat furiously onto the stage of Théâtre de l'Échiquier as he railed at his fellow actor. Sheepishly Ravaillac retreated stage right to prepare for a second offensive against the Gallic Hercules.

'Well, what is it? Why is our stage manager twitching like a scared rabbit?'

'Quick, Monsieur Leglantier, hide, it's Monsieur Vannier!'

On hearing the name of his main creditor, Edmond Leglantier rushed over to the prompter's box and opened a trapdoor, vanishing from the stage and ending up beneath the auditorium. He could hear a general commotion above him as his company scattered. He walked down a narrow passageway leading to the props room and bumped into a female figure bending over a trunk, putting away some pasteboard plates.

'You can't see a thing down here! Who's that?' he asked, feeling an ample behind.

'It's me, Andréa,' the young girl squealed.

'Well, I never. What a shapely pair of haunches you have, my lovely. You'd be an absolute knockout in a tightfitting bodice. No need for the claque, the fellows in the stalls would be crying out for an encore!'

Andréa took a step backwards, pressing herself against the wall; Leglantier's wandering hands were already exploring her.

'Don't be shy – let me look at you! Oh, what a lovely pair, and all your own,' he muttered, feeling up her bodice.

Andréa gave him a resounding slap and promptly burst into tears. Edmond Leglantier rubbed his cheek.

'A spirited wench! If you'd only stop blubbing, you'd be sure to impress the crowd.'

She could star in a classical sketch, all transparent veils and revealing robes. Nothing too deep; she's still wet behind the ears. Or a saucy pantomime with pan pipes, he thought to himself.

'You could play the Valkyrie,' he said, as an afterthought.

'Who's that?'

'A kind of Amazon, but with a winged hairstyle – daughter of the god Wotan.'

'The coast is clear,' the stage manager boomed.

'Blow your nose, you silly girl, I'm going back up,' Edmond Leglantier said to Andréa.

The royal carriage stood centre stage hemmed in by two carts outside a tavern called the Crowned Heart Pierced by an Arrow. While the actors were busy straightening their wigs, Edmond Leglantier reflected with satisfaction that he no longer needed to live from hand to mouth now that the Ambrex swindle had paid off. He was back on his feet again, but he didn't want the news getting out or else every sponger in France and Navarre would be rolling out the red carpet for him, beginning with his mistress, Adélaide Paillet, of whom he'd grown weary. I'll replace her with the luscious Andréa, he thought.

'You look like a scarecrow,' he yelled at the actor playing the Duc d'Épernon. 'Try to look intelligent, and read aloud that letter for me from the Comte de Soissons.'

'The Comte de Soissons has written to you?'

'Not to me, you dunderhead, to Henry IV! Only Henry IV has left his spectacles at home so he's asking you politely to read the blasted letter, get it?'

'Should he be reading it?' asked Ravaillac.

'As for you, you ham, shut up and concentrate. This time you must run me through shouting: "Have at ye, man of straw!"'

Henry IV and the Duc d'Épernon heaved themselves into the carriage. Lying in wait behind a barrel, Ravaillac bit his nails nervously, trying to remember his solitary line.

The Duc d'Épernon announced, 'Your Majesty, it is with great tardiness that I reply to your epistle. A rumour is abroad that the enemies of the kingdom are watching you and that your life will be in peril if you mingle with your subjects, for—'

Edmond Leglantier snatched the letter from him.

'What drivel! Philibert Dumont is a good-for-nothing hack!'

He dropped the piece of paper. Just as he was bending down to pick it up Ravaillac leapt out, roaring, 'Have at ye, man of hay!'

He lunged twice at the Duc d'Épernon who collapsed screaming, 'Help! The fool's run me through! Oh . . . the pain, it's terrible.'

Edmond Leglantier leant over him ready to shower him with insults, only to discover to his horror a bright-red stain on the actor's side.

'What's come over you?' he asked Ravaillac, in a shocked voice.

Ravaillac, whose wig had slipped off to reveal his balding pate, looked aghast at the drop of blood on the end of his dagger.

'I didn't do it on purpose,' he wailed.

'You blockhead, a moment sooner and you'd have stabbed me!' Edmond Leglantier bawled.

'He's killed me,' moaned the victim.

'There's no button on the tip of the blade. It's the props man's fault. He—'

'Don't stand there bickering! Go and fetch a doctor!' cried Maria de Medici.

The stage manager hurried off. Edmond Leglantier carefully lifted his fellow actor's doublet and confirmed the existence of a superficial wound.

'Nothing to worry about, my friend – it's a mere scratch,' he whispered, using his own shirt, which he'd taken off and rolled up in a ball, as a compress.

Bare-chested, he stood up and caught Andréa gazing admiringly at his muscular torso. He twirled his moustache and roared, 'Bravo, everybody! A magnificent performance. Stunning dialogue, sublime, a true work of art! Well done! You wreck my production then you try to kill me! I'll show you what I'm made of! For a start . . .'

With a ferocious smile he turned to Ravaillac, who shrank back.

'Fire that bungling props man! I'm going upstairs to rest. You deal with the doctor. I want Épernon back on his feet in one hour, do you hear me?'

He strode across the auditorium with great dignity, puffing out his chest.

'He's got a nerve going off like that and making us hang about!' exclaimed Maria de Medici.

'And, anyway, I'm the one who's been murdered, not him!' whined the Duc d'Épernon.

'The dagger I had yesterday was shorter with a thicker hilt. It was perfect. Who changed it?' bleated Ravaillac.

Nobody answered.

Slumped in a wing chair, Edmond Leglantier forced himself to take deep breaths. His cast was a disaster. They'd never be ready to open by the end of the month. Gradually, he began to calm down. What good would come of fretting? By way of relaxing, he conjured up images of Andréa's naked, lustful body yielding to his desires in the little love nest he would rent for her at Passy or Grenelle. His daydream was shattered by a violent knocking that shook the door.

'You rat, just wait till I get my hands on you!'

Somebody was leaning against the door so hard that it creaked and groaned under the pressure.

Edmond Leglantier's first response was to stare at the door handle, which was being jiggled fiercely up and down, and congratulate himself on having turned the key. Then he reflected that a scandal would tarnish his reputation. Still stripped to the waist, he opened the door so abruptly that the man standing there, who was tall, sharp-featured and as bald as a coot, stumbled forward into the centre of the room.

'Monsieur le Duc de Frioul! To what do I owe the honour—'

'You have the nerve to speak of honour! Here is my card, I have my seconds, choose your weapon.'

Edmond Leglantier swallowed, and curled his lip.

'Whatever is the matter, my friend? I sense animosity in your voice. Have I offended you in some way? I don't understand . . .'

'Ah, so you don't understand, you damnable vulture preying on honest men's flesh!'

Brandishing a handful of Ambrex shares, the Duc de Frioul drove Edmond Leglantier back to the wing chair.

'Monsieur le Duc, I beg you to be reasonable. I'm neither a rat nor a vulture. Why this amounts to—'

'An outrageous amount of money! You extorted a fortune out of me, and in exchange for what? A few scraps of . . . of paper fit only for the sewer. They're worthless, do you under-stand? Utterly worthless! I'm going to make you pay,' the Duc hissed.

Rage had reduced his eyes to slits.

'What! Worthless? . . . Why, that's impossible! It's an outrage! I can't breathe,' moaned Edmond Leglantier.

He fell into a swoon, taking care to land on a chair. Disconcerted, the Duc de Frioul shook him by the shoulder.

'I know your game,' he growled. 'You're sticking to your story, you rogue, and trying to wheedle your way out of it.'

'No, I swear! I invested every penny I had in this scheme . . . I'm ruined . . . I might as well end it all!' cried Edmond Leglantier, his voice quaking. 'Bring me some water . . . This is a bad dream. You must be mistaken!'

'I only wish I was. On the contrary, I've uncovered the fraud.'

'Do you mean the shares are bogus?'

'At first sight they appear flawless. The problem is the revolutionary substance they claim to be selling.'

'I don't follow you.'

'You remember the cigar holders you gave me to convince me they were imitation Baltic amber? Well, they're real. I was suspicious so I put a red-hot needle to one of them and it produced only a tiny blister. This proves beyond any doubt that they're made of pure resin! You swindled me and my associates. We'll drag you before the courts.'

'You're forgetting that I've been fleeced too.'

'It's you who sold us these worthless scraps of paper. You acted as the inventor's guarantor!'

'I'll wring his neck!'

The Duc de Frioul sneered.

'Right now, he's probably smoking a cigar on the Côte d'Azur and splitting his sides at the thought of having cleaned us out.'

'And what if you're wrong? What if this substance has the same reaction to heat as real amber?'

'How many times do I have to tell you? There's no such substance, any more than there is money that grows on trees,' the Duc de Frioul repeated, his face flushed, striking the keys of a typewriter forcefully to accentuate his words.

He composed himself, and added coldly, 'I tried to find the notary, this Maître Piard. I made enquiries at the chamber of notaries. Nobody had ever heard of him. As for the printer, the courts will no doubt deem him to have acted in good faith; you, on the other hand . . .'

'Me! Oh woe is me! I was taken in! I'm ruined!'

'Stuff and nonsense! You have your theatre.'

'It's mortgaged up to the hilt.'

'I couldn't care less.'

'It's too dreadful for words!'

Edmond Leglantier then did something which neither he nor the Duc de Frioul would ever have expected. He began to sob. He made no attempt to hide his shame. The tears rolled down his cheeks, he sniffled and drooled, the very picture of despair. Bemused, the Duc de Frioul went over to pat him on the back. But it was no use, Edmond Leglantier's howls grew steadily louder, and his face puffed up like a toad. Defeated, the Duc de Frioul beat a hasty retreat, abandoning his plans for a duel, incapable of heaping further suffering on a fellow already in such despair.

Edmond Leglantier waited for a few seconds after the door had quietly closed before grabbing his flannel waistcoat and drying his eyes and blowing his nose.

'Hell's bells! What a waste! With a performance like that I would have triumphed on stage. End of Act One. Beginning of Act Two: my great-aunt Augustine in Condé-sur-Noireau has just passed away and I will very shortly receive news that I'm her sole heir.'

He stood squarely in front of the mirror, hand on heart, and declaimed, 'Today tragedy, tomorrow farce! French farce, of course,' he concluded, smothering his face in cold cream.

The chimneystacks stood out against the pink light glowing above the rooftops. Shut up in his lodge all afternoon, Casimir Myon twisted his neck to catch a glimpse of the tiny rectangle of sky from the bottom of the shaft that rose five storeys high. During this bright spell, he could smoke his pipe and lose himself in speculations about the weather.

'Today has been thundery, but the sky is clear now, apart from a few fluffy clouds. Tomorrow will be fine . . . They look like grains of rice, no, more like tapioca.'

The idea of food made his stomach rumble and he felt a pang of hunger. It was time to prepare his supper. After filling a jug with water from the pump in the courtyard, Casimir Myon walked back into the cramped hovel allocated to him as concierge of Théâtre de l'Échiquier next to the stage door. On hearing the slosh of water in the pot, a black cat, which had been curled up on the ledge of the only window, stretched and miaowed.

'Patience, Moka, I've only got two hands! I've got to peel the vegetables while the water's heating up . . . Here, have this as an hors d'oeuvre.'

Taking his time, he cut a piece of lung into small strips and laid it on some newspaper. While Moka chewed, he sat down at the table and began peeling the potatoes and carrots which he would supplement with a piece of pork rind. The sound of hammering echoed down the corridor leading to the orchestra pit; the theatre was being renovated in anticipation of its reopening. On the left of the room, a padded door opened on to the foyer, which in turn led to the box office. Casimir Myon had put an armchair in front of it to stop the actors and props men from barging in all the time. These people hadn't an ounce of common sense; they led riotous lives and were quite capable of sending him out on a whim to buy a cigar or deliver a love letter. He wouldn't be surprised if they knocked him up in the middle of the night because they'd left a handkerchief on stage.

'This place might be a hovel, but it's my home, and I don't want to share it with the likes of you, so hop it, you lot!' the concierge was fond of saying.

And so, when somebody began pounding on his door, all he did was stifle a yawn and raise his eyes to heaven. But he put down his knife when a woman's voice cried out, 'Monsieur Myon, Monsieur Myon! Help! It stinks of gas!'

The word 'gas' had an instantaneous effect and the armchair

was dragged away, allowing in the actress playing the part of Maria de Medici.

'Calm down, Mademoiselle Eugénie. Where's it coming from?'

'From the first-floor staircase. It was one of the carpenters who warned me – he rushed up to Monsieur Leglantier's room.'

'Has Monsieur Leglantier been told?'

'Yes, he's shut himself in his office. He was supposed to come down for a costume fitting. We've been waiting for him for over an hour! The others sent me up to find out what was going on and that's when the carpenter told me to go back down on account of the gas.'

Casimir Myon hurried to the foot of the stairs where he could tell from the overpowering stench that there was a major gas leak.

'Whatever you do don't light a match, anybody. I'm going to air the place.'

Clasping a handkerchief to his face, he ran up to the dimly lit first-floor landing and opened the casement window then examined the pipes, which seemed to be in order. Behind him, Maria de Medici couldn't stop coughing.

'What about upstairs, in Monsieur Leglantier's office . . . He might have come out again and forgotten to turn off the gas,' she suggested.

They continued mounting the stairs. The concierge went over to the door of the office. He felt faint and hung on to the doorknob.

'Are you there, Monsieur Leglantier?'

There was no reply.

'Where's the fireman on duty?'

'Alfred Truchon? He's at his post in the auditorium.'

'Go and fetch him as quick as you can, and tell the police! Hurry, there may be an explosion any moment.'

Tripping over her petticoats, Maria de Medici ran down to the ground floor and returned in a flash with the fireman hot on her heels. They managed to push their way past the musketeers, stagehands, gentlemen in ruffs and ladies in hooped skirts who had gathered around the concierge, getting on his nerves with all their suggestions.

The fireman wedged a chisel between the door and the doorjamb and, with a massive shove, broke the lock. Pushing the door open proved more difficult, and only when they had succeeded did it become apparent what had been blocking it: the manager of Théâtre de l'Échiquier lay slumped on the floor, his body twisted as though he were drunk. Andréa gasped in fright. The gas fumes drove back the crowd. Casimir Myon had great difficulty forcing open the window, as the handle was jammed, and left the fireman to attend to Edmond Leglantier.

Alfred Truchon knelt down beside him. 'He's not breathing . . . Fetch a doctor, quick!' he cried out to the onlookers.

The concierge felt dizzy for a moment and held on to the back of a chair. He braced himself. His vision, which had blurred for a second, became sharp again, and he noticed a piece of paper stuck in the typewriter barrel. His duty was to read it.

'Is he . . . Is he dead?' stammered Andréa, clutching the shoulder of Maria de Medici, who remained silent.

It wasn't Ravaillac who had slain Henry IV this time, but the city's gas supply.

CHAPTER SEVEN

Tuesday 18 July

V ICTOR was in a foul mood. He was annoyed with Joseph and with Tasha for having foisted a lovelorn, flea-ridden kitten on him. Kochka's rasping miaows and scratchings at the door had woken him at two in the morning.

'Why don't you let her in?' Tasha had suggested.

'Why don't I sling her in the studio!'

'She'll claw my canvases to shreds!'

So Kochka had nestled between their pillows and promptly expressed her euphoria by purring loudly.

Victor had tossed, turned, scratched himself and wondered how such a skinny little creature could make such a din, before finally dropping off just before dawn.

The next morning, his eyes still puffy from sleep, he pushed his bicycle along Rue Monsieur-le-Prince, even though his two visits the previous day and the day before that had provided no useful information. This time he was in luck. As he walked past a building with a flaking façade, a bare-headed woman appeared and rushed over to a small boy who was diligently stirring a pile of horse droppings in the middle of the road. There were shouts, slaps and howls, but they did not deflect Victor from asking his ritual question.

'Forgive me for bothering you. You didn't happen to hear

an explosion the day Monsieur Andrésy's shop burnt down?'

The woman froze, clutching the child who struggled to get free.

'How did you know? Yes, there was a blast – *bang, bang*. It gave me such a fright I dropped my saucepan of milk; luckily it was only lukewarm. Poor Monsieur Andrésy, such an obliging man, always willing to look after this scamp for me.'

She was suddenly aware of the danger her child had escaped, and clasped him to her skirts.

'Did he have friends?' Victor pursued.

'He wasn't very sociable, but I sometimes saw him with a large, cheerful-looking bloke. They would lunch together at Chez Fulbert on the corner.'

Her son wriggled free and made a dash for it. She ran after him, caught him and, forgetting her recent surge of affection, promised him another slap if he was naughty again.

On a trestle table outside the Chez Fulbert tavern stood a row of glasses and some carafes filled with pink liquid. A slate advertised:

Grenadine – ten centimes a glass

A flabby girl offered feebly, 'Refreshments? With free ice.'

'Put a bit more energy into it, Marie-Louise, you sound like you're selling a sleeping draught,' a voice shouted from inside.

There was laughter. Victor joined a group of regulars at the bar.

'That lass is no bright spark, but she's easy on the eye,' a road worker remarked.

'Hey, Arsène, you keep your hands to yourself or you'll feel my boot on your backside.'

The landlord, a rotund little man, sliced the head off a glass of beer with a violent gesture and slapped it down in front of one of his customers.

'For you?' he barked at Victor.

'A vermouth cassis, please. I'm trying to track down anyone who knew Monsieur Andrésy. Somebody just told me that he used to have lunch here with a friend.'

'Somebody told you right. First Sunday of every month, regular as clockwork, at that table over by the window. They were old comrades – fought together in that filthy war. Talk about a tragedy!'

A customer hidden behind a newspaper raised his head.

'Do you happen to know the friend's name?' Victor asked.

'Monsieur Andrésy always called him Gustave. He lives near La Chapelle, Rue . . . Rue . . . My errand boy would know, only he's away at a wedding until the 24th. He delivered a case of table wine to Monsieur Gustave last year – a gift from Monsieur Andrésy, the real stuff, mind, straight from the vine. My brother's a winegrower in La Gironde. Here, try some – it'll tickle your taste buds more than that cassis of yours!'

He poured a slug of red wine into a glass. The regulars pricked up their ears at the sound of the pleasant glug-glug. The man reading lowered his newspaper to take a closer look at the lucky recipient of such largesse. Victor tasted the wine and clicked his tongue.

'Full-bodied, fruity with a good bouquet, my compliments to your brother.'

'It's a shame! They were here just a couple of weeks ago. I can still see Marie-Louise bringing them a cassoulet and almost tipping it over them because she tripped over her own feet.'

'Like I said, not the brightest of lasses . . .'

'I won't tell you again, Arsène, belt up or get out,' growled Fulbert. 'It's impossible to have a private conversation around here. Where was I? Oh yes, we get used to having people around and when they kick the bucket we realise that time is marching on and we're all on the same slippery slope.'

'You're getting very philosophical in your old age, Fulbert,' said the man with the newspaper.

'So I am . . . They were bachelors so they appreciated a slap-up meal occasionally. But I mustn't talk about Monsieur Gustave in the past tense – he isn't dead!'

'Have you seen him since the accident?'

'He was very upset. He wanted us to tell him exactly what happened then he drowned his sorrows with three glasses of gut-rot,' said Fulbert, wiping the counter.

Victor left, followed by the man with the newspaper, who asked him, 'Were you one of Monsieur Andrésy's customers by any chance?'

'Yes, I'm a bookseller. I used to send him books to bind.'

'That's what I thought. And if I'm not mistaken you have a Chinese colleague?'

'Japanese.'

'And your assistant is Joseph Pignot who published a serialised novel in *Le Passe-partout*. I couldn't put it down, it was so true to life. Someone said it was based on a real crime you helped solve. It was in the papers and nearly cost you your life . . .'

'You've certainly done your homework.'

'Monsieur Andrésy and I discussed it at length. It's rare to come across somebody who pursues their own line of enquiry right under the noses of the police. Speaking of which, I need some advice. Monsieur Andrésy has no living relatives and I'm wondering what I should do with his watch. I'm a watchmaker, you see, and I do repairs. Monsieur Andrésy asked me to try to fix his fob watch – it gave up the ghost this winter. He was very attached to it. Should I keep it or give it to the police? I'd appreciate your opinion. Look, it's going to pelt down. Why don't you come into my shop. It's very near.'

When Victor first entered the gloomy premises, set back from the road, he had the impression that a colony of bugs was busily gnawing away at the walls at varying speeds. Then in the half-light he made out the assortment of pendulum clocks, cuckoo clocks and carriage clocks filling every available space. The saraband of the moving hands made his head spin.

'Quite a racket, eh? A constant reminder that my hourglass is emptying. Père Lamartine was right: "It flows, and we pass."[35] Now, where did I put it? Ah, here it is. Go over to the light and have a look at the inscription on the back.'

Victor held the watch up to one of the little windows and managed to make out the words:

Sacrovir. Long live the C—

'Long live what?'

'The corps. Well, what do you think? If I take it to the police they'll only make me fill in a lot of tedious forms.'

'I'll sign to say that I've taken it, and pay for the repair. I feel sure that Monsieur Andrésy would be happy to know that Monsieur Mori, who was one of his closest friends, had inherited his watch.'

'Ah, Monsieur, you've taken a great weight off my mind. I just can't take it in, that he died so suddenly.'

Before getting back on his bicycle, which he'd fastened to a lamp-post, Victor jotted down:

Bookbinder's friend Gustave, La Chapelle. Talk to the errand boy at Fulbert's on 24th to find out his exact address.

He pedalled off towards the Luxembourg Gardens. It was so hot that his shirt was damp with sweat. He remembered the half-melted fob watch on Inspector Lecacheur's desk. An inscription in the middle of an ornate daisy design left no doubt as to the owner's identity:

To P— from his —e

'*P* was for Pierre. As for his —*e* . . .'

Puzzled, Victor freewheeled down Rue de Médicis, invigorated by the wind on his face. On the other side of the railings, some tramps were sleeping on park benches. Two watches? There was nothing strange about that. While the watchmaker was repairing one, he carried the other.

He braked and turned into Rue Soufflot. He saw a dog, its

tongue hanging out, on the edge of the pavement. A group of children lying on their fronts next to an air vent were fiercely contesting a game of marbles. Victor grabbed hold of the Courcelles–Panthéon omnibus. Its horses, in a lather, flared their clammy nostrils as they struggled to the end of their ordeal. Their hooves occasionally slipped on the cobblestones that had just been hosed down, and Victor himself narrowly avoided coming a cropper. He overtook the exhausted animals, hungry for oats and water, who were making one last effort, in a hurry to be free of the wretched harness.

Sacrovir . . . Was it a name? A place?

As he raced down Rue Sainte-Geneviève, the intoxication of his own speed drove all speculation from his mind.

Victor braked sharply in front of the bookshop, and narrowly avoided knocking over an imposing-looking woman wielding a large flowery umbrella, who looked daggers at him through her lorgnette. She was about to tick him off soundly for having such an infernal machine when Joseph appeared.

'I'll park your mustang at the back of the shop, Boss. Oh, good morning, Madame la Comtesse, look at those clouds! It'll soon be raining cats and dogs.'

The Comtesse de Salignac pursed her lips, pushed him smartly aside and swept into the shop like a ship in full sail, making for Kenji, who was talking on the telephone.

'Any news?' Joseph whispered to Victor.

'Go down to the stockroom and look up the word *Sacrovir* in the dictionary,' Victor replied softly.

'What about my deliveries? Monsieur Mori will be furious. Sacro what?'

'*Vir*, the name probably comes from the Latin *vir* meaning "man", like in *triumvir*.'

'Ah! And sacrolumbar is the lower back. I get it! It's a man suffering from backache.'

'I'm not interested in your half-baked theories; this isn't a guessing game. Go and look it up before you start blathering,' Victor ordered, putting on a charming smile as he rejoined the Comtesse de Salignac.

She was beating the air stoically with her fan, put out at having to wait for Kenji to be free.

'Would you care to sit down, dear Madame?'

'I'm quite capable of standing, I just don't want to have to stand here all day,' she retorted.

'May I be of some assistance?'

'No, it's your colleague I must see.'

Adopting what she considered a suitably dignified pose, she turned her head away, fanning herself furiously. Victor withdrew, intrigued by the in-quarto volume in yellow morocco-leather, which the battle-axe was clutching to her bosom. It looked familiar.

Joseph stumbled over something and banged his knee violently. Cursing, he finally managed to find the light switch. Since Monsieur Legris had moved to Rue Fontaine, the darkroom in the basement he had used for his photography had been turned back into a reading room and electric lights installed. Its shelves were lined with bibliographies, collector's items, catalogues and encyclopedias, which could be taken out and consulted at a table.

'These tomes weigh a ton! They'll be calling me Sacrovir when my back breaks from lugging them about.'

He leafed absent-mindedly through several volumes. What a pity his meeting with the girl in the classified ads at *Le Figaro* the evening before had ended in failure!

Regretful at having resisted the advances of the employee in the satin bonnet, he'd used the pretext of a delivery in order to enjoy Monday afternoon off. He'd gone to wait for the girl at the entrance to the newspaper's offices and had asked her politely to take a drink with him at Café Napolitain, where he hoped to catch a glimpse of Georges Courteline[36] and Catulle Mendès.[37] Emboldened by the effect of the sherry, she had told him that her name was Francine. She realised from Joseph's indifferent expression that he'd been hoping for some interesting revelation.

'You know, I've racked my brains about that death notice and it's come back to me. He was well-to-do. Middle-aged, and podgy,' she added.

'You mean fat?'

'Well, there's fat and there's fat! Let's say he was . . . well padded. And he had a squint. Yes, he had a squint.'

As she spoke, she gently pressed Joseph's foot under the table with hers. Nonchalant, she drained her glass, moistened her lips and resumed, 'He had a scar on his chin, too, and a thick Alsace accent.'

Joseph prudently crossed his legs. The wealth of detail

together with the attack on his shoe had aroused his suspicions. She was leading him on. Much to Francine's dismay, he suddenly remembered a courtesy call he had to pay to his first cousin who'd suffered a fit of catalepsy recently, and left in a hurry after paying the bill, which he considered a little steep.

'A fat bloke from Alsace with a squint and a scar my eye! She must think I was born yesterday! I swear women are a mystery to me. First they say no, then they say yes, next they're nudging you with their foot under the table while you're having a drink, and by the time the dessert comes they've shown you their stocking tops . . . A pity, though, she was rather fetching . . .'

Francine's face was replaced by Iris's in his mind.

'I must be on my guard!' he concluded.

His finger stopped at a paragraph on the history of Gaul.

'By Jove! I think I've found it! Sacrovir!'

The Comtesse de Salignac studied Kenji in sullen, reproachful silence. She'd given up fanning herself and her cheeks had turned bright red. She was visibly at the end of her tether. At last, Kenji replaced the receiver. Eudoxie Allard, alias Fifi Bas-Rhin, former cancan dancer at the Moulin-Rouge, had clearly lost none of her volubility during her stay in the north. Having no doubt grown tired of her Russian archduke, the insatiable woman was back in town and eager to renew her intimate relations with her men friends.

As Kenji hung up, he looked like the cat that had got the cream but hastily composed his expression and calmly enquired of the Comtesse to what he owed the pleasure of her visit.

'Pleasure! Ah, Monsieur Mori, it is not pleasure but disgrace that brings me here. Will you buy back this edition of Michel de Montaigne, which Monsieur de Pont-Joubert's uncle purchased from you?'

Kenji pretended to be indifferent, but Victor recognised the rare fifth edition from 1588 of *The Essays of Michel, Seigneur de Montaigne* he'd bought at auction two years before.

'One thousand nine hundred francs,' said Kenji.

The Comtesse's jaw dropped in indignation, her cheeks flushed a darker red.

'What!' she exclaimed. 'Is that a joke? The Duc de Frioul paid you six thousand francs for it! It was a wedding present for my niece Valentine!'

Joseph heard the name as he reached the landing and it brought back disagreeable memories.

'You're mistaken, Madame, he only paid five thousand two hundred francs. You should be thankful, generally speaking we only reimburse a third of the price. I'm making an exception because it is you.'

The Comtesse's mouth twisted into a bitter smile.

'Come, Monsieur Mori, I'm one of your best customers – surely I deserve better treatment than this.'

'Alas, Madame la Comtesse, shares have plummeted,' parried Kenji, 'and the book market is subject to the same fluctuations as the antiques market. Is Monsieur de Pont-Joubert experiencing financial difficulties?'

The Comtesse sniffed and tossed her fan into her reticule.

'He has suffered a reversal of fortune, his capital has been tragically reduced and he is obliged to rein in his expenditure.

The nincompoop has been ruined by the Duc de Frioul's idiocy. What is the world coming to when we can no longer even trust our own relatives!'

Hiding behind a pile of books, Joseph had been hanging on every word and was inwardly rejoicing: there was such a thing as justice!

'Do you see how far I must stoop in order to save the family reputation, Monsieur Mori? Not content to fritter away his own fortune at baccarat, that gambler Frioul had the brilliant idea of buying up a lot of worthless shares! When I think that he's my niece Valentine's uncle by marriage! And do you know what the old skinflint had the nerve to give the twins on their first birthday? Amber cigar holders – one for Hector and one for Achille. It's a disgrace!'

Victor, choking back his mirth, turned aside in case the Comtesse saw him with her eagle eye. Kenji maintained an expression of polite concern.

What a brilliant actor! Victor thought, watching him. How does he manage to keep a straight face?

The Comtesse rummaged in her reticule and pulled out a piece of crumpled paper, which she waved under Kenji's nose.

'Here's the proof!'

Victor came over to help Kenji out.

'Why not tell us the whole sorry story?' he suggested, pulling up a chair for the Comtesse.

She collapsed into it, explaining in a tremulous voice that the Duc de Frioul had been swindled by a second-rate actor, a ham, a scoundrel by the name of Leglantier – the so-called manager of Théâtre de l'Échiquier.

'The Duc wanted to use his shares as security for a loan since he was in need of ready cash. He went to his bank, Crédit Lyonnais, and what did they tell him? The Ambrex securities were fake. Naturally, he immediately contacted Colonel de Réauville, who was also in a panic. He'd just come back from his own bank. Théâtre de l'Échiquier indeed! As if anyone had ever heard of it! It was all a fraud!'

She handed the share certificate to Victor and pulled herself up out of the chair.

'I have enough of them to paper my bedroom. Frame it and hang it above your counter! Well, Monsieur Mori, what about the Montaigne?'

Victor decided to make himself scarce. Joseph beckoned to him from the back of the shop.

'The boss isn't being very charitable, is he, Boss?'

'Charity begins at home. What did you want to say?'

'I found your Sacrovir. I made notes. I'll read them to you then I'll have to dash. He was a Gallic chieftain, who occupied Autun at the beginning of the first century AD. He was defeated by the Roman legion of Upper Germania, which ransacked and pillaged his village. It would make a great subject for a play. Why all the interest? Are you thinking of writing an essay on Gaul?'

'It's something to do with Pierre Andrésy's death. Can I come over to your house tonight? I'll tell you all about it then.'

'Perfect, Maman's going to play cards at Madame Ballu's. I'll see you later.'

The Comtesse was leaving just as Victor went back to the main shop. She gave him a murderous look before she closed the door. Kenji was looking greedily at the copy of Montaigne.

'How much?'

'Two thousand five hundred. She drove a hard bargain. Incidentally, I've looked into the matter of the *Stories of the Parrot*. I went to see Esquirol, the dealer who sold that lot of Oriental books at auction at Rue Drouot. He described the seller as a short, plump man approaching fifty.'

'Is that all?'

'I went to Rue de Richelieu, but alas I couldn't confirm whether our work was among the Bibliothèque Nationale's recent acquisitions or not. I do have a theory, though, and I'm going to get to the bottom of this.'

'I don't doubt it.'

'I'm going now. Will you tell Iris that I may be back a little late?'

Alone in the shop, Victor ran his finger over the Montaigne. Something important must have distracted Kenji for him to leave it lying on his desk.

It was a calm afternoon. The washed-out sky was the delicate blue of a watercolour, without a trace of cloud. A row of sparrows on the guttering twittered gaily. The cries of a chair-rusher took on an operatic quality. Anglers were snoozing along the cool banks of the Seine.

Kenji, clean-shaven and smelling faintly of lavender, walked past the Théâtre Français. He liked to cut through the gardens of the Palais-Royal where he communed with the departed souls of Restif de la Bretonne, André Chénier, Musset, Stendhal and Cagliostro. Could any of them tell him whether the mysterious manuscript at the Bibliothèque Nationale was his? Lucien de Rubempré[38] whispered to him to stop chasing after illusions and enjoy the moment.

He dallied under the elm trees near the fountain. The shadows of the leaves dancing over the water were soothing. He felt light-hearted. What had Eudoxie said on the telephone? 'You improve with age, my dear man. You look positively dashing with white hair.' Curiously she was always quite formal on the phone although she addressed him much more intimately in the bedroom – more intimately than he could ever bring himself to address her.

He approached the arcades and studied his reflection in the window of a print shop. Eudoxie was exaggerating: his thick black hair had only a few silvery strands in it. He'd decided not to dye them because greying temples seemed to excite the female imagination. He grinned at himself and plumped up his cravat. It was six months since he'd been to Rue Alger!

As he climbed the stairs, he pictured a less youthful, less lissom body than Eudoxie's, a quizzical face with a sensual mouth. He quickly cast the image of Djina Kherson from his mind and rang the bell.

Eudoxie opened the door. Her eyes, beneath their long lashes, softened, and her slim body draped in a flesh-coloured lace negligee stirred in him the physical desire he'd been repressing for what seemed like a decade.

'Why, it's you, my dear Mikado,' she breathed. 'Come in.'

Struck dumb, he followed her into the living room, then composed himself and sat on the sofa, back straight, hands resting on the pommel of his cane. He glanced discreetly around the room that had witnessed their erotic games, and noticed a thick volume lying on the pedestal table: a work in Russian the Cyrillic title of which he was unable to decipher.

'It's for you,' she said. 'I thought you'd appreciate a deluxe edition.'

'What is it?'

'*Anna Karenina.*'

'Tolstoy? Goodness!'

'I'm not completely illiterate! True, my Russian is limited, but I've read the French translation. It's tragic. I'm outraged by the condemnation of passionate love.'

'When did you get back?'

'This morning. I asked the cab driver to go via Rue des Saints-Pères. I saw you. I didn't want to disturb you and, since you were kind enough to equip me with a telephone, I rang.'

'Are you alone?'

'Fédor is in St Petersburg. I told him I was homesick and that the doctor had prescribed a trip to Paris. I missed you dreadfully! Fédor is a sweet man, kind, thoughtful, rich, loyal; only between the sheets . . . he simply doesn't measure up, you see.'

Kenji felt a familiar demonic sensation. The symptoms were unmistakable: a dry throat, butterflies in his stomach; he recognised the face of lust. His common sense cried out, 'Say no, leave! This woman is a bird of passage.' But a second voice immediately told him, 'Go on! It's high time you put an end to your dry season!'

'It's really quite simple,' Eudoxie went on in a tremulous

voice, 'every time he took me I closed my eyes and imagined it was you, prayed that it would be you. So you see, I was condemned to live in perpetual darkness.'

'I very much doubt whether such an immoral prayer has a hope of being answered,' he remarked sardonically. 'All you had to do was stay in Paris.'

'Don't mock me, you wicked man. It was a prayer that came from the depths of my soul, and I'm sure it'll be answered. I'm here now, aren't I?'

'For how long?'

'That depends on a certain Monsieur Mori, a book dealer in Rue des Saints-Pères,' Eudoxie whispered, wriggling closer and closer to him.

He stood up without touching her.

'Well,' he murmured, 'I'll be sure to mention it to him. Are you planning to take up dancing again?'

'Fédor wants to marry me. I'm tempted. I'd be the Archduchess Maximova. Only St Petersburg is freezing in winter and I can't live without heat.'

Kenji sighed.

'I'm free this evening,' he said.

'So am I! Come at six o'clock. You'll see, I won't let you down.'

Fifteen minutes later, Kenji was walking up Rue de Rivoli.

'Pleasure controlled increases tenfold,' he sang softly to himself.

He felt like skipping along the street, blowing kisses to the shop girls in Magasins du Louvre. Fifi Bas-Rhin was waiting for him. He would go home and smarten up then do some shopping and be back at Rue Alger at the appointed hour. His first thought was to take her to Drouant's. But he decided they should dine alone together in her apartment – a gourmet meal accompanied by fine wine – no, by champagne. He mustn't forget to buy flowers. He would show her the difference between her vulgar Kulak and a red-blooded gentleman like himself.

Joseph was rereading with delectation his *Rip-roaring Tales from Rue Visconti*. There was a knock at his study door. He went to open it and stood there, stunned. The man facing him bore a distinct resemblance to Monsieur Legris, but with one important difference.

'Aren't you going to ask me in, Joseph?'

'Boss, is it really you?'

'Who else could it be? The Negus?'

'But . . . your moustache!'

'I shaved it off. Any objections?'

'I'm sorry, it's just that . . . you look like a butler!'

'Have you something against domestic staff? Tasha says when it doesn't prickle it tickles. Don't you like me like this?'

'Well, if it's what Mademoiselle Tasha wants . . . no wonder you obeyed. It's the women who wear the trousers! But if you want my opinion? I preferred the old look, it was more . . . More dignified. And what about the customers? Have you thought about that?'

'Why should they care? Why should you for that matter?'

Victor caught sight of his reflection in a cracked mirror

propped up against a volume of the civil code. The respectable gentleman had vanished, wiped out by a pair of scissors and a razor. He'd grown attached to his moustache; it had been part of his personality – without it he felt naked, younger-looking.

You're thirty-three but you don't look it – even with those crow's feet, he thought to himself.

'Well, I think I look rather debonair, Joseph! And, since you're having a go at me, can I remind *you* that you never thought to ask my permission before foisting that cat on me!'

'Touché, Boss! Let's change the subject. We'll talk about Sacrovir. What's he got to do with the price of tea in China?'

'I went to Rue Monsieur-le-Prince and found Pierre Andrésy's watch.'

He handed the box to Joseph, whose face suddenly darkened.

'You promised we'd investigate this case together,' he grumbled, keeping quiet about his meeting with Francine at Café Napolitain.

'Isn't that what we're doing? What does Sherlock Pignot think?'

'He thinks that Monsieur Andrésy had a strange nickname. Maybe that's what they called him in the army. *Long live the C*— Long live the corps or the camp?'

'Or long live chiropody, chicanery or comedy if the inscription refers to a doctor, a lawyer or an actor. How can we be sure?'

'You disappoint me, Boss. The *C* could stand for itself. Don't you know about Elliptical Style?'

'What's the connection?'

Joseph moistened his forefinger and flicked through his notebook.

'In my serialised novel *Thule's Golden Chalice* I drew inspiration from Dumas *père*. I will read to you from *The Lady of Montsoreau*.[39]

> '"I have another idea," said Saint-Luc.
> "Let's hear it!"
> "What if . . ."
> "What if . . . ?"
> "No."
> "No?"
> "Yes!"
> "Explain!"
> "What if it was Monsieur le duc d'Anjou?"'

'Fascinating, but I don't see how it is relevant to our inscription.'

'What if it was created by the author of a serialised novel using the great writer's method? Why not? It's paid by the line. I went the whole hog. I'll read it to you:

> 'The mastiff was slavering near the Saint-André cross.
> "Éleuthère, you dirty dog!"
> "Woof! Woof!"
> "Does this keep hold the Knight Templars' treasure?"
> The mastiff froze, paw raised, and sniffed the air.
> "Grrr . . . Grrr . . . Grrr . . ."

"What's that foul stench? My God, it's . . . the dreaded amber!"

The mastiff fell to the ground in a heap, tongue hanging out, eyes rolled upwards.

"We're done for," murmured Frida von Glockenspiel.

Before losing consciousness, she was able to scratch in the dust: VAIVODE.'

'Have you lost your mind, Joseph? You're leading us miles away from the investigation with these circumvolutions. I certainly didn't come here to discuss how many lines are in your serialised novel.'

'You don't like my writing.'

'Too many *woofs* and *grrrs*.'

'That's what builds up the suspense. You always have to criticise. Do you like it or not? I've been slaving over it for months.'

'Yes, well done, you'll go far because in literature, as in cuisine, the simpler the recipe the more predictable the outcome. Why that particular word?'

'Vaivode? I wanted to give it a Gothic feel.'

'No, not vaivode, amber. It's strange that you should have chosen amber.'

'It was on account of that robbery at Bridoire's Jeweller's. I read you the article or have you forgotten? Of course you never listen to anything I say – I might as well be talking to myself!'

Victor smoothed out the Ambrex share certificate the Comtesse de Salignac had left at the shop, and studied it thoughtfully.

'Oh, the famous slip of paper!' declared Joseph. 'That numbskull Frioul and his pompous nephew got what they deserved. It reminds me of John Law's credit system and the French East India Company. In *The Hunchback*,[40] a crooked man from Rue Quincampoix tells speculators they should touch his hump for luck. The Duc de Frioul should have touched mine then maybe his scheming would have amounted to more than a hill of beans!'

He snatched the share certificate and studied it carefully. Something caught his eye.

'What's this? Léopold Grandjean . . . Grandjean . . . Look, Boss! There, on the left, one of the director's signatures . . . Hang on a minute.'

He waved his notebook in the air excitedly.

'Grandjean, Léopold Grandjean, the enamellist who was stabbed to death in Rue Chevreul! This is more and more convoluted. That fellow was one of the Ambrex directors!'

Victor skimmed the articles glued into the notebook and mumbled, 'Like amber, musk, benzoin and incense . . . Léopardus, the leopard . . . How is this connected to Pierre Andrésy's death?'

'And the other director, Frédéric Daglan, who is he?'

'Wait a moment, let me think. Who did the Duc buy the shares from? . . . From a ham actor . . . Théâtre de l'Échec!'

'De l'Échiquier, Boss. We must find this Daglan fellow before he goes the same way as Grandjean. Let me go to the theatre and nose around. If you ask me, something's rotten in the state of Denmark.'

Victor nodded. In the meantime, he would go to La Chapelle

to look for Pierre Andrésy's lunch partner, even though he only had the man's first name to go on. Gustave.

Worn out after traipsing the city streets, Josette Fatou finally glimpsed the columns of La Nation calling her like twin beacons above the tree-lined Cours de Vincennes. She breathed in the fragrant humidity before turning into Rue des Boulets. She still had to open the gate to the building, which always reeked of soup and slop buckets, and put away her cart. Then finally she would be able to rest her strained arms.

Evening had set in and there was no trace of the early-morning showers in the dappled sky. Even so, Josette quickened her pace, convinced of an invisible presence advancing through the grass on the nearby patch of wasteland. She was losing her mind. She was suspicious of every man she saw. How would she recognise the man who was following her? She thought she heard a mocking whisper.

'You won't recognise me, but I know who you are. I'm watching you. You can't escape from me. Each time a man buys your flowers you'll ask yourself: is it him? You'll never be sure. Bad things happen to people who find themselves in the wrong place at the wrong time.'

She saw a rat scurry along the wall, fleeing before the clogs of a potbellied woman laden with baskets. Josette always tried to avoid the tenant on the second floor, who lived with her husband, a brocade weaver whom she nagged from dawn until dusk. This evening, Josette felt relieved to be able to follow her up the stairs, and almost happy when the woman gave a deep grunt that passed for a greeting.

The half-light cast ominous shadows on the landing. Josette hurried on up to the third floor and locked herself in her room. Leaning against the wall, she caught her breath and walked over to the window. Darkness was slowly creeping over the street. A few couples had fled the furnaces of their garrets and were out strolling. The lamplighter would come along soon. Comforted, she adjusted her lamp in order to use up as little fuel as possible. She didn't feel like preparing a meal and instead made do with a piece of bread and dripping, an apple and a glass of water. She couldn't help going back over to the window that was glowing with the bright-orange rays of the setting sun. At the foot of a lilac bush, a shadow lengthened then drew back. It was a man. He was smoking a cigarette. He'd followed her and now he was spying on her. Josette leapt away from the window. She must control her fear or it would engulf her. She steeled herself to take another peek. This time the courtyard was empty.

'I'm just imagining things. I'm losing my mind.'

She would calmly undress, have a quick wash then fall into a deep, healing sleep. Yes, that's what she would do.

A knock at the door surprised her as she was unbuttoning her blouse. She felt a cry rising up her throat and her pulse quickened.

'Mademoiselle Fatou? It's me, your neighbour, Madame Cartier . . . Little Christophe has spilt all my flour. I was wondering, could you lend me some? Mademoiselle Fatou, are you there?'

With a trembling hand, Josette opened the door. A tiny

moonfaced woman barged in. Apart from a pair of threadbare slippers she was dressed only in a thin shift.

'I hope I'm not disturbing you . . . That brat keeps badgering me to make pancakes. I'll pay you back next week, as soon as my Justin gets his pay packet. Forgive my state of undress, this heat is killing me. Oh, while I'm here, lend me an egg and some sugar, would you?'

Her head spinning from the woman's chatter, Josette helped Madame Cartier carry back her spoils. She left the woman, reluctantly, and in the gloom of the landing peered over the banister. At the bottom of the stairwell, the large copper ball on the newel post transformed into a leering face. She cried out in fright and hurled herself into her apartment, double locking the door.

There he was, standing in the middle of the room, smiling.

She thought her heart would stop. A red cloud engulfed her as she lost consciousness.

CHAPTER EIGHT

Wednesday 19 July

THE heatwave had shrivelled the leaves on the chestnut trees on Boulevard de la Chapelle.

'Does the name Monsieur Gustave mean anything to you?' Victor asked a woman sweeping the pavement.

She gave him a quietly mocking look.

'I know as many Gustaves as there are scorched leaves.'

Victor also drew a blank from some children playing leapfrog. One of them had fun chasing after Victor's bicycle, bellowing through a rolled-up poster. A salt-meat seller busy scraping knuckles of ham scratched his head and declared, 'There was a Gustave who had a café near Rue Pajol, but he snuffed it last week.'

Disheartened, Victor decided to turn back. He'd covered every inch of the neighbourhood, from the freight train station of the Northern Railway to the grim-looking gasometer in Rue de l'Évangile, via the workshops of the Eastern Railway and the depot of the Compagnie des Petites Voitures in Rue Philippe-de-Girard. He'd spoken to about thirty Gustaves, none of whom counted a bookbinder from the Latin Quarter among his friends. The sight of the ramshackle buildings and their impoverished inhabitants depressed Victor, and he felt the urge to take himself off to more pleasant surroundings. If he wanted to find his man, he'd just have to wait until Fulbert's errand boy came back on the 24th.

He decided to make one final attempt in Place de la Chapelle and slipped through a huge carriage entrance. As he pedalled past an enormous building, he was astonished to hear a voice calling out his name.

'Monsieur Legris! Fancy seeing you here! How are you? Do you remember me? You look different.'

Victor stared at the man leaning out of a window low enough to climb through. He recognised Pérot, whose whiskers would have put Vercingetorix to shame.

'Monsieur Pérot![41] Do you live here?'

'This is where I work. Welcome to La Chapelle police station.'

Victor walked into the entrance where he propped up his bicycle so that he could shake the hand of the fellow who led him through to his office.

The gloomy decor of cracked tiles and brown paint would have brought to mind a hospital waiting room had it not been for the glass-fronted cabinet lined with books.

'Are you still an exponent of free verse, Monsieur Pérot?'

'I've religiously preserved your Jules Laforgue, a priceless gift, and I continue to serve my muse. I've even had the pleasure of seeing some of my poems printed in *La Plume* under the pen name Isis. Léon Deschamps[42] and I have become friends. It's only the beginning. My dream is to be published in *Gil Blas*. What fair wind brings you here?'

'I got lost . . . I was on my way to value a collection of books.'

'Ah! Books, books!'

'You're not growing tired of your profession, are you, Inspector?'

'Assistant Chief of Police, please, I've been promoted! I've stepped into the shoes of Oscar Méténier[43] and Ernest Raynaud,[44] two talented men of letters who filled this position before me. The Chief is furious at being landed for the third time in a row with an assistant who has a passion for literature. He doesn't know I've been published, so mum's the word.'

'And how is your tortoise . . . Nanette?'

'I couldn't find a home for her so I adopted her myself. Our office boy Lucien takes devoted care of her and the Chief's stray dogs – despite his aversion to literature, the Chief has a kind heart. You must come back one day and watch Lucien reviewing his recruits all decked out in their caps and capes.'

Outside, a noise grew louder. Victor noticed a crowd had gathered at the window. Raoul Pérot frowned.

'It's impossible to have any privacy around here. You can hear everything in this house. It's made worse by the fact that we have no local police stations and so no local police, just two inspectors and . . .'

He was interrupted by the arrival of an old man with a white beard, and a cheerful-looking youth. Between them was a fellow holding up his trousers with both hands in order to stop them falling about his ankles.

'A fight in Rue du Département. We caught this pimp on the point of slicing up some other blockhead so we stepped in quick before any of his friends came to join in the fray, and as we'd left the handcuffs behind we pulled all the buttons off his breeches to stop him escaping.'

'Thank you, Inspector Gaston, and you, too, Lucien. Please feel free to stay, Monsieur Legris. Sit down,' Raoul Pérot ordered the knife wielder. 'Lucien, tell those people to move along. Your name?'

'Roger, but they call me the Tick. I didn't do anything, I swear, Inspector. It was the other bloke who started it.'

'Who is this other bloke and what exactly did he do to you?'

'He came into my territory; he's from La Villette. While I was in La Santoche[45] he had his way with my Léonie and now she's expecting. How am I supposed to get by with her in the family way? Léonie's my other half. No one can hold a candle to her! And look at her now, useless!'

The Tick suddenly leapt to his feet, spitting with rage, eyes bloodshot, and banged his fists violently against the wall, crying out, 'Ah, Inspector, I'm so angry! I won't stand for this!'

His trousers slipped right down to his ankles, revealing a pair of spindly legs. A window on the ground floor opened partially and a hairy man leant out, his face puffy from sleep.

'Shut your trap before I do something I regret. Damn it, I work nights, you numbskull. What's all this racket about anyway?'

The Tick leapt over to the window.

'What the hell's it got to do with you?'

'Nothing!' retorted the disturbed sleeper, prudently closing his window.

Just then, a side door opened and in strode a tubby middle-aged man wearing a suit and a bowler hat. Ignoring Raoul

Pérot, he pounced on Roger, who immediately looked down at the floor.

'Hey, you, pipe down,' the man in the bowler thundered. 'They can hear you yelling a mile away. As for your sorry tale, save it for the examining magistrate.'

The man in the bowler rushed out into the corridor, vanishing as swiftly as he'd appeared.

Raoul Pérot leant over to Victor.

'That's Corcol, the other inspector, a man with a firm hand, not known for his subtlety. Come on, Roger, hitch up your trousers and sit down. Did you intend to eliminate your rival?'

'It all depends on what you mean by that. I just wanted to jump him, to give him a fright on account of my Léonie being lumbered with a kid – it's going to cramp her style something awful. I'm a law-abiding man, Inspector, as peaceful and inoffensive as can be.'

'Inoffensive . . . That's a matter of opinion – your breath alone could kill a fly at ten paces.'

A soprano voice echoed sweetly through the courtyard.

'Long live wine, love and tobacco!'

Victor gave Raoul Pérot a surreptitious sidelong glance and bit his lip. Raoul Pérot smiled craftily.

'Light opera, Monsieur Legris, cares nothing for law and order. We're fortunate enough to work next to a tavern where operatic companies rehearse. It permits us to mete out justice to the sound of music while pondering Verlaine's question: "Is life really such a solemn and serious affair?" Roger,' he said, addressing the Tick, 'there's no point in me giving you a warning, I'm simply going to confiscate your knife. Kindly keep a low profile, do you understand?'

'What about my trouser buttons? They took my trouser buttons!'

'That'll teach you a lesson. Lucien, accompany this sans-culotte back to Rue du Département.'

Victor looked amazed.

'Aren't you going to arrest him?'

'What good would it do? A week in jail won't turn him into a choirboy. We're better off saving our energy for more judicious cases, for are we not all destined to perish?'

'You're a funny sort of policeman!'

'No doubt it's the influence of literature, Monsieur Legris. Why not join me for lunch? Your bicycle will be safe under the watchful eye of Inspector Gaston; he never leaves the office except to go home to bed.'

They crossed the courtyard and slipped through a concealed door into Madame Milent's establishment, where the table reserved for the assistant chief of police was screened off by a partition.

The place was already full, and laughter and curses rang out in the smoke-filled atmosphere. Victor studied the elegant handwritten menu and ordered the braised veal.

'A good choice, both filling and economical. I'll have the same, Madame Milent, and a pitcher of red!'

Behind Victor, Inspector Corcol sat alone, a newspaper open next to his napkin.

'Don't look round, Monsieur Legris,' whispered Pérot.

'It's my colleague whom you met just now. He's ignoring me.'

'Why?'

'Nobody likes to see younger men step on board, especially when they have seniority. He was after my post. We've settled for armed peace. Incidentally, Monsieur Legris, where's that collection of books you were going to value?'

'Rue . . . Oh, how silly, the name escapes me, it must be the wine . . .'

'I heard about your friend.'

'What friend?'

'The bookbinder in Rue Monsieur-le-Prince. Chavagnac and Gerbecourt who were under me in the sixth arrondissement happened to be there.'

'Pierre Andrésy. Yes, a dreadful affair. Do you know the results of the investigation? Inspector Lecacheur hinted it might be arson.'

'Did he? No. I've no idea. How's your assistant?'

Pérot's colleague's chair creaked. He brushed past Pérot as Victor sliced into his veal and replied, 'He's very well. He's writing another serialised novel.'

He raised his head, about to take a mouthful of food. Inspector Corcol was saying goodbye to the landlady. He straightened his bowler and gave Victor a brief, hostile look. He seemed in a hurry to leave.

Madame Milent went over to clear his table. She hadn't missed a word of Pérot's conversation with that clean-shaven stranger – what was his name again? Monsieur Leblanc? No, Monsieur Legris, that was it.

'He's every bit as handsome as Monsieur Daglan. I wonder

who he is . . . Monsieur Daglan will be proud of me for being –
how did he put it? Oh yes! "His eyes and ears."'

As he reached Rue de la Lune, Joseph caught a delicious whiff
of butter brioche and gave in to temptation. In the words of
Monsieur Mori: 'Empty stomach, empty head'.

He pushed his way through the swarming, bustling crowd
on the Boulevard, zigzagging across streets teeming with
packed omnibuses, long carriages piled high with parcels,
hansom cabs with their oil-cloth hoods, and jittery hackney
carriages. He loved the lively atmosphere, the cafés, the
theatres. He let his imagination run wild: one day soon, one of
his serialised novels would be adapted for the stage and play to
full houses, catapulting him to stardom.

Thule's Golden Chalice, featuring Réjane or Sarah Bernhardt
as Frieda von Glockenspiel. As for Éleuthère the mastiff, that
could wait. And why not have it performed at Théâtre du
Gymnase? The play would cause such a sensation that everyone
with a telephone would listen to extracts on the théâtrophone.[46]
Not to mention patrons of the smart clubs and guests at the
grand hotels who could simply put fifty centimes into the magic
box and enjoy the best lines.

He imagined Monsieur Mori, so keen on the latest inven-
tions, with his ear glued to the receiver, nodding with delight as
Éleuthère's barks ascended the scale (could Monsieur Coquelin
Cadet be persuaded to make himself up to look like a dog?).

Sated on brioche and daydreams, he reached Théâtre de
l'Échiquier.

This doesn't look very promising. It wouldn't be my first choice, unless of course they offered me a nice fat advance, he told himself.

He walked across the foyer and knocked on a padded door with a sign saying CONCIERGE. A crabby voice rang out.

'What is it now?'

'I have a manuscript here to be delivered in person.'

There was a grating sound and a pointed nose poked warily through a crack in the door.

'Do you have an appointment?'

'Naturally. Joseph Pignot's the name, author of *Thule's Golden Chalice*, a sensational serialised novel soon to be printed in *Le Passe-partout*, which previously featured the outstanding *The Strange Affair at Colombines*.'

'Who's your appointment with?'

'The manager.'

'That's impossible. Monsieur Leglantier has been dead since Monday.'

The nose was retracted and the door closed.

'The silly old fool!' Joseph declared loudly, somewhat taken aback. However, he was now in possession of a vital piece of information: the infamous actor referred to by the Comtesse de Salignac had shuffled off this mortal coil. Could it be through natural causes?

An alluring young woman rushed in through the main doors. He followed her into an Italianate auditorium, which was dimly lit apart from the stage, where a few oil lamps were burning. A group of men and women were having a lively discussion in front of a set designed for a swashbuckler. Joseph, hoping not to be noticed, slipped among them nonchalantly. To no avail.

'You're not part of the cast,' a man declared.

'I'm a journalist. I'm here to find out more about the death of your manager.'

'You're the first person besides his creditors to show any interest in poor Monsieur Leglantier,' muttered the stage manager.

'And yet he was such a nice man!' affirmed the winsome young woman Joseph had followed.

'Could you tell me any more, Mademoiselle . . . ?' he asked, pencil poised over his notebook.

'Andréa's the name. He told me I had the makings of a star.'

'A shooting star, no doubt,' quipped a plump woman.

'He said something about an Amazon,' the young woman parried.

'An Amazon on an old nag? He must have meant in Fernando's Circus!'

'Eugénie, you're a spiteful old bitch!'

'And you're a common little tart!'

'Ladies, please! Show a little decorum, if only out of respect for Monsieur Edmond. Suicide is an act of deep despair that takes great courage.'

'And what would you know about courage, Monsieur le Duc d'Épernon!'

'What? You mean he killed himself!' exclaimed Joseph.

They all began chattering and gesticulating at the same time. Joseph took advantage of the confusion to usher Épernon into the wings.

'Did he really kill himself?'

Flattered that a journalist would want to interview him, Épernon whispered to Joseph, 'Between you and me, he was crippled by debt. Still, I'd never have believed him capable of ending his own life in such a tragic way. He was so intent on getting his theatre up and running again! I'll let you into a secret: he was counting heavily on my performance.'

'You say he had debts?'

'Apparently l'Échiquier was mortgaged. Do you think that might explain why he began his farewell note with a verse from La Fontaine: *a monkey and a leopard made money at the fair*?'

'A leopard?'

'Yes, I copied it out while nobody was looking. It goes on: *Cleaned out and completely ruined, I'm leaving this sewer. Farewell. My condolences to the other mugs. E. Leglantier – misunderstood genius*. Ah! Money is the root of all evil! Strange, though, that Jacques Bottelier should nearly run me through with his dagger when he was supposed to be stabbing Henri IV – I mean Leglantier. Would you like to see my dressing?'

'Hang on a minute, who's Bottelier?'

'He plays Ravaillac. The police are holding him for questioning. You're not leaving already, are you? Hey, Monsieur, don't forget to take down my name. Germain Milet – like the painter, only with one '*l*'!'

As Joseph was walking past the concierge's lodge, a woman's voice called out.

'Mr Journalist!'

Andréa appeared, looking very appealing with her heaving chest and flushed cheeks.

'Monsieur, I don't know what Germain's told you, but did he say anything about the bald bloke Monsieur Leglantier quarrelled with just before he died? I couldn't help overhearing them – they were making such a racket. They were calling each other all the names under the sun. I distinctly heard Monsieur Leglantier say, "I've been fleeced." I'm sure that bald bloke is not to be trusted. In my opinion, if anyone's to blame it's him. Ravaillac, I mean Jacques, wouldn't hurt a fly – he's the sort who faints if he sees a spider. He takes care of his mother and what'll become of her if he loses his job? You should stick that in your newspaper.'

'Are you in love with him?'

'Who with?'

'With this Jacques Bottelier.'

'Come off it! I don't like injustice, that's all. I missed my chance with the manager, Monsieur Leglantier, though. He fancied me, only I don't like sharing and he had an insatiable appetite. He'd already had Eugénie. She told me he had an official mistress, Adélaïde Paillet – a woman of at least thirty-five who runs a shop selling the latest fashions in Place Clichy.'

'Thank you kindly, Mademoiselle . . . You'll make a splendid Amazon.

'A sight for sore eyes in a tight bodice!' he muttered under his breath.

'The leopard and the Ambrex shares hold the key to this affair, don't you think, Boss?'

Down in the basement, out of earshot of Kenji, Victor listened to Joseph's account of his visit to Théâtre de l'Échiquier.

'That actor . . .'

'Épernon, Boss.'

'Yes, well, he says Leglantier wasn't the sort to have taken his own life, but he breathed in enough gas to put him six feet under.'

'He was broke, terrified of scandal. From what I could gather, the Duc de Frioul – the bald bloke has to be him – wasn't exactly gentle with him: threats of repossession, a lawsuit, a duel . . . Do you think it was murder? The scheming white-gloved hand of the aristocracy? Yes! Murder made to look like suicide.'

'Don't jump to conclusions.'

'But, Boss, it all fits! It's simple. Frioul goes to see Leglantier, they quarrel, Frioul tampers with the gas meter, types out a letter that he leaves in the typewriter, then departs, locking the door behind him. Frioul's the leopard!'

'Why would he choose a spotted feline as an alias?'

'No doubt he's got some ancestor who was loyal to the King of England. The Hundred Years War, and all that . . . Oh, I've got it! He owns a country seat at Quercy. I'll bet his coat of arms has a leopard passant or a spotted lion on it. I saw one once in a book on heraldry.'

'Your reasoning is a little far-fetched, Joseph. Do you really think Leglantier would have waited patiently to be gassed?'

'A good clout on the head might have helped.'

'It's possible. Your scenario would make a perfect plot for a serialised novel. Unfortunately the Duc de Frioul hasn't the gumption or the imagination to be a murderer.'

'You underestimate those toffs.'

'Let's be serious, when the Duc de Frioul was born, the good fairies rummaged through their sack and gave him the dross: a title, an estate in the sun and very little else. No, Joseph, our Léopardus is a notch above the rest in the brains department.'

'All right, you win, but how about this for a scenario? Leglantier cooked up a scheme to sell fake shares, did away with one of his accomplices – the enamellist Léopold Grandjean – then took his own life when the swindle was exposed.'

'And where does your clever theory about the arson attack on Pierre Andrésy's shop fit in? You're not thinking straight.'

'Will you stop criticising me? I'm fed up with it! What about you? What information have you brought to the case?'

'Drat, I'm late. I'm taking Tasha to a concert. We'll drop in on this Adélaïde Paillet woman tomorrow morning. Hopefully she'll be able to tell us more about her lover. Go on up, I'll follow.'

'You're in charge,' Joseph muttered, hiding the satisfaction he felt at having shut his boss up.

I'll go to Rue Monsieur-le-Prince next week. The errand boy at Fulbert's will be back by then, and he's bound to remember where he delivered the wine for this Gustave fellow, Victor thought to himself.

Joseph emerged from the basement and bumped straight into Kenji.

'Now that your secret assignation in the catacombs is over, I'm going out. You're dining here tonight.'

'What do you mean I'm dining here?'

'Have you forgotten? You're supposed to give the Balzacs and the Diderots a polish and arrange them in the window. We discussed it a fortnight ago. Your mother is making fried tomatoes and creamed spinach – she'll bring it to you down here. Good night.'

'Spinach! I can't stand that muck!'

'You're wrong there, pet,' Euphrosine shouted from the top of the spiral staircase, 'spinach cleans out the bowels.'

Thursday 20 July

Kenji, his eyes closed, gave his vow of abstinence the final coup de grâce as he made his way in a cab towards the Bibliothèque Nationale. He felt rejuvenated after his night with Eudoxie. He had replenished his energy with a seafood platter and some chilled white wine at Prunier's,[47] and was now focusing on his inner sensations, allowing his mind to drift freely – an exercise he practised whenever his attention was not needed elsewhere.

The cab dropped him off at Rue de Richelieu where he re-engaged with reality.

He spotted the fellow whom the clerk with the paper knife had mentioned at the far end of the second row of tables to the right of the main desk. Dressed in a wide-sleeved tunic, a pair of baggy trousers and a green skullcap, the Armenian was fast asleep behind a mound of folios, his arms crossed over a thick volume. Miraculously, the seat next to him was free. In fact, the reading room was almost deserted on account of the heat. Kenji quickly began leafing through a catalogue he'd chosen at random. He filled in a form specifying where he wanted to sit and the reference number of the books he wanted to consult, handed it to an assistant librarian and went to take his place next to Aram Kasangian.

Kasangian sat up slowly, his doleful face half hidden by an imposing black moustache and flowing beard. He looked Kenji up and down with suspicion, and shifted the pile of folios to conceal the volume he'd been using as a pillow. Shielding his work with his arm, he began taking notes.

Aware that he was under observation, Kenji started meticulously polishing his spectacles. He was wondering how to initiate a conversation with his neighbour, when the man muttered, 'You are in great danger, Monsieur.'

Kenji, alarmed, thought that he was about to reveal some terrible secret about the Persian manuscript.

'Please explain.'

'If you persist in this harmful habit you will be afflicted by unimaginable suffering. Constricting the blood vessels can lead to a blocked artery. Deprived of blood, the heart starts struggling and slows down until it stops completely.'

'To what are you referring?'

'To your cravat.'

The Armenian leant over his book again as abruptly as he'd sat up.

Just my luck. The man's a raving lunatic, Kenji thought, as the librarian brought over an octavo volume.

'I see you're keen on Africa,' his neighbour resumed in a low voice.

'Not really.'

'Then why are you consulting Stanley's *Through the Dark Continent*?'[48]

'I'm interested in the sources of the Nile. And what is the nature of your research, Monsieur?'

Aram Kasangian chewed his penholder and studied him.

'If anybody asks, tell them you don't know.'

Exasperated, Kenji stood up, walked behind the Armenian and tried to catch a glimpse of the book he was so zealously guarding. The man responded by flattening himself over it completely.

'Could you tell me the name of the manuscript – I assume that's what it is – which that wild-eyed fanatic is consulting?' he asked the assistant librarian.

'Shh!'

He'd spoken too loudly and a few heads were raised.

'I'm afraid that's confidential. Monsieur Kasangian is a renowned philologist. He's been coming to the library for the past twenty-five years and is honouring us by drafting on these premises what will be the definitive Persian–French dictionary. In their eagerness to assist him the librarians have done everything in their power to acquire as many Arabic and Persian texts as they can. Ah! If only we could compete with the libraries of Mecca and Constantinople!' the assistant added, ruefully.

'May I at least have a look at this rare work when he returns it at the end of the day? I myself am an expert on Sufism.'

'As well as on Africa?'

'The one does not exclude the other.'

'Monsieur Kasangian stays right up until closing time and will reserve for first thing tomorrow the books he's been consulting today.'

'But surely they're not his exclusive property!' Kenji exclaimed.

'Please try not to raise your voice above a whisper, Monsieur!'

Kenji gave up. He went back to his seat and spent the next hour devising strategies to glimpse the famous manuscript. He dropped his pencil under the Armenian's chair, asked to borrow a rubber, sat sideways on his seat in an attempt to force him to rearrange the wall of folios shielding the coveted treasure. To no avail – his neighbour never lowered his guard.

As the minutes ticked by, Kenji resigned himself to following each arduous step of Stanley's journey in search of Dr Livingstone, whilst dreaming of Eudoxie's charms. As six o'clock approached, he leant towards the Armenian, who had begun gathering up his folios, and stood on tiptoe in a last attempt to see over the stack of books. But in a sleight of hand worthy of a conjuror, Aram Kasangian had already spirited the manuscript away under an encyclopedia. Refusing Kenji's offer of help, he triumphantly carried his hoard of books over to the main desk.

Kenji stared at him, screwing up his eyes, and, with a cat-like expression on his face, vowed silently, I'll get the better of you yet.

'I hate those great big statues with their arms sticking up in the air!' Joseph said, pointing to the monument glorifying General Moncey's heroic stand.[49] For his part, Victor was busy studying an enormous poster depicting an Arab standing with his camel opposite a chap in colonial dress who was admiring an Oriental carpet. On the side of the same building, a shop sign inspired by

Chéret featured a woman swathed in lace, her foot perched boldly on a tombstone inscribed in letters of fire:

TO DIE FOR
The New Fashion Store

Adélaïde Paillet's shop, although unpretentious, nevertheless boasted a foyer lit by a glass cupola, and an open fretwork staircase leading up to the first floor. The manageress oversaw two sales girls on the ground floor, which was devoted to lingerie and the latest Paris fashions. An affable male assistant was in charge of accessories on the first floor, catering to ladies wishing to liven up their outfits with a velvet flower, a feather boa or – the height of luxury – a fox fur or sable stole.

Madame Paillet's professional sycophancy changed to marmoreal coldness as soon as Victor explained the reason for their visit.

'We're from *Le Passe-partout*. We've been assigned to write a portrait of the manager of l'Échiquier, who recently took his own life. I believe he was a friend of yours.'

'I can see that discretion is a thing of the past. Please have the decency not to discuss my private life in front of my customers.'

None of the young ladies busy fingering the various fabrics appeared to have overheard. One of the sales girls was measuring a length of silk against a yardstick attached to a copper rod descending from the ceiling. The other whispered, 'Monsieur Edmond killed himself! That's not possible, Madame!'

'It is both possible and true, Camille. Monsieur Myon telephoned me last night to give me the news.'

'Oh, Madame, how awful for you! I'm so sorry.'

'Thank you, Camille. Now go and help poor Lise – I know those infuriating customers who make you unravel twenty yards of surah only to end up buying half a yard of cotton.'

'You are remarkably self-possessed for somebody who is in mourning,' commented Victor.

Adélaïde Paillet looked askance at him, trying to detect any hint of irony in his voice. Having decided that he was sincere, she dabbed her brown eyes and patted her bun ruefully.

'Displays of grief won't bring Edmond back. Since Monsieur Paillet was taken from me by an inflammation of the lungs. I belong to the ranks of the widowed. I've made my own way in life. Edmond was attentive, but alas that was all. He was a miser and a skinflint who only wanted me for the pleasures of the flesh. Do you know what he had the nerve to give me two months ago? A complimentary ticket for a seat in the tenth row of Les Folies-Belleville. Can you imagine my embarrassment surrounded by a lot of flashy foreigners and oglers of half-naked flesh! When I think that he was about to pull off a deal that would have given him the means to finish renovating his theatre. Apparently he'd achieved the impossible! I was hoping he'd pay me back the money he owed me before we parted for good. I can kiss that goodbye now!'

'Did he ever mention Léopold Grandjean or Pierre Andrésy?'

'Do you imagine he confided his secrets to me? He took me for mussels and *frites* on a Sunday then back to his place, where all I got was a sore back from his lumpy mattress. I don't want to know about his schemes. We agreed to break off our relationship last month. It's the 20th today, isn't it? That makes it an anniversary. Hurrah for freedom! You can see yourselves out, gentlemen.'

She left them standing there, and went over to serve an old crone in raptures over an artistic window display featuring a light-blue dress, a scarf twisted round a chair and a few parasols.

'This one in cerise satin with the matching forget-me-not tassels is the height of fashion and perfect for the seaside, Madame.'

'Perfect for scaring off the seagulls, more like,' muttered Joseph.

'Come along, we're wasting our time here,' Victor announced.

A woman dragging a tearful child by the arm bumped into them. Joseph noticed a tuft of fur sticking out of the boy's jacket and gestured to Camille, who ran into the street after them. She returned a moment later, flushed, holding a muff.

'Just look at that!'

'What is it?' asked Joseph.

'Siberian grey squirrel. Madame, thanks to this gentleman here, I nabbed a thief who was using a kid as a decoy,' she explained to the manageress. 'She got away, but I managed to recover the merchandise.'

The customers and the two shop girls broke into loud chatter.

'It's a disgrace using kids like that! They hide the stolen items on them, pinch them until they cry, then scarper,' Camille explained.

'Not to mention the ones who work in pairs, where one

sends you up a ladder to fetch a bolt of cloth while the other nicks half the shop,' Lise went on.

'And that trick of dropping a fine piece of lace on the floor and hiding it in their shoe,' added Camille.

'Where will it end!' Adélaïde Paillet exploded. 'The government, the middlemen and the public are ruining us and unfair competition will finish us off for good. How can we compete with stores like the Palais du Travailleur[50] which covers six thousand square yards and sells everything from the latest fashions to hire-purchase furniture and even milk at sixty centimes a litre? Gentlemen, I'm hugely indebted to you.'

She asked the two men to follow her up to the first floor where she scolded the sales assistant for his inattention before leading them into a changing room.

'There are one or two things I didn't tell you. But you've done me a favour and fair's fair. Just don't mention my name. I've enough worries as it is.'

'We give you our word,' Victor promised.

'Every other Sunday Edmond would come to my place. About a month ago, on 18 June, I told him I'd break off our relationship if he didn't pay me back the ten thousand francs he owed me. He swore on his life – ill-fatedly as it turned out – that he'd have the money for me the following Thursday. He was a very good actor and a little bird told me not to trust him. So I decided to follow him. He didn't go very far – just to Muller's brasserie, at 60, Rue du Faubourg-Montmartre. I watched him through the window. He walked up to a man who handed him a cake box. He didn't open it and the man left. Another of his shady deals! I thought to myself. The following Thursday he handed me five thousand francs in cash and promised to give me the rest in shares. Naturally I refused. That is all, gentlemen.'

'What were the shares in?'

'Ambrex.'

'Can you describe the man he met at Muller's?'

'A nondescript fellow of about fifty, poorly dressed, wearing a terrible checked bowler, below average height, with a slight potbelly, the sort of person you wouldn't look twice at in the street.'

'You're very observant, Madame.'

'I have to be in my line of work.'

When they descended, the old crone had given in to the temptation of the cerise parasol and was feverishly fingering a bathing cap trimmed with little bows.

They strolled down Avenue de Clichy past the restaurant Père Lathuile. Victor was staring down at the pavement as if he thought he might find the answer to his questions there. He stopped dead in his tracks; he'd suddenly remembered Kenji's description of the man who'd sold the lot of Oriental manuscripts to Esquirol. Could it be the same fellow who was at Muller's brasserie? If so, then perhaps he was the link between Pierre Andrésy and Edmond Leglantier. He shared his reflections with Joseph, who had been wondering whether he was going to take root. They walked back the way they'd come and turned left.

'Why do I have the feeling you're not telling me everything, Boss?'

'You're imagining things, Joseph.'

'Don't try to pull the wool over my eyes. You didn't tell me what Monsieur Mori was up to. I'm the last to know, just a shop assistant, no better than a slave! How are we supposed to make progress if you won't let me in on anything?'

'It went clean out of my head.'

'You're becoming very forgetful in your old age.'

'Well, now you know. Monsieur Mori's investigations ended in failure. This leaves two possibilities: either the manuscript miraculously escaped the flames or . . . somebody started the fire deliberately in order to steal it.'

'It was only worth fifteen hundred francs.'

'Our knowledge of human nature tells us that people will be tempted by less.'

'It's absurd. Pierre Andrésy would never have become involved in . . . No, Boss, you're talking through your hat!'

Joseph kicked a pebble and sent it flying over the iron bridge which rose above Montmartre cemetery. The boss was right. Even Iris had fallen off her pedestal.

'It's still early,' said Victor. 'I'm going to *Le Passe-partout*. I'm sure if I try hard enough I'll manage to wheedle some information out of them.'

'But they don't know anything!'

'They know the name and description of the person who witnessed Grandjean's murder.'

'And what about me? Are you leaving me in the lurch? I suppose I'm to be relegated to Rue des Saints-Pères.'

Joseph looked dolefully at the sombre avenues of the cemetery where two of his favourite authors, Stendhal and

Murger, were buried. Life was a trick, love an illusion and his boss's promises hollow.

'Come on, Joseph, what's happened to your usual optimism? You're not being relegated anywhere! Antonin Clusel is an old friend of mine. Seeing him on my own will save a lot of chitchat. And, anyway, Kenji will object if one of us doesn't return to the fold.'

'I'll volunteer – you go and run rings round that wily fox, Clusel. But don't forget I'm the one who started this case.'

'What I regret having forgotten, Joseph, is my bicycle.'

He rummaged in his pockets and pulled out a handful of coins. 'Here, we'll split this and take a cab each.'

A constant stream of pedestrians held up the traffic in Passage Jouffroy. By the time he reached the offices of *Le Passe-partout* in Rue de la Grange-Batelière, Victor felt stifled, as much from impatience as from the heat. His entrance amid the ceaseless animation of the newspaper aroused no comment and he walked straight up to the office of the editor-in-chief. He didn't even need to knock, simply slipping through the door on the heels of a typographer who had come to ask for advice about the page layout. Antonin Clusel, perching on a corner of a table, circled a few freshly printed lines in pencil while an amply proportioned secretary tapped away on a typewriter. It was only after the typographer had left that Antonin noticed Victor.

'Just the man I need! Am I right in thinking that you're a cycling enthusiast? Eulalie, my dear, stop that racket for a moment, would you? Go and find something else to do while we talk.'

She complied grudgingly, and slammed the door.

'A sweet child, I've often thought of marrying her, but in the words of Alfred Capus: "How many couples are not torn apart by marriage!" Help me with this, will you? I'm devising a questionnaire aimed at the man in the street. No doubt you're aware that since 28 April a tax has been levied on bicycles.'

He read aloud, '"Ten francs for every bicycle, plus five centimes per franc, plus another three centimes for the tax collector." This is something that affects many of our readers. The tax raised on a hundred and eighty thousand bicycles will be one million nine hundred and forty-five thousand seven hundred francs gross a year. As a sportsman, what is your opinion of this?'

'I think they ought to put a tax on feet – one sou per toe. Imagine the amount of money that would bring in to the treasury.'

Antonin Clusel stroked his chin.

'What a pity you refuse to work with me! I need clever men like you. I've just hired two new reporters whose copy is as dull as ditch-water. I'm taking the newspaper in a new direction: less debate, more detailed reports and interviews. I want to go back to the last editor's methods. He inspired readers with features like "A Week with . . ." during the Universal Exposition of 1889.'

'I don't much hold with the present vogue for printing people's opinion on anything and everything. Ministers, murderers, actors, priests, soldiers. The problem is they're encouraged to talk about things they know nothing about: the priest rants against the theatre, the actor criticises the army, the murderer applauds amnesties and the minister laments the condition of the worker. It's impossible to escape the torrent of words: opera, murder, sardine fishing, vaccination, the immortality of the soul, war, corsets; anything goes so long as it fills the daily columns!'

'What passion, what eloquence! You deserve a glass of curaçao. I'll pour you one while I have a cigar.'

Antonin Clusel blew out a flawless smoke ring.

'You've summed up perfectly the problem facing today's press. Events cause people to ask questions. However, if they refuse to act, it's up to us to shake them out of their lethargy. The people we interview are chosen not because of what they know, but because of how well known they are. The average man or woman, far from sending the *Passe-partout* journalist packing for asking strange or intrusive questions, opens their door to him and shows him round the house, inviting him to admire their fine curtains and valuable artwork. You see, my friend, people nowadays like to show off. Everybody dreams of being in the papers.'

'I scoured *Le Passe-partout* in vain for the name of the witness to Léopold Grandjean's murder.'

'Ah! I smell a case! Be careful or you'll have Inspector Lecacheur on your back. Of course you didn't find the name; printing it would endanger the witness, and if there's anything yours truly the Virus detests it's breaking his word. I have yet to sink so low. However, I will give you a clue: the witness is a woman.'

'And Grandjean's address?'

'You're insatiable! What are you getting yourself mixed up in this time? I shouldn't really tell you, but I will because I like you: 29b, Rue des Boulets.'

Victor gulped his curaçao down in one and was preparing to leave when he suddenly changed his mind.

'Is there any news about Edmond Leglantier's death? Did he leave a suicide note?'

'Not as far as I know. You're a walking encyclopaedia of news stories, my friend! His so-called suicide looks suspiciously like murder. Your Leglantier was knocked senseless before the gas fumes got to him. The police have grilled an actor by the name of Jacques Bottelier, but he has an alibi: at the time of the crime he was dressed as Ravaillac waiting with his fellow thespians for Henri IV to arrive. However, it appears that the Duc de Frioul – no less – is heavily implicated. The police are handling him with kid gloves because of his noble lineage. He categorically denies hitting Leglantier over the head and shutting him in with the gas on. As for yours truly the Virus, you'll quite understand that he refuses to question the honesty of one of his newspaper's main shareholders . . .'

CHAPTER NINE

Friday 21 July

VICTOR felt a heady sense of elation that morning as he cycled across Paris, despite his remorse at having told lies to the two people dearest to his heart. It was the longest bicycle journey he'd ever undertaken, and he felt invincible. He let nothing stand in his way; he avoided every obstacle as if he were one of those genies in the fairy tales. In fact, there was very little traffic that day and the only hold-up he encountered was a couple of carts blocking the entrance to Rue du Faubourg-Saint-Antoine. The mild night had dispelled the dampness of the past few days, and the air had a spring-like feel. Victor whistled, forcing himself to stop thinking about the fibs he'd told Tasha and Kenji. Tasha thought he was meeting a fellow photographer with an interest in itinerant traders, and Kenji believed he had an appointment with a book collector in the eastern suburbs of the city.

"'The end justifies the means, O mother of mine, long live the students!"' he sang. He watched his reflection in the windows as he pedalled past first an upholsterer and then an ironmonger and saw a man in a slim-fitting jacket with trousers clasped by bicycle clips.

Throngs of workers spewed forth from every building, their knapsacks slung over their shoulders. Housewives were hanging their washing out to dry and children were making their way to school. The stench of tanned leather wafted through Rue des Boulets. Victor was looking at the house numbers as he rattled across the moss-covered paving stones, when his bicycle slipped and began to weave dangerously. He managed to regain control and smiled at a little girl tying a piece of rag round a puppy's neck. But then his front wheel hit a piece of broken pavement and his bicycle tipped forward. His hands flew from the handlebars, his feet from the pedals and his backside from the saddle. He sailed through the air and landed with a thud. He lay sprawled in the gutter, winded. He'd sustained a few grazes but no broken bones. Kneeling beside his machine, he weighed up the damage. The chain was still on and the handlebars weren't bent.

'A lively steed!' a man's voice cried out. 'Needs taming, perhaps?'

'He's calmed down. He does get a little skittish sometimes,' Victor replied.

'You're bleeding,' the man said. 'Come inside and stretch out on the tiles. They're cool; it'll calm you.'

'I'm all right, really,' mumbled Victor, pressing his handkerchief to his nose.

Victor followed the man in grey overalls into his workshop.

'Fulgence,' he shouted, 'go and park this gentleman's bicycle, and keep an eye on it.'

The boy sitting in front of the tall machine with cogwheels that was winding up a roll of wallpaper didn't need to be told twice.

'A glass of hooch, that'll lift your spirits,' said the man in the overalls. 'Mine, too, for that matter – I'm parched. Bottoms up!'

'I apologise for the disturbance.'

'Oh, it breaks the monotony. We're slaves to work! If we take Monday off it's because we've worked all day Sunday. My name's Père Fortin.'

'I was on my way to Monsieur Grandjean's – I placed an order with him before he was . . .'

Victor had scarcely uttered the enamellist's name when Père Fortin wiped his moist whiskers and launched into a detailed diatribe.

'Grandjean, I was always bumping into him. It's only natural when you work in the same trade and you live in the same neighbourhood. He worked in Passage Gonnet, about two minutes from Rue des Boulets. His sons, Polyte and Constant, thirteen and fifteen, are friends of my son Évariste. I can't understand why anyone would want to kill Léopold – he was a generous soul and liked by everybody. You should have seen the turn-out at his funeral! He was buried at Père-Lachaise; we had a whip-round for the wreaths and the blonde negress supplied the flowers.'

He leant towards Victor and confided, 'She found the body, she even saw the killer – from a distance, mind you, she couldn't describe him. More's the pity. A rotter like that should be skinned alive. Ever since, the poor girl's been scared the murderer will find her, which wouldn't be difficult.'

'Why?'

'She sells flowers. She can't afford to lie low until things die down. Mind you, the newspapers behaved decently; they didn't publish her description or her name and her address, which is almost the same as mine – I'm number 12 and she lives at 29b.'

'She's a negress and she's blonde?'

'Well, not exactly, more coffee-coloured with lightish hair – a pretty girl, if a bit wild. I don't suppose life's been very kind to her.'

Victor thanked him before leaving on foot, wheeling his bicycle.

An iron gate at 29b led into a courtyard overgrown with weeds where a few hens pecked. The building resembled an army barracks with its forbidding wall and tiny shutterless windows. A woman with a double chin was walking towards him, carrying a basket. She opened the gate and glanced suspiciously at Victor, who doffed his hat.

'Excuse me, Madame, is this where the flower girl they call the blonde negress lives?'

'Josette? Yes, she has the flat above ours. She gives herself airs because she found a body and it was in the newspapers. As if she didn't get enough attention! She's a brazen hussy if ever there was one. My Marcel has a docile nature, but even his eyes pop out on stalks whenever he sees her. It makes you sick, a half-white creature like that.'

Having vented her malice, the woman gathered up her basket.

'Where does she sell her flowers?'

'How should I know? On the streets or at the flower markets – girls like her are right little streetwalkers!'

Victor was considerably less elated on the return journey than the outward one. He felt slightly sick as he recalled the fat woman's words; was it an effect of the heat or the alcohol, or were the dealers in English furniture and the makers of Renaissance dressers and demi-Louis XV wardrobes sneering at him from their shop doorways as he walked past?

I just hope Iris, Tasha or Kenji are never on the receiving end of such bile, he said to himself as he reached Place de la Bastille.

By an unlucky twist of fate, one of the customers when he arrived at the Elzévir bookshop was that overgrown nanny-goat Blanche de Cambrésis, who always had something unpleasant to say on the subject of foreigners. This time, however, she had other matters on her mind and was busy running down her friend Olympe de Salignac for the exclusive benefit of Kenji, trapped behind his desk.

'What a perfect coward! When she heard that Valentine's uncle by marriage was mixed up in a murder, she shut herself away at Rue Barbet-de-Jouy, with that poor Adalberte whose health is so frail and whose husband, incidentally, is no better than the Duc de Frioul! Réauville may be an ex-colonel, but he's no less of a ninny. He also cleaned himself out in order to buy those Ambrex shares! Adalberte will have a fit. You wouldn't catch me making such a risky investment. I've put some of my money in Russian bonds – at least you can rely on them!'

Taking advantage of the situation, Victor whisked Joseph out from under a customer's nose and gave him a brief summary of the information he'd gleaned. The Hachette guidebook showed them where the flower markets were: two of them were at La Cité and La République on Wednesdays and Saturdays. There was a third flower market at La Madeleine on Tuesdays and Fridays.

'You'll have to dash over to La Madeleine as soon as you've had lunch,' concluded Victor, before going to Kenji's aid.

Joseph hurried off to La Madeleine. On the pavements outside the church, the flower sellers stood under their tarpaulins serving elegant customers or their servants. Tea roses, white gardenias, variegated carnations and brightly coloured gladioli were arranged next to simple daisies and pots of sweet peas. The shimmering colours filled him with joy as he sniffed the air, trying to identify the different perfumes that had mingled into a single heavenly scent. A gardener's daughter wearing a dress with braid trimmings gaily pointed out the blonde negress's stall to Joseph, whom she tried without success to interest in a beautifully composed bouquet.

When she glimpsed the young man striding towards her, still attractive despite his slight hunchback, Josette Fatou was filled with a sense of foreboding that was quickly justified by his blunt declaration.

'Mademoiselle Fatou, my name is Joseph Pignot, novelist and bookseller. I was hoping that since you were a witness to a murder you might be able to help me reconstruct . . .'

Josette's shrieks were already drawing a crowd before he had time to finish his sentence. A plump woman wearing a mantilla hurried to her aid, spurring on the little brown dog trotting along at her feet.

'Bite him, Sultan, bite!'

The animal merely lay on the ground and yapped at Joseph.

'What's all the fuss about, Josette?' her neighbour called out.

'This man is making indecent proposals.'

'Shame on you! Libertine, lecher!'

Joseph took the insult with the composure of a hero in a Dumas novel: hands on hips, resigned yet proud, he was the image of a victim defying adversity.

'Silence that wild beast, Madame, I am withdrawing.'

A constable was coming over, and Joseph thought it best to beat a retreat.

Alone once more, Josette managed to control her fear, but she could not stop her hands from shaking. The man's face still haunted her. She relived the fear she'd felt when she regained consciousness, stretched out on her bed, a cold compress on her forehead. Had it been a nightmare or had she really felt a hand caressing her breasts while she was still semi-conscious? She couldn't be sure, though her blouse was half open. The stranger had apologised for giving her a fright, he'd had no business entering her bedroom. If he'd dared to importune her it was because she was the only one who could help him – that is if she agreed to describe the man who'd stabbed Léopold Grandjean. She had cowered, convinced that he was enjoying her terror and that he would beat her, violate her, kill her even. But instead he had sat down beside her and gently handed her another compress. Then she'd told him falteringly that she could only remember two things about the murderer: his hair was grey and he liked music, because when he'd stabbed the enamellist he'd started singing a song.

'Mademoiselle, you've just given me a priceless piece of information,' the man had said, getting up to leave. 'See you soon!'

She jumped as a voice whispered to her through the openwork fence behind her stand.

'Mademoiselle, it's me, Joseph Pignot. Please don't scream. I don't want to hurt you! I lied, I'm not really a novelist, I'm a trainee journalist and this is my assignment. You see, my future depends on your willingness to help me. All I ask is a few details you haven't already given the newspapers.'

'What good will it do if I tell you?'

'I'll avoid a dressing-down from my boss!'

She smiled weakly at Joseph's forlorn expression and his lopsided bowler.

'All right,' she sighed. 'Here we go again. I was on my way back from Les Halles – it must have been about seven in the morning. I often passed Monsieur Grandjean and we'd say good morning to each other. He was a very kind man, and good to his wife, he was always buying her bunches of carnations.'

'Did you see his attacker?'

'He had his back to me. He was wearing a felt hat and a sort of greatcoat. I think he was quite old because when he ran off I saw a lock of grey hair sticking out from under his hat. Monsieur Grandjean clutched his stomach, and fell to the ground. It seemed to happen so slowly, like a bad dream, but it can't even have been five minutes. I couldn't move. The killer bent over and laid something on his chest then he started singing.'

'Singing? What?'

She paused. She'd told the other man. But telling a journalist . . . What difference did it make?

'"The Cherry Season", my mother's favourite song. It was strange the way he stood right over the corpse and started singing, like you'd sing a child to sleep. I crouched, hidden in the doorway. I waited until he'd gone before running over to Monsieur Grandjean, who was curled up in a ball. For a moment I thought he was still breathing because he was holding a scrap of paper between his fingers and it was moving. And then I saw the blood. I screamed and everyone came running. A coalman went to fetch the coppers. The policeman arrived. That's all. Please, whatever you do, don't mention my name. I'm terrified the murderer will come for me!'

'I swear on my mother's life! How tall was he?'

'About the same height as you, five foot seven. I couldn't say whether he was fat or thin with that big coat on.'

'Mademoiselle, you've saved my bacon! Here, I'll buy one of your gardenias; it'll make a pretty buttonhole.'

Bravo lad, a cake-walk. You're becoming a right little Romeo! Right, grey hair, 'The Cherry Season', five foot seven, a fine harvest!

Iris was waiting in the hallway of the School of Oriental Languages on the corner of Rue de Lille and Rue des Saints-Pères. She had just attended a conference on *Genji Monogatari* and, as she'd been one of very few women in the lecture hall, and no doubt the youngest and the prettiest, all the men's eyes had been on her. A few months earlier, she would have felt pleased as punch, but now her success with men infuriated and repulsed her. A curse on her beauty, if all it did was bring her unhappiness! Why couldn't she be like those plain or even ugly girls who dazzle people with their intellect! Then she would not have fallen for Maurice Laumier's smooth-talking charm and would have avoided the rift with the man dearest to her heart. The moral of this unfortunate story was enough to make a poor innocent girl faced with life's dangers cynical: it was better to lie, or to leave out one or two important facts, rather than risk disaster.

She heard the echo of voices and footsteps behind her; the conference, which she'd left just before the end, must be over. She put her parasol up and left the place. The sound of running feet made her quicken her pace. Her pursuer, far from being discouraged, also speeded up. Exasperated, she swung round, ready to give the bounder a piece of her mind. She was unable to utter a word. The man whom she'd been studiously avoiding and who for his part had been giving her the cold shoulder stood motionless before her. Joseph, his cheeks bright pink, his hair tousled beneath his bowler, embarrassed at having chased her in that way, tried desperately to find the right thing to say. Who knows what guardian angel whispered to Iris the expression that would defuse the situation, but without pausing to weigh her words, she observed hurriedly, 'Between love and friendship there is but one small step: backwards!'

Her words swept away the resentment that had built up between them. The words hung in the air, the corners of their mouths twitched and suddenly they were in fits of laughter.

'Where . . . where did you get that from?' hiccuped Joseph.

'I read it in a magazine,' she managed to reply before choking with laughter again.

Having finally composed themselves, they stared at one another for a long time, oblivious to the silence that was devoid of any awkwardness. They were together again! The invisible wall that had grown up between them had crumbled! How absurd their lovers' tiff now seemed! Joseph stifled his urge to kiss Iris, although he sensed that she would have overlooked the impropriety of the gesture and let him. He was content to hold her hand. He took her to the Temps Perdu café, where he and Monsieur Legris occasionally went for some refreshment when they were out on one of their investigations. Sitting side by side, they marvelled at the sights on Quai Malaquais, where booksellers hoped to attract the attention of the strollers drawn to the cool shade under the trees.

'I have but one wish, and that is to take a step forward,' he said.

'Do you still love me?'

'I've never stopped adoring you!'

How wonderful life seemed all of a sudden! The love they thought had died, withered on the vine, was in full bloom like the flowers at La Madeleine . . . Blast! He had to tell the boss about his talk with the shapely flower girl. And then invent a good excuse for staying out with Iris until the evening.

'I'm going to telephone your brother to tell him we'll be late.'

'Are we going out? Where?'

'Wherever you like. Choose your drink as well. I'll be back in a tick.'

And too bad if it breaks the bank! he thought.

A little jaunt together, somewhere in the city Kenji and Victor didn't know about. How romantic and at the same time devilishly daring. Iris swelled with pride, convinced that she embodied the ideal of the *fin-de-siècle* young woman, emancipated, yet in control of her destiny. As if to prove it to herself, she ordered two quinquinas, and reflected on where she would like to go. By the time Joseph came back, she'd decided. He flopped down beside her, clutching his jaw.

'Officially, I've got terrible toothache, on account of the heat. You and I ran into one another, and you kindly offered to accompany me to the dentist. The bosses weren't convinced, your brother made a sort of clucking noise, and I could hear your father complaining about my frequent absences, so I was forced to howl down the telephone!'

'You poor thing. Is it dreadfully painful?'

'I'm all right now, but it was awful for a while.'

She blushed, and stammered, 'One day, I was studying a dragonfly's flight in Place du Panthéon. Attracted by a ray of sunlight, she'd lost her way and was in danger of being crushed by the traffic and the pedestrians. A gust of wind saved her from disaster . . . Will you ever forgive me?'

'The war is over; we're throwing in the towel. This moment marks the beginning of an era of peace.'

I must remember to put that in one of my novels, he thought.

'Is there anywhere in particular you'd like to go?' he added, hoping that she would ask him to take her to the nearest secluded doorway.

'Tasha's father is very enthusiastic about the praxinoscope in his letters from America. I'd love to go to Théâtre Optique at Musée Grevin. They have showings until six o'clock.'

'Why not? It's certainly better than having a tooth pulled,' he replied philosophically.

As he was counting up the few coins competing for the honour of a place in his pocket, he noticed that he'd lost his gardenia.

Of the three animated pictures advertised, Iris chose *Poor Pierrot* – although *The Clown and His Dogs* and *A Good Beer*[51] looked equally amusing. She clapped excitedly throughout, like a little girl, and Joseph took the opportunity to put his hand on her knee to rein in her ardour. Forty minutes later they tore themselves away from the Cabinet Fantastique. Iris read out in a soft voice the programme of events advertised on the poster by Chéret:

> POOR PIERROT, A PANTOMIME
> *Characters:*
> *Pierrot, Harlequin, Colombine.*

Harlequin is Laumier, Colombine is me, and poor Pierrot is . . . she said to herself.

The same thought had no doubt occurred to Joseph, because he yanked her away.

'I've never seen anything so mesmerising!' she declared.

'There's no mystery about these projections, Mademoiselle

– or should I say Madame,' remarked a man with a blond moustache in a light-coloured suit.

'Mademoiselle, soon to be Madame,' Joseph replied abruptly.

Iris was so captivated that the announcement went right over her head.

'Do you know how it works? Oh, do tell me, please!' she implored, to Joseph's dismay.

'Monsieur Émile Reynaud perfected the zoetrope, which an Englishman named Horner invented. Sketches of a figure in different phases of a movement are placed on the inside of a cylinder at the centre of which is a rotating mirrored drum. When you look through one of the holes it gives you the illusion of movement.'

'It's childish,' remarked Joseph.

'You're right, the eye quickly tires of these simple, repetitive images, which is why Monsieur Reynaud's idea of a strip of celluloid containing a series of drawings is so brilliant; the perforated images pass from one bobbin to another and are reflected onto a mirror which then projects the carefully drawn hand-coloured scenes through a lantern onto a screen.'

'Do you work here?' asked Joseph, jealous of the spellbound expression on Iris's face.

Am I becoming worse than Monsieur Legris? He pulled himself up.

'No, I'm a journalist at *Le Temps*.'

'How marvellous! My fiancé writes for a newspaper, too. *Le Passe-partout*! He's a well-known author of serialised novels.'

At these words, Joseph's heart soared. Iris had called him her fiancé, and referred to his works! She'd atoned for her impulsiveness and the hack's impudence.

'Really? Why don't we discuss it on the Boulevard? Allow me to invite you to dinner,' the stranger proposed.

Joseph, his wallet almost empty, accepted gratefully.

How easily he'd snared these lovebirds, Frédéric Daglan thought to himself as he studied the clumsily written menu. A little technical knowledge gleaned from the newspapers together with the gift of the gab had been all it took.

'It's a simple, unpretentious place that suits my modest income. The lamb is delicious. I recommend it.'

'Have you read *The Strange Affair at Colombines*?' Iris asked.

'Alas, Mademoiselle, I'm a financial columnist. Numbers distract me from literature – which as a lover of the arts I lament. What is the story behind this strange affair?'

The author of serialised novels began to relate a muddled plot, which was soon lost on Frédéric Daglan. He thought back over his day: the flower market at Place de la Madeleine, Josette Fatou looking particularly appealing amidst her roses, despite their prickles. He'd been about to introduce himself when this journalistic oaf had sprung out of nowhere and caused a fracas. And then, judging from the conspiratorial look on their faces, he'd come back to wheedle information out of the blonde negress. So when he'd leapt on an omnibus, Frédéric Daglan had followed close on his heels, his hat pulled down over his eyes. Then, on Quai Malaquais, he'd had to put up with the couple's endless billing and cooing, after which he'd followed them in a cab to Rue Montmartre, where they'd taken in an animated spectacle. That was the price he'd had to pay in order to pin down the misguided scribbler.

'And just then Dr Rambuteau orders the nurse to wash poor Félix Charenton,'[52] concluded Jojo.

'What a wonderful story, brilliantly constructed. And who is the author of this absorbing work?'

'Joseph Pignot at your service, but you exaggerate, I'm just an amateur.'

'Don't listen to him, Monsieur . . .'

'Renard, Cédric Renard.'

'Joseph is always putting himself down, Monsieur Renard. Not only is he a published author, he's also a bookseller.'

'An excellent combination, Monsieur Pignot. Where do you exercise your talents?'

'At 18, Rue des Saints-Pères. You may have heard of one of my bosses? Victor Legris. He's solved a number of difficult crimes. I'm his right-hand man.'

Frédéric Daglan felt a knot in his stomach. Legris . . . Legris . . . The fleeting image of Madame Milent came into his mind. She was reading back to him a conversation she'd noted down between Inspector Pérot and a clean-shaven fellow . . . Legris? Yes, Legris. They'd lunched together at her place on . . . on the 19th.

'Monsieur Legris is very clever,' the fair-haired youth enthused. 'But he wouldn't be anywhere without me. Why, only today . . .'

Joseph bit his lip.

Frédéric Daglan heard his voice reply as though it belonged to somebody else.

'Only today what?' he echoed, helping himself to mashed potato.

Chatter on, my friend, chatter, blow your own trumpet. If I could tell you one thing, it would be: you're not half as clever as you think, and there shall be weeping and gnashing of teeth.

'I'm sorry, Monsieur Renard, my lips are sealed; nothing's been solved. But you can expect the bomb to go off any minute!'

'The bomb? Joseph, surely you haven't . . .' Iris began.

The waiter eyed them suspiciously.

'Monsieur Renard, tell him not to worry, my fiancé is only joking.'

'He was referring to an ice-cream bombe, my friend,' Daglan explained to the waiter. 'Speaking of which, what are your desserts this evening?'

He threw himself into studying the dessert menu. Legris, Victor Legris. Yes, I remember now, the bookseller who fancies himself a sleuth. You thought you were acting alone, Daglan, but it appears you've got company. You'll need to play a close game from now on.

'Waiter! Three slices of nut tart and the bill, please!'

Victor nibbled on the biscuit he was holding in one hand while he turned Pierre Andrésy's timepiece over in the other. He was only half listening to Tasha, who was leaning over the table where she kept her paints and charcoals.

'It's a beautiful story of love between an older man and a pure-hearted young girl, who is old for her years,' she mumbled, a paintbrush between her teeth.

She chewed on the end of it, remembering how as a girl she used to nibble her pen while a French governess tried to din into her the basic rules of her language. The paintbrush joined its brothers and sisters in a pot next to the palette.

'My favourite part is when she gives herself to him. "Take me then, since I give myself!" And then Zola writes: "Theirs was no fall from grace – glorious life raised them aloft; they belonged to one another in the midst of great joy." He's cocking a snook at morality, wouldn't you say? Are you listening to me, Victor?'

'Of course, darling,' he assured her, closing his hand round the watch.

He felt something click, as though the casing had opened.

'So, what was I saying?'

'Goodness, you sound like a teacher interrogating her pupil. You were talking about . . . a book by Zola,' he ventured, in a hurry to turn back to the fob watch.

'Yes, but which one? You see, you weren't listening! If you'd been paying the slightest attention to what I was saying, you'd have immediately said *Doctor Pascal*. Only you're all the same, you men. The fact that a woman is capable of profound thought upsets your preconceived ideas.' Wounded to the quick, she snatched at her paintbrushes.

'Surely you and I are above these generalisations about men and women, darling. Forgive my inattention – blame it on this unsettled weather. In my eyes you're Zola's equal. Remember, I sacrificed my moustache for you, kitten,' he whispered, placing his arms round her neck.

Had Kochka picked up the word 'kitten'? She leapt straight

onto Tasha's shoulder. Not wanting to disturb her unbidden guest, Tasha walked slowly over to the recess. Victor took the opportunity to peep inside the watch. Engraved in minuscule letters was an address: *4, Rue Guisarde*. Tasha returned without the cat, which was now chasing its little brush tail on the bed. He quickly stuffed the fob watch into the pocket of his jacket hanging on an armchair.

'I must be having an acute attack of feminine intuition: you're as skittish as a foal. Are you tempted to embark on a new case?'

'I'm tempted by your charms.'

'I've known you for four years now and I can read the signs. You haven't taken a photograph in days. And . . .'

She nibbled her thumbnail, unsure whether to continue.

'And I bumped into Antonin Clusel today. We had a little chat. He told me you'd managed to wheedle some information out of him about a murder. Are you at it again?'

'How could you think such a thing? You know how Antonin loves to embroider the stories he runs in his newspaper. Didn't I promise?'

'Promises are snares for fools.'

'I see that Kenji has a salutary influence on you.'

'What's the news about the bookbinder? Is he being buried?'

'The case is closed. Kenji is arranging for his cremation at Père-Lachaise. He'll keep the ashes in case the cousin turns up.'

'Good. You and Kenji were his closest friends.'

'I'm close to you, too, so close, in fact, that I'm happy to know that under that smock you're completely naked.'

She allowed him to undress her, lead her over to the bed and explore her curves feverishly with the expertise of one who knew her body's secret geography intimately. He waited for her to welcome him in with a moan of pleasure.

They shooed away Kochka, who had been circling them during their gentle combat.

'You've exhausted me,' he murmured.

'It was you who molested me! My poor Samson, deprived of his strength, is it because of me or because he shaved off his moustache?'

'I sacrificed it on the altar of your love. But if you're going to be like that I'll let it grow back down to my feet!'

'It'll catch in the wheels of your bicycle,' she protested, stroking Kochka.

'You prefer that ball of fur to me!'

'At least she has hair all over!'

'That's mean! I still have some,' he protested, taking her hand and placing it on his chest.

She put her arms round him and began to recite, ' "He accepted the supreme gift of her body, as if it were a priceless treasure he had won through the power of his love." '

'Not Zola again!'

'Do you know how he described his protagonists' first night together? He called it their wedding night.'

'Our first night was a long time ago.'

'But we're still novices where wedding nights are concerned. I've thought about it a lot; there might be a solution.'

He sat up straight.

'Do you mean to say that you accept . . .'

'This autumn, nothing fancy, just two witnesses, and only provided that the big event is kept under wraps.'

'Darling, I'll see to everything!'

'In return I have two requests. First, grow back your moustache; Joseph and Kenji aren't happy about you flying in the face of convention. And, secondly, forget about Pierre Andrésy.'

'*Da, koniétchno*,[53] consider it done!' he assured her, crossing his fingers.

No. 4, Rue Guisarde, next to Place Saint-Sulpice, he had time to think before rolling onto her.

CHAPTER TEN

Saturday 22 July

Victor and Joseph stepped off the yellow omnibus at Carrefour de l'Odéon and walked up Rue Saint-Sulpice, which was lined with shops selling religious paraphernalia. Jojo pretended to be interested in the window display of a church vestments shop then in one selling candles, night lights and candle-snuffers. He was trying to think of a suitable way of telling his boss that he and Iris had patched things up.

'Why have you stopped in front of that candle shop? You're not planning to install night lights in the bookshop, are you?'

'I was just wondering whether your sister might not like that oil lamp, because . . .'

'Because the flame of your undying love has been reignited?'

'Oh, Monsieur Legris, I couldn't have put it better myself. I ought to . . .'

'Use it in one of your novels, I'll bet. All right, you have my permission. Don't give away your lover's secrets. I've some of my own. I have a feeling the coming months are going to be good to us, Joseph. Come on, I'm impatient to get to the bottom of this.'

On the left-hand pavement, in front of Église Saint-Sulpice, a man with no legs was hawking religious images, his hoarse voice intermittently drowned by a barrel organ grinding out a slow waltz. Some children were chasing one another round a tiered fountain, while their nannies sat watching the flurry of vehicles: big brown omnibuses from La Villette, little green ones from Panthéon, cabs parked next to a public convenience charging five centimes.

A procession of seminarians entered Rue des Canettes. Victor and Joseph brought up the rear, turning off almost immediately into Rue Guisarde. They nearly collided with a pair of handcarts blocking the narrow street under the calm gaze of a spaniel. Number 4 was a squat building with a cracked façade next to a shed full of barrels of cider and perry.

'What's the plan, Boss?' Joseph asked, suddenly feeling thirsty.

'There's nothing for it but to knock on every door and ask if anybody's heard of this Gallic chieftain.'

'We're asking to get a basting!'

'Fear is a mad bird that must be caged, Kenji would argue.'

'Thank heavens there are only three floors.'

There were two apartments on each floor. The long faces that greeted them grew even more sullen at the mention of Sacrovir. They'd reached the top floor when a limping gait shook the stairs. A woman of about thirty with an angular but kindly face appeared carrying an enormous bundle. Victor rushed over to help her.

'I'm much obliged, Monsieur. Those stairs will be the death of me. It's not very clever living on the top floor when you've got one leg shorter than the other, I have to admit.'

'Where . . . where would you like me to put this?' Victor gasped, his knees beginning to buckle.

'Hang on a moment while I open the door. There, put it down on the table.'

He threw rather than put down the bundle, which was like a lead weight.

'You wouldn't think linen weighed so much, even when it's dry. It's much worse when it's wet! I had terrible backache when I was a laundress. After I fell into the washhouse tub three years ago, and especially after my husband was killed falling from some scaffolding, I started taking in ironing and mending. I'd be happy to add your names to my list of satisfied customers.'

Victor and Joseph looked at one another awkwardly.

'The fact is we came here looking for a man named . . .'

A small boy, half dressed, with jam all over his chin, emerged yawning from an alcove.

'You haven't washed your face!' his mother scolded him. 'Have you been a good boy?'

He nodded, stuck his finger up his nose and stared at Joseph.

'That's my Jeannot. Say hello to these gentlemen. He's shy. You said you were looking for a man named—'

'Sacrovir,' Jojo blurted out, deliberately ignoring the brat, who was poking his tongue out at him.

'Sacrovir? Yes, I remember him. A fine lad. Always cheerful and obliging. He lived on the first floor. He was from Autun originally. But that wasn't his real name. It must have been a nickname.'

'What was his name?'

'You first, what's your name?' the child answered back.

'Victor Legris, bookseller, and this is my assistant, Joseph Pignot,' Victor said hurriedly.

'Nice to meet you. Please take a seat, gentlemen, in this heat! Jeannot, go and shut the door. My name's Mariette Trinquet. Would you like a glass of water? I have some chilled in a jug.'

'That's very kind of you, I'm absolutely parched,' Joseph replied.

Victor stifled a gesture of impatience. The woman was already filling the glasses.

'Do you know Sacrovir's real identity?'

'Heavens, no. I was only little – eleven or twelve at the time. He must have been in his twenties. But now we're talking about him I can picture him vividly. He was tall, well built, with soft brown eyes and curly black hair. The truth is I was in love with him – a childish crush. My heart would beat wildly whenever I saw him. He used to chant: "Mariette, Mariette, on her way to the fête." He was teasing, of course. I was a serious child, I used to help my mother with her washing. She was a laundress too and a widow, talk about history repeating itself!'

'Did Sacrovir have a job?'

'Yes, he worked at a printer's. His fingers were always stained from the ink. The day of my first communion at Saint-Sulpice, he gave me sugared almonds and threatened to smear his hands on my dress. He told me it was to get back at God for having made a right old mess of things. I turned bright red and ran away!'

'Pinot's a wine!' Jeannot cried out, standing right beside Joseph.

'Where did you hear that?'

'At the cider seller's.'

'Pignot, not Pinot,' muttered Joseph.

'Go over there and play – you're in the way,' Mariette ordered.

'What happened to him?' resumed Victor.

'After the defeat, he came back from the front – all the time he was away I went to church and prayed – and then the Prussians surrounded Paris. The siege was terrible. A few months later – I remember because it was my birthday, 1 March 1871 – the provisional government allowed the Boches to enter Paris in exchange for Belfort and peace. That bastard Thiers!'

'Maman, that's a rude word – you'll get a smack!' cried Jeannot gleefully.

'Plug your ears. But it's true, isn't it? He was a crook. He was so terrified of the people that he refused to arm them and win the war. He preferred to make a pact with the invader. You don't need me to tell you what happened next.'

'It's ancient history,' agreed Victor, who hated raking over the past, unless it was his own.

'What year were you born, Monsieur?' Mariette enquired softly.

'In 1860.'

'I was born in 1859. A year makes a difference. That's probably why it's so fresh in my memory. A twelve-year-old can understand that when a section of the regular army and the National Guard refuse to stand by and do nothing when the enemy invades their city it can only lead to disaster. Thiers was livid. He sent troops to take over the cannons at Montmartre, but they mutinied, and two of his generals were shot by those refusing to hand Paris over to the Prussians. After that, things escalated, the government withdrew to Versailles, Thiers gave the order to retreat, and the Paris Commune was declared.'

'Maman, what's "scalated"?' Jeannot asked, a spinning top between his finger and thumb.

'Seventy-two days of freedom, no more. Then they cracked down.'

'The Communards were no saints either,' remarked Victor.

Joseph gave in to his urge to speak.

'They dreamt of a better world, where the rich would be less rich and the poor less poor!'

'That utopia simply reverses the roles, Jojo, and, when all's said and done, there's nothing new under the sun.'

'Even so, your friend is right, Monsieur; they wanted justice. Justice doesn't come from asking politely – it must be taken by force. The Communards lost the battle and the followers of Thiers, Mac-Mahon and Galliffet showed them no mercy. Thousands were slaughtered without trial, for a mere trifle. They weren't sentenced, just lined up against the wall and bang! In the end, even the most enthusiastic of the Versailles Army soldiers were calling for the killing to stop. There were so many corpses in the streets, the Seine, the gutters and fountains, and swarms of flies everywhere, and the stench . . . Well-to-do folk were scared of catching cholera.'

'Maman, are we going to die?' wailed Jeannot.

She hugged her child to her.

Victor persisted. 'And Sacrovir?'

'He vanished. I only found out later. He was a Communard and printed posters for the central committee. Maybe he escaped, maybe he was executed. Those were crazy times. Maman and I only just escaped the firing squad. The bitch on the second floor was married to a policeman and she was jealous of Maman. Maman was pretty and had all the men hanging around her. The bitch spread rumours about us associating with Communards. As soon as we heard the police were looking for us, we went into hiding. Père Derave, the manager of a bistro in Rue des Canettes, let us stay in his cellar. He was a good man. We were holed up there for nearly a fortnight. Through the cellar window we could hear gunfire and soldiers from the Versailles Army shouting: "Get in the queue!"'

'The queue?'

'Yes, queue up and wait quietly for us to put a bullet in you. In the end they were all machine-gunned.'

'Boss, it's awful!'

'Yes, Joseph, it is awful,' echoed Victor, trying his best to console the sobbing Jeannot.

'Here, little boy,' he whispered, slipping him a coin, 'buy yourself some sweets.'

'Aren't you shocked?' Joseph bawled.

'Of course I am. But I realised from a very early age that human beings are more savage than the most ferocious animals.'

'Oh, here we go. Next you'll be saying it's just dog eat dog!' Joseph declared.

'Let's leave the proverbs to Kenji and get back to Sacrovir. Tell me, Madame, did he have any family?'

'I've no idea. That year my childhood ended. You grow up quickly after seeing all those dead bodies. Have you ever seen a dead body? The swollen flesh, the staring eyes that nobody has closed . . . I couldn't stop thinking about Sacrovir. I was afraid he might have been killed. The thought drove me to distraction

. . . Oh, Jeannot my love, I'm scaring you! Blow your nose, it's all over. It's scandalous; most of the murderers and informers kept their positions. They're having an easy time of it. Some of them are even magistrates. They sent thousands of poor souls to their death and now they represent the law! It's enough to turn you into a revolutionary!'

'Besides you, is there anybody else who might be able to tell me about Sacrovir?'

'You might try asking the old butcher's son – he worked at the same printer's, as a typesetter, I think.'

'Where can we find him?'

'He moved out of the neighbourhood a long time ago.'

'What was his name?'

'I've forgotten. He must be about sixty by now – if he's still alive. I'm the only tenant left from that time, all the others moved away after the war. The bitch and her husband took off in a hurry – they were scared of reprisals. Now I come to think of it, there's Monsieur Fourastié, the cobbler. He lived at number 1 but he's near the Louvre now, Rue Baillet. Thanks for the coin, Monsieur. By the way, why are you looking for Sacrovir?'

'I have something which belongs to him and which I'd like to return.'

She showed them to the landing.

'It would be a miracle if you found him. Tell him . . . No, don't tell him anything.'

Kenji had taken particular care over his clothes: a semi-fitted jacket, a white shirt and grey trousers. He'd forced himself to swap his cravat for a bow tie and had put on a brand-new pair of brown suede gloves. So when he asked Iris to stand in for him at the bookshop, she imagined he was off to see one of his latest conquests. This wasn't the right time to tell him about her having made up with Joseph. She'd wait for a more suitable moment when Victor and Euphrosine were also there.

The cab stopped near Église Saint-Eustache. The piles of vegetables and fruit blocking the maze of side streets around Les Halles created such chaos that it was quicker to walk.

Kenji loved this vibrant neighbourhood where the flood of foodstuffs inundated the shop windows, spilt onto the pavements and overflowed into the costermongers' barrows. Lemons, cheeses, confectionery, the first fruits and vegetables of the season, all made bright splashes of colour at the base of the opulent buildings, their shop signs written above in gold lettering.

He narrowly avoided colliding with a trolley pushed by a strapping lad in a striped sweater, and turned into Rue Mandar, unexpectedly calm after the torrent of cries and expletives. He had no regrets about having slipped Hagop Yanikian a banknote in exchange for an essential piece of information: Aram Kasangian, whose address the cousin had also provided, spent Saturdays at home, where he gave Arabic lessons at two francs an hour.

It was unusual to see a concierge at his post before dawn, but the one at number 15 was already sitting in the gloomy entrance to his building peeling Jerusalem artichokes and tossing them into a bowl. Without pausing or glancing up, he informed Kenji that Monsieur Kasangian lived on the fifth floor in the apartment overlooking the courtyard.

Judging from the musty odour, the stairwell hadn't been aired since the building was put up. The plaster on the walls was flaking off and the ceiling on the top floor was so low that Kenji was obliged to stoop. He knocked for a long time before the Armenian, dressed in a collarless tunic, deigned to open the door. Aram Kasangian gave a slight start, which could have been mistaken for a bow, and raised his hand to warn his visitor not to speak. A silent scrutiny followed, ending in the pronouncement, 'Given the extreme improbability that a citizen of Japan with a passion for the sources of the Nile would have the slightest interest in the study of Arabic literature, the answer is no, despite the fact that I have no pupils at present.'

'I've followed your advice and stopped wearing a cravat. Moreover, as I have yet to ask anything of you, I cannot accept this flat refusal.'

Unnerved, the Armenian began tugging at his beard, as though expecting it to come up with a rejoinder. Finally, he motioned to Kenji to step inside the attic room.

Besides a cracked leather pouffe, a salamander in front of the fireplace, and a few piles of books, the room was filled with masses of newspapers stacked against the walls or spread across the bare floor in layers of varying thickness.

'Are you intrigued by my furniture? It is most economical and easy to clean. When it becomes too dusty I simply chuck it away and get some more. It costs next to nothing to replace at Rue du Croissant if you are a subscriber. They have loads of the previous days' unsold editions. Other advantages of newspaper are that it keeps you warm in winter and keeps out the heat in summer, and is soft enough to stand in for a mattress and blankets. Excuse me while I get dressed.'

He slipped on his green skullcap and some Oriental slippers then sat cross-legged on the pouffe.

'I am all ears.'

'I've brought you a gift.'

'Please be seated.'

Kenji hesitated before constructing a makeshift chair for himself out of several piles of periodicals. He handed the Armenian a sextodecimo.

'*The Persian Language*, by Narcisse Perrin,'[54] the latter read from the spine, which was decorated with fine cord. 'There are six volumes missing.'

'This is the only copy I have. It's an essay on Persian literature, which should be of interest to you.'

'I have skimmed the work. It is superficial.'

'It is bound in half-calf,' Kenji insisted. 'This blue would look striking in any bookcase.'

'I have none. Look around my room: the works I use are dotted all about me. What is the point of owning books when the Bibliothèque Nationale will lend them to me? Books are made from trees, and enough forests are cut down already without me adding to the destruction. The trees are our friends, our brothers. Just as they lose their leaves, so we lose our hair as soon as we get past a certain age. Our blood, like their sap, no longer flows into our limbs, our skin wrinkles, our roots grow stiff and we become paralysed – wretched, useless stumps. And then we die.'

Chilled by this speech, Kenji lightly touched the strands of hair he had been thinking of dyeing. At a loss for an argument, he made one last attempt.

'Seeing as it's a gift, you are at liberty to sell it if you don't care for it.'

The Armenian lifted his tunic and scratched his leg, clearly indicating that he was deep in thought.

'In short, you wish to get round me. What is the meaning of this gift otherwise? What is it you really want?'

'A title: the name of the manuscript you managed to hide from me when we spoke in the reading room.'

A paternal expression came over Aram Kasangian's face.

'Since it means so much to you, I could ask a lot more than the price of this simple volume.'

'That would be unworthy of you.'

The Armenian immediately put on an appearance of uprightness.

'You have touched a nerve. I am a man of honour. I will tell you what you are so desperate to know.'

He half rose from his pouffe and, bringing his face close to Kenji's, mumbled a title.

'So, it was *Touty Namèh*, after all,' Kenji said in a solemn voice.

'That really takes the biscuit, Boss!' exclaimed Joseph, without making it clear which of his employers he was addressing.

The Elzévir bookshop was closed for lunch: fried aubergines, which they had wolfed down after Iris had eaten and left for her watercolour class at Djina Kherson's. Kenji was preparing a cup of green tea while Jojo and Victor drank their coffee.

'It's quite simple,' declared Victor. 'Either the bookbinder sold the manuscript . . .'

'Impossible,' Kenji interjected.

'. . . Or it was stolen from the shop after the fire.'

'Equally impossible – everything was reduced to ashes.'

'No, it *is* possible!' objected Joseph. 'Whoever set fire to the shop could have taken it before letting off the firecrackers!'

'But Pierre Andrésy would have tried to stop him,' declared Victor.

'Where's the problem? The criminal knocked him out just like he did Edmond Leglantier.'

They went quiet suddenly, aware of Kenji's astonishment.

'What on earth are you two talking about? Why are you so sure that Pierre Andrésy was murdered? And what does it have to do with this Edmond Leglantier?'

'Boss, it's time we made a clean breast of it,' said Joseph contritely.

They gave Kenji a brief summary of their investigations, both interrupting each other.

'That explains the reason for all your absences. I congratulate you on once again being such discreet and devoted sleuths. However, I would have appreciated being kept informed of these developments in view of my friendship with Pierre Andrésy.'

'But, Boss, we wanted to catch the culprit first!'

'Don't count on my collaboration. Your last case nearly got us all into deep trouble. I'm not going along with it this time.'

He savoured his tea, avoiding their eyes. Despite his resolution, as he placed his cup in the sink, he muttered, 'There's another possibility you haven't thought of. Pierre Andrésy might have been alive when the manuscript was stolen, and, not wishing to throw me into a panic, he tried to find it and was murdered.'

Victor slapped his forehead.

'Of course! Why didn't we think of that?'

Kenji left the kitchen.

'Joseph, I'm going straight to Chez Fulbert. I must at all costs find the last man to have spoken to the bookbinder.'

'The famous Gustave . . . You're not leaving me behind again, are you, Boss?'

'I'm sorry, I prefer to work alone rather than make a blunder. I promise to give you a detailed account this evening.'

'He'll see, when I'm his brother-in-law he won't be able to fob me off with a lot of bedtime stories!' howled the abandoned Jojo.

The old lady was struggling to hang out her washing on the clothesline, which stretched from one side of the courtyard to the other. Victor propped his bicycle against a wall and finished pegging up her sheets, for which he received a string of thank-yous. He discovered that Monsieur Gustave wasn't home from work yet, but that he wouldn't be long.

The errand boy at Chez Fulbert had been unable to give him Monsieur Gustave's exact address, but he was sure that there was a mattress maker's workshop next door on the ground floor. Armed with this information, Victor had wandered around La

Chapelle until he'd finally located Rue Jean-Cottin. He now stood watching the carding machine relentlessly chewing up and swallowing the wool and cotton. His life was falling apart, he thought, overcome by a sudden wave of melancholy. Tasha agreeing to marry him had filled him with joy to begin with, but now the prospect was preying on his mind. What if she'd been right when she'd refused to marry him? What if formalising their commitment undermined their love?

Steam engines puffed in the distance. A short, portly fellow in a check bowler was making his way towards Victor, who was instantly on the alert. He fitted Adélaïde Paillet's description of the man who had handed the cake box to Edmond Leglantier. As soon as he entered the courtyard, Victor recognised his face; he'd seen him at the police station with Raoul Pérot and then again briefly at the restaurant where the two men had lunched. Crocol? No, Corcol. Inspector Corcol.

'Excuse me!' he cried out, drawing level with the man, who swivelled round with cat-like agility.

He, too, recognised Victor – the fellow at Madame Milent's, he thought. Both men feigned indifference.

'Monsieur Gustave? I believe you were a friend of Pierre Andrésy's?'

'I still am.'

'Even though sadly he died in a fire recently.'

'Yes, the news came as a terrible shock.'

'I was – am – also a close friend. He mentioned your name.'

'Really?' Corcol said, frowning.

'Certainly. He was most insistent: "Dear Gustave, now there's a true friend!" But how rude of me. Allow me to introduce myself,

Victor Legris, bookseller. Monsieur Andrésy did all my rebinding. I found your address through Fulbert. I came to you because there is something bothering me and I'd like to get to the bottom of it. Have you seen this?'

He showed him the death notice from *Le Figaro*. Corcol looked at it, his face betraying no sign of emotion.

'Yes, I've seen it. It puzzled me, too. I thought about it and came to the conclusion that it must be a tribute to his brother who passed away on 25 May last year. Pierre was in a terrible state about it.'

'What about the cemetery, could it be Saint-Ouen?'

'Possibly. It's quite near. Ah, fate can be so cruel . . .'

'It's strange that the notice should appear on the eve of the fire . . . almost as if . . . as if he'd foreseen the tragedy.'

'Maybe Pierre had left instructions in the event of his own death. His health wasn't good, his heart, he only told his close friends about it.'

Victor ignored the insinuation that Pierre Andrésy hadn't considered him close enough to confide in.

'The fire was an accident. How could he possibly have foreseen it?'

'After sixty we start being on first-name terms with death; we can sense it, we cultivate it.'

'The notice refers specifically to *his* funeral not his brother's. How long had you known him?'

The courtyard was gradually filling up with children frolicking and playing hide and seek using the old lady's washing. They were joined by housewives discussing the price of vegetables, dogs sniffing the wind, workers and craftsmen released from their labours. Shouts rang out above the general hubbub and an exasperated mother pulled up her youngest and gave him a slap on the backside.

'Nearly two years. Let's get away from this racket,' grumbled Corcol.

Victor followed him to the end of a passageway next to a blind alley filled with refuse.

'We used to drink at the same bar,' he resumed. 'We ended up becoming acquainted and would swap reminiscences. He often visited his brother at Hôpital Lariboisière, where the poor fellow's lungs finally gave out, the result of a bad wound he'd got in 1871.'

'That's strange. He never mentioned he had a brother,' remarked Victor.

'Poor Pierre, he was very close to his brother. I did my best to comfort him. It's common among war veterans; war brings us together – it's a real joy! I was at Gravelotte and he was at Reichshoffen. He was shot in the hand by a Prussian sniper.'

'What was his brother's first name?'

Corcol blinked. 'How stupid, I can't remember offhand. Age is affecting my brain. I didn't see him for a while after his brother died. Then one day I dropped in at his shop. And I went back there. Occasionally I'd stay and watch him operate the presses. We arranged to meet once a month for lunch. It's distressing imagining him trapped by the flames. It was a terrible blow. What grieves me most is not being able to visit his grave and pay my respects. They assured me at the morgue that there was nothing left of him, or so little . . .'

'Did he have a cousin, as the death notice implies?'

'If he had any relatives, he kept them well hidden. He only mentioned his brother to me. Frankly, this Léopardus is a mystery.'

'Inspector, do you have any idea what the word Sacrovir might mean?'

'No. Could it be a new swearword? Delighted to have made your acquaintance, Monsieur Legris. Leave me your card in case I remember the brother's name.'

Victor returned to his bicycle just in time to save it from being dismantled by a group of kids, and rode off in the direction of Rue des Roses. Was Gustave Corcol a brilliant actor or had he been telling the truth? If so why couldn't he remember the name of Pierre Andrésy's brother?

By the time he rode past the artesian well in Place Hébert, Victor was convinced the man was a liar.

Gustave Corcol gulped the smoky air greedily. He was worn out after climbing three flights of stairs. He stood there panting, surveying the industrial landscape at his feet, the railway tracks and workshops, the stations linking the Ceinture lines, where engines stood belching out steam. Infuriated, he tore himself away from the window and paced up and down his two-roomed apartment, which years of living alone had transformed into a hovel. The place had a sour smell of stale sweat and grime, and was strewn with dubious-looking garments and greasy plates. Still, Corcol had decided against hiring a cleaning lady for fear she might stick her nose into his shady affairs.

'And to think things were going smoothly and now this idiot

bookseller is threatening to muck everything up!' he bawled at his own reflection in the centre of a dusty mirror.

Did Legris know about the part he'd played? It was unlikely. They'd met because of an unfortunate set of circumstances, that blasted Fulbert had given him his address, that was all! No, there was more, otherwise the fellow wouldn't have been so thick with the Chief of Police's assistant, that wretched Raoul Pérot. He must come up with a counterattack, and quickly.

He took off his jacket and wiped his brow. This situation was about to turn very nasty. He unlocked a desk drawer and took out a file full of press cuttings. They all implicated Daglan. Daglan was the mysterious cousin Léopardus who had murdered Léopold Grandjean, the designer of the Ambrex shares; Daglan was responsible for the fake suicide of the loud-mouthed actor Leglantier and for the disappearance of the printer Paul Theneuil. He had signed his nickname to this string of crimes and embellished it with cryptic messages that were meant to be humorous. For God's sake! Why was he getting so worked up when all of these hideous crimes could be laid at the door of the leopard of Batignolles?

His first aim must be to put Daglan out of action before the police got hold of him.

Inspector Corcol hadn't a cowardly bone in his body. Only recently he'd taken on a band of thugs down by the gasometer in Rue de l'Évangile, an exploit that could have cost him dear. He wasn't afraid of hard work, despite the scant respect it earned him from his superiors. And yet, at that moment when he clutched in his hand the few short paragraphs bearing the leopard's signature, fear clouded his judgement, preventing him from thinking clearly. He would have preferred a bloody fight to this uncertainty in the face of an absurd situation.

He screwed up the cuttings and dropped them in the ashtray. His hands were shaking so much that he had difficulty striking a match. He reassured himself as he watched the paper burn, 'Once Daglan is dead, nobody will be able to trace anything back to me. How ironic that, if I'd stayed on, the Chief of Police might have congratulated me for ridding society of such scum! An act of bravery! Only in four days time, I'll be far away.'

Gustave Corcol closed his eyes. He imagined his colleagues' faces when they realised that he'd gone. The miserable wretches, if they only knew!

They would never know, sadly, for he'd have liked nothing better than to show them his contempt. Too bad, his triumph would go unnoticed. Everything he'd always aspired to was within reach. The women who made fun of his physique, ignorant bigwigs, self-important bosses – he'd got them all where he wanted them now. Money bought respect, honour, comfort and pleasure. And he had money. It was waiting for him snug and warm in Brussels, a tidy sum: more than two hundred thousand francs, a hundred and eleven years' salary! Why worry now that he was almost home and dry?

'Only four more days and you'll be gone.'

He pushed back his chair, and slipped on his jacket. He made sure he stepped across the threshold of his hovel right foot first, smiling at his own childish superstition. He knew the fellow's address on the outskirts of Batignolles. He'd find that petty thief and cook his goose.

Sunday 23 July

Frédéric Daglan had spent the morning wandering from stall to stall at Carreau du Temple market. He'd got hold of a greasy old cap, a pair of down-at-heel army boots, some woollen trousers and, after much searching, an army greatcoat.

He tried them on behind the locked door of Mother Chickweed's shed. In less than five minutes he was transformed into a shaky old fossil. The worn uniform was too tight, and the cap so big it fell down over his eyes, but the regular strollers who were used to the familiar appearance of the park keeper wouldn't be able to tell the difference. Brigadier Clément would spend part of Monday snoozing in his hut while Théo kept watch outside, and once the operation was over, his uncle would take up his place again.

Frédéric Daglan slipped out of his rags, then, stripped to the waist and wearing only his drawers, he set to work on the key part of his plan.

Smoking a cigarette, he opened a book at the page indicated by a bookmark and began numbering the lines. When all this was over, he wouldn't return to Rue des Dames or Porte d'Allemagne. He would wait quietly at the lodgings of his latest conquest until things blew over. Nobody would ever think of looking for him there.

Monday 24 July

As usual, Joseph was singing a brisk marching song at the top of his voice as he took down the shutters and opened the shop. This morning's recital was 'The Goodbye Song'.

'"From north to south the warrior's trumpet . . ."' Jojo bellowed, his foot slipping on an envelope on the floor.

He bent down to pick it up.

'Who put that there? I nearly came a cropper!'

'Grumbling already? You'll wake Kenji and he'll be in a bad mood,' warned Victor, who had just that moment jumped off his bicycle.

'Ah, there you are at last, Boss! I've been waiting for you since the evening before last!'

'I was worn out. I went straight back to the stable.'

'That's nice, comparing Mademoiselle Tasha to a horse,' muttered Joseph, removing the last shutter.

'If you're going to be grumpy I'll keep my lips sealed.'

Victor wheeled his bicycle to the back of the shop. Annoyed, Joseph pocketed the letter. Victor reappeared leafing through a novel by J. K. Huysmans and began singing a couplet of his own.

'Dear Monsieur Gustave, as he drew near, looked straight at me, and said with a leer . . .'

He stopped and glanced mischievously at his assistant.

'Come on, Boss, you're dying to tell me what the fellow said.'

'And you're on tenterhooks. All right, I'll tell you.'

At the end of Victor's account, Joseph picked up his pen and stroked his cheek with it, distractedly.

'Something's not right. Pierre Andrésy couldn't have been wounded at Reichshoffen, since I happen to know he was nowhere near the battlefields. I remember him telling me as clearly as if it were yesterday. He'd lent me some books by Erckmann-Chatrian:

Madame Thérèse, *Story of a Conscript in 1813*, *Waterloo* and *Fritz's Friend*. When I gave them back, I asked him about 1870 and he told me: "War is a dirty business. I'm on the side of those who prefer not to take part in that great celebration of nationalism, thank you very much."'

'What does that prove?'

'Hold on. I told him my father was in the National Guard and spent two months freezing to death on the city ramparts.'

'I know all that, but what about Pierre Andrésy?'

'There's a connection, because as soon as I asked him whether he'd taken part in the fighting, he told me that he'd refused to serve an emperor. "The Republic at a pinch, but the Man of Sedan,[55] never!" he declared. In short, he went to England and sneaked back into France during the siege.'

'I knew it! Corcol is a bare-faced liar. He had the nerve to refer to Pierre Andrésy's war wound!'

'The war . . . The siege of Paris . . . The Com— Hang on, Boss! I've got it! The inscription on his watch! It must be: "Long live the Commune"!'

Victor gave a whistle of admiration. Joseph feigned humility, but inside he was jumping for joy.

'That means Pierre Andrésy was almost certainly Sacrovir,' he concluded. 'In any event, I don't believe that story about his brother dying in Hôpital Lariboisière for one moment. The bookbinder didn't have a wife, or children, or any brothers or sisters – just a cousin in the country.'

'Congratulations on your brilliant deductive reasoning. My only criticism is that you should have told me all this before. I hadn't a clue you knew anything about his family.'

'It came out during the course of our conversations. Monsieur Andrésy often confided in me, but it was all jumbled up and I had to piece it together. While I remember, somebody slipped a letter under the door last night.'

While Victor was tearing open the envelope, Kenji, wearing a dark-red dressing gown with white polka dots, leant over the spiral staircase.

'Is this a bookshop or a drama school? One of you singing, the other declaiming . . . Has the post come already?' he muttered.

Squeezing up beside Victor, Joseph was reading the text at the same time.

'God in heaven, Boss, a coded message!'

Kenji came down to join them, unconcerned about appearing in front of potential customers in his dressing gown.

'Read it aloud,' he ordered.

Victor cleared his throat.

'Dear Monsieur Legris

Will you play with me?

He grew up in Faubourg Saint-Jacques. His elder brother was called Abel. His other brother died insane. The annus horribilis. WHOSE FAULT IS THIS?

Come to Batignolles park on Tuesday 25 July between two and six o'clock. I'll be waiting for you.'

'Then there's a series of numbers in groups of four: 5815, 0405, 0303, etc. There are loads of them.'

Joseph managed to snatch the piece of paper and quickly ran up his stepladder in order to ponder this mathematical puzzle. With a shrug of his shoulders, Kenji made for the stairs.

'I hope you have the sense not to walk straight into what is clearly a trap. However, if you should be tempted to do so, I wash my hands of you,' he declared, as he went back upstairs.

A door slammed on the first floor and Victor leapt over to the ladder, eyeing the piece of paper like the fabled fox eyeing the crow's cheese.

'Do you think you can crack it, Joseph?'

'Of course! I had a go when I was reading a spy novel set during the War of Secession. The secret services played a crucial role during that campaign, it was fascinating!' he exclaimed. 'It's dead easy!'

'Well, since you're the expert why not show me?'

'I will if you let me get down. Here's how it works. You choose a book and then decide on a page to be used for the coding. Each group of four numbers in the scrambled message corresponds to a letter. The first two numbers refer to the line the letter is in, and the last two to the position of the letter in that line. Are you with me, Boss?'

'Yes, no, but carry on.'

'If the number of the line or the position of the letter is less than ten, a zero is placed before the number.'

Joseph scratched his neck.

'The problem is finding out which book he's using.'

'Yes, Monsieur the expert, that might be a help,' Victor jibed.

'In any event, the person in the riddle lived a long time ago because he's referred to in the past tense. Wait a minute, the *annus horribilis*, that's 1870–1871! And why is "Whose fault is this?" written in capital letters?'

'It could be the title of a book . . . Can you dig out *The Life and Times of Victor Hugo* by Alfred Barbou[56] for me?'

'I think we sold it.'

The door bell tinkled, and reluctantly Jojo had to stop deciphering the message and attend to a professor in search of essays on the Renaissance. Victor took the opportunity to scour the bookshop from top to bottom. He was almost certain that 'Whose Fault is This?' appeared in *L'Année Terrible*[57] by Hugo. He found an old edition, and followed the method advocated by his assistant, but he made a hash of it because the poem was interleaved with a couple of engravings. Finally rid of his scholar, Joseph came to the rescue.

'What if we just use an anthology? We have a standard edition. Yes! I've found it! Here, on page 37: "Whose Fault is This?" Grab something to write on.'

Victor reached for an old order book.

'The poem has fifty-nine lines, Boss. You said 5815. The first two digits give me line 58: *And you would destroy all this*. Are you with me?'

Joseph was thoroughly enjoying playing the role of teacher to Monsieur Legris's humble pupil.

'The next number is fifteen, isn't it, Boss?'

'Fifteen.'

'Fifteen, fifteen . . . Only the letters count – no apostrophes or other punctuation. The first letter is *t*. Next?'

'Next we have 0405. Oh, this is a fine kettle of fish!'

'Be patient! *Yet what a curious crime!* Fourth line. The fifth letter is *h*.'

An hour later, they were poring over the following sentence:

The leopard is innocent.

'The madman chose this poem intentionally.'

'Of course he did, Boss. Victor Legris, Victor Hugo. He lived at Faubourg Saint-Jacques, had two brothers, one called Abel and the other Eugène, who died insane.'

'I'm more interested in the verses. Listen. The author of the message jumps from line 8 to line 54, but this is what the poem says if it's read in the correct order:

'1 Have you just burnt down the library?
2 "Yes.
3 "I set fire to it."
4 Yet what a monstrous crime!
5 A crime against yourself, you wretch!
6 For you have put out the fire in your own soul!
7 It is your own flame that you have extinguished!
[. . .]
55 Books are your riches! They are knowledge.
56 Justice, truth, virtue, duty,
57 Progress and reason that banishes all folly.
58 And you would destroy all this!
59 "*I cannot read.*"'

'I don't see what you're getting at, Boss!'

'How did Pierre Andrésy die?'

'He was burnt alive.'

'What did his shop contain?'

'Books. Ah! Then the text confirms our suspicions! Arson!'

'And the person who, according to the messages printed in the newspapers, is implicated in this and all the other murders is trying to convince us of his innocence and wants to meet us.'

'Provided he really is the author of this letter.'

'The only way we can find out, Joseph, is by keeping the appointment tomorrow.'

'The two of us this time, Boss?'

Victor tore the page out of the order book and folded it in four.

'The two of us, I promise.'

'Blast, Boss!'

'What now?'

'It doesn't work. Remember what Mariette Trinquet said. She was eleven or twelve at the time and Sacrovir was in his twenties.'

'So?'

'Do the sums. What year is it now?'

'It's 1893. And?'

'Think about it, Boss, the 1870–71 war, the siege of Paris, the Commune . . .'

'Heavens, Joseph! It was twenty-two years ago . . . Twenty-two plus twenty is forty-two, and Pierre Andrésy was nearly sixty, then Sacrovir . . .'

'If it wasn't Monsieur Andrésy, who was it?'

CHAPTER ELEVEN

Tuesday 25 July

Hiding in an empty shed, Frédéric Daglan had waited until the middle of the night for Inspector Corcol to leave. His surveillance had been all the more unpleasant because he was dressed as a woman and in order to look the part had squeezed into a corset. He wondered how the fair sex could bear to have their bodies compressed into such armour day in day out. He'd studied his figure with a critical eye in Mother Chickweed's pier glass and seen the attractive image of a slender seductress with an ample bosom, whose moustache was hidden under a fine white linen scarf. And so when Corcol had gone and he knocked at the door of 108, Rue des Dames, he was delighted when the concierge held his candle aloft, stared at him through his window and said, 'Fine time of night to be going up to Monsieur Daglan's! You shameless hussy!'

He bounded up the stairs of the old town house divided into flats, and shut himself in his first-floor apartment on the left, frantic to get out of his tart's clothes. He took a deep breath then lay down on the settee, which he used as a bed. Three hours later he awoke with a start feeling refreshed; he was used to making do with brief snatches of sleep. He felt thirsty, but the water in the jug was stale and so he wet his face with it and took a swig of claret instead.

The room was lined with books and magazines, most of them devoted to the libertarian cause. Works by Mikhail Bakunin,[58] Élisée Reclus[59] and Jean Grave[60] had pride of place. In addition, Frédéric Daglan was the proud owner of ninety-one editions of *L'Endehors*, published between February 1891 and May 1893, for he was a great admirer of its founding editor, Zo d'Axa,[61] who described himself as an anarchist beyond anarchy. The furnishings were completed by two chairs, an oil lamp on a pedestal table and a military trunk, from which he now removed the locks and unfolded a gold-buttoned uniform.

Half an hour later, a park keeper, his face lined with age, a battered old army cap over his snow-white hair, slipped out of a window and onto the roof of the lodge at the front of the building. He leapt cat-like into the street, and after a few paces assumed the stumbling gait of an old man.

Dawn was lighting up the façades of the houses. The neighbourhood had changed beyond all recognition. It was no longer every Parisian tradesman's dream to retire there and live off his savings. You could still see those dubious characters lounging about in cafés from dawn till dusk, their fat bellies splayed out in front of newspapers such as *Le Constitutionnel* or *La Patrie*, or playing dominoes with others like them, the enemies of progress, freedom, socialism and Victor Hugo!

The developers, attracted by the cheap land, had gradually pulled down the modest dwellings with their kitchen gardens to make way for blocks of flats. Another breed of people had invaded the sleepy provincial haven that was still protected from the demands of the toll office. Paris had spilt over into this neighbourhood, too, invading its quiet streets with noise and pollution.

Frédéric Daglan almost preferred the potbellied pensioners he'd once reviled. He despised the new breed even more – the civil servants with their briefcases bulging with files, the shop girls and book-keepers flocking like sheep into the city centre, filling the cafés and bakeries at dawn. He had always refused to sell his labour to the employers, and he despised these wage slaves.

But he was careful not to let his contempt show, and people took him for a sophisticated chap. As for the park keeper he had become this Tuesday morning, he trotted along the pavement, head nodding slightly, watching the city come alive and respecting the order of things. In Rue Darcet, he politely greeted a washerwoman, and on the Boulevard he smiled at a tailor who was airing out his shop.

His back to Montmartre, where the basilica was still under construction and framed by scaffolding, he caught the omnibus that was turning onto Rue des Batignolles and would drop him opposite the public garden where, as arranged with Brigadier Clément, he would be on duty until evening. He had the whole morning to get into character before facing the bookseller whom he was certain would keep the appointment. But would the bookseller be willing to believe him? That was another matter.

'That Alphonse Allais[62] is too amusing! His jokes have me in stitches. Impossible to have the hump with him around, if you'll pardon the pun, Monsieur Pignot, and you see we're really in the same business, so I absolutely must get hold of a copy of *The Regimental Umbrella* recently published by Ollendorf.'

'We haven't received any copies yet,' Joseph replied coldly. 'Try again next week.'

Kenji noticed that his assistant was busy with Monsieur Chaudrey from the dispensing chemist on Rue Jacob, and muttered some garbled explanation before hurrying out of the shop.

There goes the boss dressed up to the nines. He must be in love, deduced Jojo, whose reignited passion had made him a little more indulgent. However, he didn't realise the full implications of Kenji's sudden departure until the pharmacist left and Victor appeared to inform him that they couldn't both go to Batignolles. Joseph felt the ground tremble beneath his feet.

'All right, you don't have to spell it out, I'm the mug who has to stay behind!'

'Why don't we toss a coin? Tails I win, heads you lose,' Victor suggested.

That old trick, he must take me for an idiot, Joseph thought, and retorted, 'Did you know that in London blind people are able to see in the fog . . . ?'

'Do I take it that means yes? Here goes, then.'

He tossed a coin into the air and slapped it down on his wrist.

'Tails. I win. Sorry, you watch the shop.'

'Very clever, Boss.'

Victor put up no defence; he had already left.

'I should have guessed last night when he gave me his word. False promises!'

Joseph leant on the counter and gazed mournfully at the notebook containing his ideas for his new novel. He hadn't the energy to get down to any work, and anyway he was stuck on the epilogue. Should he hurl Frida von Glockenspiel into the arms of the cruel but virile Otto von Munk after they dug up the famous chalice, or give her a more passionate future with Sublieutenant Wilkinson – a kindly protector of widows and orphans? He buried the unfinished work under a pile of newspapers and quoted one of Kenji's favourite proverbs: 'Lucky is the mole who can only see as far as its nose.'

A figure swathed in cream organdie and lace danced around him.

'How do you like my Empress Eugénie bodice and my printed straw hat? They're all the rage this year!'

'You look ravishing,' whispered Joseph, catching hold of Iris as she twirled, and drawing her close to him for a moment.

She struggled free, laughing.

'You're no longer afraid someone will walk in on us?'

'On the contrary, I'm proud of you – I want everybody to admire you. For instance the battle-axe, I mean, Madame de Flavignol, she'll be here any minute with her friends Madame de Gouveline and Madame de Cambrésis to pick up some books. I'd love to slip off and leave you four to discuss the latest fashions and advise each other on the best shops.'

'You think I don't know what you're all up to? Where are you going? To snoop around Rue Monsieur-le-Prince?'

'I'm going to watch over your brother.'

'A fine bunch! You, Victor and my father smelling of lavender water a mile off! Men . . . ! Well, run along, since Victor's safety is at stake. It's lucky I'm here to look after the shop.'

Scarcely had she uttered the words before Joseph was pelting towards Boulevard Saint-Germain to catch the Odéon–Clichy–Batignolles omnibus.

*

As he walked past the tiny covered market at Batignolles, Victor mused over the sad fate of Hippolyte Bayard[63] who had photographed it forty years earlier. He paused as he remembered the self-portrait of the artist, which he'd seen at the French Society of Photography. In it, Hippolyte Bayard depicted himself as a drowned man slumped in an armchair, with a caption below, written in 1840:

The corpse you see here is that of Monsieur Bayard, inventor of the technique whose marvellous results you have just witnessed. The government, having given far too much to Monsieur Daguerre, claimed it could give nothing to Monsieur Bayard, and the wretched man drowned himself.

Victor continued on his way. Life could be so cruel. Would anybody remember the lowly civil servant from the Treasury, a lover of art and the first person to successfully print positive photographs directly onto paper, whose discovery was attributed to Daguerre?

A crowd drew his attention away from his reflections. He slipped through to the front of the circle of onlookers. A strongman in hose was haranguing the spectators.

'Ladies and gentlemen, your attention please. You are about to witness an unparalleled display of strength. Your humble servant, the Parisian Rock, will lift half a hundredweight as easily as if it were a set of juggling balls.'

Victor was amused by how credulous people were. The strongman lined up six or seven weights at his feet then picked out the middle one, which weighed no more than ten or twelve pounds. He lifted it confidently above his head before stretching his arms out straight. Then, to prove that there was no cheating involved, he invited the onlookers to pick up one of the other weights, which really were heavy. Coins fell thick and fast onto his mat.

Fraud really is the mother of wealth and fame, Victor reflected as he walked away.

A sudden downpour cooled the air. Victor took shelter in Église Sainte-Marie behind a crescent of tall houses. He sat down near a confessional and heard murmurings from within. A woman nearby counted the stitches on her knitting needles while another was praying. He closed his eyes and was transported back to Rome where he'd spent two weeks in the summer of 1887 and where, fleeing from the insufferable heat, he'd studied the paintings and frescoes in every sanctuary along the way. The heat and the paintings had become fused in his memory. A vision of Tasha half naked in front of her easel came unbidden to his mind. The loud clickety-click of knitting needles shattered the image and forced him to leave the church.

The rain had stopped. The air smelt of wet road and damp grass. At the entrance to the public garden a puny-looking lad was tinkling a bell.

'Tuppence for a stick of mint rock!' he chanted to the mothers and their children, eager to begin skipping and digging in the grit.

Victor walked straight towards the artificial rock, down a narrow pathway beside a waterfall and into a sandy walkway leading to a miniature lake. He glanced around. Would the leopard suddenly appear? Or did he want Victor to find him?

The sun had come out and a crowd of ladies had hurriedly occupied the benches and chairs. Under the distracted gaze of nannies in ribboned hats, children played with balls or hoops or jumped about from the sheer joy of being alive. Their squeals of delight drowned out the sound of women eagerly gossiping about their neighbours' bad behaviour or habits. Besides an old park keeper maintaining a discreet watch over this little corner of the world, there were no men in sight.

Victor strolled by the lake pretending to look at the ducks, aware that his presence was causing a stir amongst the old ladies parked in the sun. One dropped her glasses, another turned down the corner of a page in her book. The advance of the nonchalant stranger broke the all-powerful spell of boredom.

He walked back the way he'd come, hoping to find a secluded spot. He paused under a tree and lit a cigarette. A rustle made him jump.

'Don't look round, Monsieur Legris. You didn't hang about, did you? Go to the top of the grotto; I'll follow you.'

He obeyed without trying to catch a glimpse of the man.

When he reached the meeting place, all he found was a nanny in a printed cotton dress. She was gesturing to a child standing next to the railings separating the park from the tracks, which converged towards Saint-Lazare station. As soon as she saw Victor, she blushed and scurried away. When the coast was clear, the park keeper appeared, twirling his moustache.

'You're punctual. I'm grateful for that,' he said in a youthful voice.

Victor, taken aback, quickly composed himself.

'I wasn't expecting such an elaborate disguise.'

'Well, it suits my purpose perfectly. Who would ever suspect a humble representative of the law?'

'Will you please explain why you sent me a coded message?'

'Let's just say I have a fondness for numbers. I wanted to test you. Did you decipher it?'

'*The leopard is innocent*. Now prove it to me.'

'Bravo, you've a good nose and plenty of pluck. But you occasionally get involved in dangerous cases.'

'Am I in danger now?'

'Not with your accomplice over there to protect you and our friends with webbed feet.'

Victor was annoyed to see Joseph breaking a piece of bread to feed the ducks and stirring the old ladies from their stupor again.

'I suggest you call him over before he draws too much attention to himself.'

It took Joseph a while to comprehend that the hand waving in the distance was gesturing to him to approach. Nervous about the reception he'd get, he speedily obeyed.

'A fine display of discretion!' muttered Victor. 'And who's watching the shop?'

'Mademoiselle Iris, Boss,' replied Joseph, his eyes riveted on the keeper, who was surveying the park.

'Gentlemen, I need your help,' the man declared calmly.

'Oh, it's you!'

'Indeed, young man, I do believe that I am me. Monsieur Legris, if you agree to help me I'll provide you with some remarkable facts. You're fond of solving mysteries, according to what I've read.'

'I'll need to know all about you.'

'A man's life begins at birth, and to recall every episode would be an impossible task. If I could give you an account of my whole life, would it not inevitably be suspect? The main thing is that I chose to live on the fringes in order to disobey the rules of a society stinking of the sewer. The world is a prison, with gilded bars for some, but a prison all the same. I am a free citizen of Batignolles, born under the splendour of an Italian sky. My father was a staunch Garibaldian by the name of Enrico Leopardi.'

'Leopardi, as in the poet?'[64]

'You are a cultivated man, Monsieur Legris! Yes, Leopardi like that melancholic, Giacomo Leopardi.'

'So, you're the leopard!' Joseph cried.

'What powers of deduction! Bravo, young man! However, in this land of freedom and the rights of man it is preferable not to have an Italian name. I am called Frédéric Daglan.'

'The name on the Ambrex shares!' exclaimed Joseph.

'Such a keen sense of observation in an admirer of Émile Reynaud doesn't surprise me, young man.'

'But how did you . . . ? Of course, Cédric Renard! The journalist! Very clever!'

'You are more perceptive than most, Monsieur Pignot.'

'What made you choose the passage from Victor Hugo about burning books?'

Without hesitation Daglan responded.

'Victor Hugo was a defender of the weak and downtrodden

of all races and nations. He had a great spirit and I admire him. "Whose Fault is This?" is one of my favourite poems. How can a man who is an outcast of society, exploited and deprived of knowledge, respect the written word? Does that answer your question, Monsieur Pignot?'

Daglan went on to give them an account of his everyday life, complaining that his profession barely provided him with enough to eat and pay his expenses.

'However, love costs nothing. Women give themselves to me without asking anything in return – I don't know why. They are unfairly accused of being venal,' he added, curling his moustache again.

'And this is enough to prove your innocence?'

'Of course not. I'm attempting to paint a general picture of my situation. As an art lover you should appreciate that. Your portraitist is really pretty!'

'You've been spying on us!'

'I love gathering information about people who take an interest in me. If I tell you who the real culprit is, will you help me?'

'Tell me first why you wanted to meet me.'

'A calculated risk. The mastermind behind this mess is impossible to unseat but together we might bring him down. I was contacted a while ago by a police officer, on 11 June to be precise. We met one Sunday in the suburbs. He asked me to steal some amber cigar holders. Curious about what he wanted them for, I asked a pal of mine to follow him. When someone hires me to do a job I like to cover my back.'

'And the name of this policeman?'

'Gustave Corcol.'

'Boss, that's the fellow who . . .' whispered Joseph.

Victor gestured to him to be quiet. Daglan went on.

'The following day, the 12th, Corcol turned up at the police station as usual. At lunchtime he took an omnibus to Rue des Boulets, where my friend Théo saw him enter an enamellist's workshop, Léopold Grandjean & Fils. There was a sign above the door. He came out half an hour later. The following day, Théo tailed him to a theatre in Rue de l'Échiquier. He and the manager, Edmond Leglantier, left together.'

Joseph choked, bursting to express his astonishment, but he was scared of Victor's wrath and dared not utter a word.

'They had a long discussion in a bar on the corner,' Daglan added. 'In the afternoon of Wednesday 14th, Corcol went back to Grandjean & Fils. This time he came out carrying a portfolio under his arm. From there he walked to Passage Thermopyles in the Petit-Montrouge district, where he slipped in to Paul Theneuil's printing works and came out again empty-handed.'

Joseph was gasping by now and Victor looked daggers at him.

'On the 15th Corcol didn't leave work all day. In the meantime, I began to set up the robbery. I left the crates, the cart and the donkey with a friend who has a market garden. That evening, Corcol paid another short visit to the printing works, this time carrying a brown leather briefcase, then he took an omnibus home. Intrigued by all these comings and goings, I resolved to get to the bottom of it. The next day, the 16th, I broke into his house while he was at work. It was easy as there's no concierge and his apartment is at the far end of a courtyard on the top floor. I had to know what was in that briefcase. I found it hidden under his mattress. Inside was a file stuffed with a thick stack of share certificates in the name of Ambrex. Now I understood why he wanted the cigar holders. The scoundrel hadn't shown much imagination in the choice of name. But imagine my astonishment when I read the names of the directors! One was me and the other Grandjean! I put everything back in its place. What he was up to exactly was a mystery. But I knew I was being set up. On Saturday 17th, as agreed, I stole the cigar holders together with a few cheap trinkets that would be easy to fence. By two o'clock I'd done the job without a hitch.'

'Bridoire's Jeweller's! Boss, you must admit I've got a nose for news items!'

'Yes, you have,' Victor conceded, remarking to Daglan, 'The crate was a clever idea.'

'Tricks of the trade. On Sunday 18th, I took the stolen goods to Chatou in a cake box. Corcol gave me my two hundred francs. I left, but I followed him to Muller's brasserie where he gave the box to the theatre manager.'

Victor and Joseph looked at one another – Adélaïde had been right.

'I stopped tailing the inspector and began following Leglantier. On the 21st he went to a club on the Boulevards. There I saw him deliver a patter worthy of any charlatan. The shares sold like hot cakes. Leglantier was set to make a tidy profit, which he would no doubt split with Corcol. The problem was that with my name on those shares I was in it up to my neck. I decided to move to the country and pluck chickens, to take a break from my criminal calling. Two weeks passed. I'd begun to breathe more easily when I read about Grandjean's murder in an old newspaper. I thought it over. If they were killing off the directors I'd be next. The irony was that they were trying to pin his murder on me, because they'd left a scribbled note on the body with some cock-and-bull story about a leopard and its spots. Grandjean had been stabbed near his workshop the day Leglantier sold his phoney shares. And then there was the disappearance of the man who'd printed them, Paul Theneuil, and the letter addressed to his book-keeper. Again, it pointed the finger at the leopard.'

'Has Paul Theneuil disappeared?' exclaimed Victor.

'Yes, vanished into thin air.'

'How did you find out about it?'

'From a news item in *Le Passe-partout*. "Remember, Paul. The leopard, light as amber, says: 'Merry month of May, oh when will you return?'"' he recited.

'Sherlock Pignot's nose must have been blocked that day,' Victor said under his breath.

'I can't be expected to read everything down to the notices about run-over pets!' Joseph protested, kicking himself for having missed the article.

'And then,' resumed Daglan, 'Leglantier took a lethal dose of municipal gas. What's funny is that they suspect an aristocrat, who was a victim of the swindle, of staging the fake suicide. In the meantime, I tracked down the witness to Grandjean's murder – a flower girl – who didn't tell me much, except that the killer was about five foot seven and that she'd noticed a lock of grey hair sticking out from under his hat. I watched over the girl in case the murderer came back looking for trouble. That's when I noticed a fair-haired young fellow snooping around the flower market at La Madeleine. He was either a policeman or in cahoots with Corcol. Or else he was a womaniser. I saw his little game with a young brunette whom he invited to the Théâtre Optique.'

Joseph, suddenly bright red, forced himself to look nonchalant.

'Did Iris enjoy the show?' Victor asked him.

'I approached them and discovered that the man was an assistant at Victor Legris's bookshop. The name was familiar. I remembered you'd nearly come to a sticky end last year, and that you'd solved some difficult cases. I decided to get in touch. Now I've confessed everything, it's up to you to help me out of this mess. True, I'm a thief, but I'm no murderer.'

'This is serious. Why don't you go to the police?'

'They'll take one look at my record and throw me behind bars, convinced that I've made the whole story up in order to clear myself of a crime which I in fact masterminded. The police are only human. Their occupation shapes their behaviour: you can judge a book by its cover. And you're forgetting that Corcol is one of them. I'll be safe behind bars, it's true, but I prefer my freedom. You're my only chance, Monsieur Legris.'

'What do you expect me to do?'

'To provide some evidence: in the beginning there were four men, now only Corcol is left.'

'You're still here. And Theneuil is running around out there somewhere. Isn't there something else you have to tell me?'

Frédéric Daglan remained silent. Suddenly, without warning, he stepped back, gazing fixedly towards the foot of the rock. Victor turned round. Two policemen were strolling across the park, talking.

'Nothing, Monsieur Legris. There's trouble ahead. I've given you enough clues to lead you to the culprit. Just don't go after the wrong man,' Daglan warned, before making his way back down towards the waterfall.

Victor and Joseph walked slowly over the iron bridge crossing the railway tracks. On the left three tunnel openings gaped. The arrival or departure of convoys of fifteen or twenty wagons was heralded at regular intervals by shrill whistles and clouds of steam. To their right, overlooking the tracks, was Batignolles station, where the Normandy trains passed through without stopping, and which served only the Ceinture line.

They stopped to look down at the people filling the platform and the stairs leading up to the waiting room.

'Boss, did you notice that Daglan never mentioned the fire at Pierre Andrésy's shop? Do you think he was bluffing, or does he not know about his death?'

'It's hard to say. The man's a paradox; you don't know whether to suspect him or to feel sorry for him. His disguise was shady enough – it was impossible to get a good look at his face under all that make-up. His voice sounded genuine, but I wouldn't trust him any more than I would Corcol.'

'We have two suspects, then.'

'Three. If Paul Theneuil has gone into hiding, then he's just as likely to be the puppet master behind this sinister farce. I suggest we go to his house.'

'Providing we know where he lives.'

'Joseph, either you need a holiday or you're not concentrating. Daglan gave us his address: a printing works in Passage des Thermopyles. I'm busy tomorrow – we'll go on Thursday morning.'

'Mmm, unless you leave me high and dry again!'

'Now that my sister's eating out of your hand again you can pass the reins over to her.'

A plume of smoke enveloped them.

'And what if Monsieur Mori complains, Boss?'

'Pretend you have a delivery.'

Joseph gasped and stopped dead in the middle of the pavement.

'Hell's bells! We're a right pair of bumbling detectives! I'm not the only one in need of a holiday.'

'Why?'

'We didn't ask Daglan about Sacrovir.'

Kenji's expression, while always remaining polite and composed, could sometimes darken in a way that broke a man's will. Adolphe Esquirol finally cracked.

'Do you intend to stand there all day long staring at me in silence? What do you want from me, anyway? I've told you everything I know!' he bawled, screwing up his rodent-like features.

'You omitted one important detail: the address of the man who sold you the lot.'

'He didn't give it to me. How many times do I have to tell you?'

'As many times as you like. I'm in no hurry. Attend to your customers. Business is sacred and must always come first,' retorted Kenji, examining his nails.

Esquirol glanced uneasily at the two eminent sinologists waiting to be served and hissed furiously, 'All right, you win. Monsieur Fourastié, Rue Baillet, near the Louvre. Satisfied? Now get out!'

Kenji carefully opened out a map he kept in his pocket.

'It's very close . . . I'll walk,' he murmured.

A tune from childhood came into his head and he began singing:

> *'Niwa no sanhyô no ki*
> *Naru suzu fukaki . . .'*

A quarter of an hour later, he was knocking at the door of a cobbler's shop. The shutters were drawn and a sign hanging on the doorknob said *Temporarily closed*.

'Will Monsieur Fourastié be long?' he asked a pretty young woman at a tobacconist's shop.

'That depends on his sciatica. When he gets one of his attacks he goes to stay with his daughter. He's not young any more, poor fellow.'

'And where does his daughter live?'

'Somewhere in Marne.'

'A lovely part of the world,' Kenji remarked with a sigh that implied he'd like to explore the region in the company of the opposite sex.

'That's all I can tell you, seeing as Père Fourastié and I aren't married. In fact, I'm not married at all . . .'

He flashed a charming smile at her. She looked vaguely like Eudoxie. Would the ex-queen of cancan be at Rue Alger at this hour? What if he paid her a surprise visit? He bought a cigar and turned to leave, showing the woman his best profile.

On the second floor of a small building, a curtain was drawn aside. A pair of cross-eyes peered out, fixing at length on the Asian gentleman carrying a cane with a handle in the shape of a horse's head.

Gustave Corcol felt for a box of matches. The flame of the candle stuck in the neck of a bottle lit up the impossible shambles of the bedroom, and showed the damp patches mottling the walls. He glimpsed a fat naked man reflected in the pane of the open window.

'Look at me,' he said.

He hated his overly wide body, a size bigger than average. Whenever he saw it he thought it looked bloated and grotesque, like a troll. He was confused for a moment. What day was it? What time? The rhythmical ticking of a clock echoed in the sultry night. He turned and looked; it was two thirty. His trip to Rue des Dames had ended in failure. Frédéric Daglan hadn't been home in over a week. What a lousy joke! Was he losing his touch? Gustave Corcol had never fulfilled his aspirations. He had cultivated bitterness and begun despising everybody around him. Life had thwarted him. When he joined the police force he dreamt of being promoted to chief of police, or even, why not, commissioner of the Sûreté? Twenty years on, he was still languishing in the lower echelons, bundled from station to station at the whim of servants obedient to an administration whose tentacles reached into people's lives, deciding their fates. The only son of a penpusher at the town hall, he'd avoided conscription by paying someone to take his place. The war, the defeat, the imprisonment of Emperor Napoleon III and the proclamation of the Republic had had no effect on him. He took little interest in politics, considering it preferable to remain on the winning side. The Commune had given him an opportunity to show his zeal. This had not gone unnoticed by his superiors, and he'd climbed a few rungs on the ladder. From police constable on an annual salary of one thousand two hundred francs, he had risen to the rank of sergeant and finally to that of inspector on one thousand eight hundred francs. He had quickly learnt how to sail with the prevailing wind. He was clever at discovering the weaknesses of his superiors and concealing his own from his subordinates. However, his efforts hadn't promoted him to the post he coveted. The recent appointment of that third-rate scribbler Raoul Pérot to assistant chief of police had crushed his hopes.

To think that he was under the thumb of a man of barely thirty! What made him angry, what disgusted him most was the lack of appreciation of his ability. Not one of his colleagues could hold a candle to him. He was a good *flic* with years of experience. During an interrogation something would click and he'd know when a suspect was guilty. His colleagues were surprised.

'How did you guess, Corcol? Talk about a fool's luck!'

They were the fools! Being a good policeman meant paying attention to every detail, however seemingly insignificant, but more importantly it meant trusting one's instinct. Today, his instinct had betrayed him. He was weary, sick of everything relating to his job. Most of his colleagues were like sheep – they toed the line and waited for a chance to win the respect of their superiors. Others simply obeyed out of fear of punishment. Gustave Corcol despised them all. He'd broken the sacred commandments of the law and the sky hadn't fallen on his head. What sweet revenge!

His rage ebbed away like the tide, leaving only a twinge of humiliation.

He walked a few paces then lay down. His mind was in turmoil. He tried to put things into perspective. He found himself talking aloud.

'It's over. Tomorrow I'll be free.'

A month before, Gustave Corcol had established close ties with a skilled forger of documents, who was unaware of his true identity. Now he could go and see the Manneken-Pis for himself. Once in Brussels he would become Monsieur Cappel from Gand – a respectable widower and pensioner with no children who lived off private means. There, he would have all the time in the world to dream about the future.

He looked with an admiring eye at the tailored suit hanging over the back of a chair.

'Tomorrow, tomorrow . . . Gare du Nord . . . Monsieur Cappel . . .' He sank into oblivion.

*

Gustave Corcol came to, sweating. He was wide awake. He couldn't understand why his muscles, his limbs, refused to obey him. He imagined he felt a presence nearby. No, it was a trick of the dying candle flame. His pulse gradually slowed and he managed to persuade himself that he'd had one of those particularly vivid nightmares that send you into a panic.

He propped himself up on one elbow.

'Is anybody there?'

A distant memory from childhood, at once strange and familiar, came back to him suddenly.

He realised how foolish he was being. Who could possibly have entered the front door, which was double locked? A ghost?

He remembered a book of fairy tales which had kept him awake at night for months, a gift from his uncle, a thick red book inhabited by monsters, ogres and dragons, which he felt compelled to open every evening.

He could just make out a shadow; it seemed to glide towards the bed where he lay.

'Who's there?'

He tried to hide under the sheets.

'Speak to me,' he implored.

The apparition began to sing:

> *'And if Lady Luck should smile on me*
> *She will never soothe my heart*
> *I will for ever love the cherry season*
> *And keep its memory in my heart!'*

Gustave Corcol's moans turned into a gurgling sound as the blade sank into his heart.

CHAPTER TWELVE

Thursday 27 July

THE only thing moving beneath the chestnut trees on Square de Montrouge was a herd of donkeys trotting towards the Luxembourg Gardens. Then came deserted streets with their whitewashed façades, where the cry of a glazier or a knife-sharpener brought an occasional face to the windows.

Halfway down Passage Thermopyles, Victor and Joseph hurried through a hall at the end of which stood Paul Theneuil's printing works. A young apprentice of about twelve, preceded by a ginger cat, was blocking their way.

'About time! Have you brought us some copy?' he demanded rudely.

'Is Monsieur Theneuil here?'

'The boss? He's done a vanishing act!' the apprentice announced, sniggering.

'Move aside, kid, you're in the way.'

The boy crouched down and, shooting Joseph a murderous look, picked up the tomcat by the scruff of its neck.

In contrast to the silence outside, the workshop was a hive of activity. Victor and Joseph walked towards one of the typesetters, who was standing beside his typecase mounted on a stand. From time to time he glanced at a manuscript before picking characters out of little compartments and placing them on a composing stick he held in his left hand. Furious at having been sent packing, the apprentice hurled the cat at their feet. The animal leapt up onto a typecase, sending the letters flying, before landing nimbly on a marble tabletop where the layout man had arranged his formes. There was a general outcry, while the boy beat a retreat, shouting, 'It wasn't me, it wasn't me!'

'I'll give you what for, Agénor! You've wrecked my layout!'

'He dipped his paws in my ink!'

'Throw that alley cat in the cooking pot!'

'That wretched Agénor! He's the master printer's son, and he takes advantage of it to drive us all crazy. The latest victim of one of his pranks was Père Flamand, our oldest proofreader. On account of a well-earned slap, Agénor nailed his slippers to the floor so securely that when the poor old fellow tried to move he fell flat on his face,' explained the typesetter.

'Forgive me, but where is Monsieur Theneuil?' Victor enquired.

'That's what we'd all like to know. He's never decamped for this long before. We're beginning to miss him.'

'Does he often go away?'

The worker exchanged a knowing look with another typesetter.

'Let's just say that he strays from the conjugal nest from time to time, when the urge takes him. Everybody knows why, including his wife, but seeing as he always comes quietly back to the fold after two or three days, she indulges him. This time, though, he's been gone three weeks, and he sent a letter which makes the claptrap in your average *fin-de-siècle* novel look like child's play.'

'This letter, was it addressed to his wife?'

'No, to his book-keeper, Monsieur Leuze, the lanky fellow with the glasses and the peaked cap sitting over there at the back.'

'By the way, have you printed any share certificates recently?'

'We don't do that sort of thing here. We only cater to men of letters and historians.'

Monsieur Leuze pushed his spectacles to the end of his nose and peered over the top of them at the visitors. When Victor informed him that they were journalists, he replied gruffly that he'd already spoken to the gentlemen of the press.

'We're writing a feature about mysterious occurrences, and we'd like to include the message Monsieur Theneuil sent you,' Joseph improvised.

'It was typewritten and unsigned. There's nothing to prove that Monsieur Theneuil wrote it,' muttered Monsieur Leuze, handing them a piece of paper on which was written:

Remember, Paul. The leopard, light as amber, says: 'Merry month of May, oh when will you return?'

'Yes, why would Paul Theneuil tell himself to remember something?' Victor mumbled.

'That's what I said when Madame Theneuil called the police a week after what we'd been assuming was another amorous adventure,' agreed the book-keeper, neatly folding the piece of paper. 'If Monsieur Paul had meant to inform us of a lengthy absence why this enjoinder to recall the passing of the seasons? It's completely idiotic.'

'What did the police make of it?'

'They think it may be a hoax, an elopement or a kidnapping. In short, they can't do anything. We'll have to wait and see.'

'Didn't the word *leopard* arouse their interest?'

'No more than our apprentice's accursed cat,' grumbled Monsieur Leuze. 'I'm sorry, gentlemen, but my time is precious. This situation has caused us a lot of trouble because Madame Theneuil hasn't the necessary experience to replace her husband, although she's doing her best.'

'Where can we find her?'

'Up on the first floor, in the glass-fronted office.'

The woman who opened the door to them had the drawn features of a person who hasn't slept for several days. Her unkempt hair and crumpled dress betrayed her distress more than her faltering voice and her deceptively formal manner. Almost immediately, her self-control broke down and she collapsed onto a chair, burying her head in her hands. She pulled herself together and apologised.

'I'm very distressed . . . My husband is no saint, but I put up with his peccadilloes. When he feels the need to go off, he lets me know, and arranges things so that the business won't suffer because of his escapades. The last time I saw him was on the evening of 4 July. I was making his favourite dish, jugged hare. He stopped by the haberdasher's to tell me that he'd be home a bit late because he had a meeting with a customer who'd ordered some posters.'

'I thought he only printed books.'

'Oh, he'd occasionally do a favour for an old friend.'

'Who was he meeting?'

'I don't know. It was raining and he'd forgotten his umbrella.'

'What was he wearing?'

'A brown jacket. I told the police.'

'Did he wear spectacles?'

'Yes, half-moon spectacles, but only for reading. Now . . . I'm afraid, I'm so afraid!'

She stood up and pointed to a pile of papers scattered over the table.

'I can't cope any more . . . You see, I run a haberdasher's down the street. I could have stopped working a long time ago because business is going well, only I wanted to save up for a rainy day. Paul is so unreliable! But he loves me, I know he does. I don't know why I'm telling you all this. Did the Chief of Police send you?'

'No, we're from the newspaper.'

'Oh! You're not going to repeat . . .'

'Don't worry. We're also trying to find out the truth. Did your husband ever receive any threats?'

'He never said anything. He would have told me. He still confided in me – despite our relationship being more like that of a brother and sister. Over the years physical attraction had turned into deep affection. I was his old pal, yes, that's what he would call me, either that or his pet . . . He'd stopped calling me "darling". And yet . . .'

Marthe Theneuil twisted her lips into a pitiful smile.

'And yet, our love was once so passionate that we believed it would last for ever. When we first met, he showered me with gifts, and I gave him presents too. And then I no longer fulfilled his needs. No doubt he didn't find me attractive enough.'

Victor and Joseph examined the gaunt face framed by a mass of dishevelled hair and reflected that in her normal state Marthe Theneuil was undeniably still appealing. Victor couldn't help exclaiming, 'And aren't you jealous of these other women?'

She remained silent for a moment then looked him straight in the eye.

'Why should I be? He always comes back to me. That part of Paul's life is not my concern. Besides, it makes him happier. Men seem to have an inborn need to seduce. When they're deprived of that, they become depressed and God knows what else. You're still young, Monsieur, but the same will happen to you.'

'Oh, no, certainly not. That would be immoral!' he cried.

Joseph was overtaken by a sudden fit of coughing, which he muffled with a handkerchief before saying, 'Monsieur Leuze showed us the famous note. Does this leopard bring anybody to mind?'

'No. It might refer to a friend or relative, or to one of his mistresses, although most of them are ill-bred tarts. I went through all his papers and correspondence with a fine-tooth comb and, apart from our early love letters, the only others of any interest were those he exchanged with Ernestine Grandjean, the sister of a childhood friend whom he courted before he met me.'

Joseph scratched his head furiously to allay suspicion.

'Grandjean?' he repeated.

'Yes, Léopold Grandjean. He and Paul saw a lot of each other despite the difference in their ages. My husband thought of him as the little brother he'd always wanted; he was a youth of seventeen at the time. Ernestine must have been about twenty, and from what I've read Paul was besotted with her. She was flattered by his attentions, but felt no attraction for him.'

Victor was surreptitiously leaning over the table trying to glimpse the bundle of letters tied with a blue ribbon which Marthe Theneuil was covering with her hands. He noticed a few bills, engravings of the latest mechanical presses, paper samples and some other letters with a flower for a signature. She realised what he was up to.

'I couldn't help rereading some of our old letters dating back to 1873 when we were first in love. Paul was forty but looked ten years younger. I was a young girl of eighteen from the provinces, mesmerised by the big city and by this quiet, serious man to whom my father had introduced me – they'd belonged to the same regiment. It took me months to get to know him, months to discover that underneath that calm exterior he was a womaniser. But I won't lose him,' she exclaimed vehemently.

'Don't despair. We'll track him down,' said Joseph, who was beginning to feel concerned.

And then immediately he added, matter-of-factly, 'Would you consent to give us Ernestine Grandjean's address?'

'I only know the one Paul used to send his letters to: 5, Rue Villedo, next to the gardens of the Palais-Royal. I'd be surprised if she's still there; it was where she worked, an army outfitter's.'

'Could you let us have a photograph of your husband?'

'Yes, it was taken last year. I gave the most recent one to the police.'

'Is Monsieur Theneuil a tall man?'

'A head higher than you.'

Victor and Joseph took their leave, eager to compare notes. When the door had closed, Marthe Theneuil walked over and stood in front of the glass wall, her figure silhouetted against the backdrop of the bustling workshop. She crossed her arms, pressing them tightly to her chest.

Djina Kherson listened to her daughter's footsteps dying away down the corridor. Love suited Tasha. It gave her a golden glow, like a freshly baked brioche straight out of the oven. Without acknowledging it, Djina envied her. She crossed the empty studio where her pupils had left the odd glove or scarf strewn about. She gathered up the abandoned palettes and paintbrushes and returned to the sanctuary of her apartment, which she was reluctant to leave. Despite the attention she received from her daughter and her daughter's lover Victor – should she call him her fiancé now? – she felt dreadfully lonely. She missed Ruhléa, to whom she'd always been closer than to her elder daughter. And Pinkus . . . Although he'd been little more than an occasional companion these past few years, the fact that she'd refused divorce and that they'd kept up their correspondence had helped Djina to cope with the vagaries of her own life. Then there had been exile, the time spent in Germany, her illness. Tasha had persuaded her to come and live in Paris. That prospect, so enticing from afar, had lost its appeal as soon as she came face to face with everyday life. Pinkus lived thousands of miles away on the other side of the Atlantic, and Ruhléa was somewhere in the depths of central Europe with a husband she had never met, whose portrait, confined in its wooden frame on the mantelpiece, sized up his mother-in-law with a mysterious expression. Yes, Tasha and Victor were very attentive and she owed them a great deal, and yet . . .

What had she learnt? That exile and separation were a means of understanding, day after day, with great difficulty and forbearance, the things she had felt and thought since the day she was born. This introspection surreptitiously revealed what had up until then been only a vague intuition. The end result of all those joys, struggles and disappointments seemed so trivial that she felt a sense of apathy and despair.

She went and stood in front of the mirror. Forty-seven, a few silver hairs. Some wrinkles, a slightly saggy neck. She'd kept her figure. Could a man still find her attractive? She slowly undid her blouse, unbuttoned her skirt, removed her under-wear, and unlaced her corset. Standing in the middle of the pile of clothing, her nakedness appeared to her as frail as a winter flower. She let her hair down and shook it out; it looked better loose. The soft light took years off her: a Djina with firm breasts, her waist slightly hollowed above the curve of her buttocks, stood exposed, awakened, filled with longing and desire. She stroked her belly. Would a man's hands caress her skin again? Would his voice whisper words of love in her ear as he pushed against her gently? She'd only known Pinkus; would she dare make love to another man?

She couldn't say exactly when she'd allowed Kenji Mori to

become so prominent in her thoughts – no doubt when she began to notice that her pulse quickened whenever she saw him. Absurd! A Japanese man . . .

She gathered up her clothes and buried her face in them.

'Too late,' she said to herself, slipping into a petticoat. Then she decided that at that point in her life she could allow herself to dream.

She put on her skirt and looked out of the window. Beyond Buttes-Chaumont, the city seemed so close it felt oppressive, like some vague threat.

Displayed in the shop window was a pair of scarlet breeches, a sky-blue fur-trimmed cloak, a plumed helmet and boots so shiny you could see your reflection in them.

'We're in luck, Boss, it's still an army outfitters!' Joseph observed, turning the door handle.

A smell of mothballs and shoe polish caught in their throats. Surrounded on all sides by uniforms, caps, shakos, epaulettes, sabres, tasselled sword-knots and red velvet saddles for general officers, they ventured over to a counter. A woman with white hair worn in a bun was spreading out on the varnished wood surface the finest collection of stirrups Victor had ever seen. A captain with a tapered moustache handled each pair as if it were a priceless jewel, while he enquired in hushed tones about the July promotions and transfers.

'Monsieur Nervin isn't back from the Ministry yet,' the woman whispered. 'If he's had wind of any nominations, he'll send you a telegram.'

'I'm sure of it. They say he can probe the mysteries of the yearbook better than an astrologer and is in on the secrets of the powers that be,' murmured the captain.

'How may I help you, gentlemen?' enquired a stooped shop assistant.

'A simple piece of information,' said Victor, stepping away from the counter. 'Do you remember having employed a woman by the name of Ernestine Grandjean after the war?'

'That's going back to the time of Methuselah! I only started working here in '86. Only Madame Rouvray will be able to tell you.'

The captain paid for his spurs and the woman with the bun was free.

'Ernestine Grandjean? She left us a long time ago, my good man. She married a notary's clerk who took her to Tourcoing. She sent us an announcement from there on the birth of their first child and after that we heard nothing. I was surprised.'

'That she stopped writing?'

'No, that she married a civilian. Not to put too fine a point on it, she had a penchant for men in uniform, and thanks to her the whole army came through here. It has to be said she was a sight for sore eyes.'

'Was there a Paul Theneuil among her admirers?'

'My good man, if I could remember the names of all her conquests I could write a directory of Paris society!'

'She had a brother called Léopold. He's the one we're looking for; it's a family matter.'

'Léopold, yes. I don't know what became of him. He worked at a printer's in Rue Mazarine. He was a bit wild, with his mistresses and his debts; his sister was fed up with it. I'd be surprised if he managed to hold down his job.'

'Rue Mazarine? A printing works?'

'Next door to a café where he spent the evenings in merry company playing bouillotte.'[65]

The printing works where Léopold Grandjean had started out in the days of the Empire had been turned into a playing card factory. A cart full of bundles of watermarked paper from the National Printing Works was parked outside the entrance. Two porters were unloading it under the watchful eye of the owner, a ruddy-faced man from the South of France. Victor explained to him that he was looking for the heir to the recently deceased Madame Grandjean, native of Jouy-en-Argonne, Meuse.

Cyprien Plagnol wiped his brow with a large handkerchief and answered him in a sing-song voice, 'I'll be with you just as soon as these two lumbering oafs have finished carrying their stuff inside.'

The shed they entered was taken up by large tables where workers were busy sticking sheets of grey chiffon paper onto sheets of card printed in intaglio, which formed the backs of the playing cards. Cylinder presses were used to fuse the sheets together, and others printed the shapes and colours onto them before the finished product was dipped in a special varnish and cut into individual cards. Joseph was sneezing incessantly, the fumes of the chemicals irritating his nose, and he paid little attention to Cyprien Plagnol's proud exposition of his *métier*.

'Huh! It may look easy, this business, but the authorities have us jumping through hoops. The number of sheets they deliver, which are manufactured exclusively for the State in Thiers – why Puy de Dôme and not Patagonia? I ask myself – must tally with the number of sheets of aces or jacks of clubs we produce!'

He lovingly tapped a pack of cards, the corners of which one of the workers had just gilded using a special glue.

'But when you see the result . . .'

'It's the same method as the one used for gilding the edges of books,' remarked Victor.

'Quite so, Monsieur! I see you're well informed. I bet you can't guess what happens to the rejects.'

'Are they donated to schools?' ventured Joseph.

'Wrong! The tax office sells them by weight to manufacturers of nougat boxes and fireworks. Come and meet Maman.'

They filed down a corridor leading to a kitchen where a small swarthy woman wrapped in an enormous gathered apron was cooking delicious-smelling dishes seasoned with garlic and peppers.

'Magali, where's Maman?'

'I think she's in the sitting room.'

Joseph, whose nasal passages had enjoyed a brief respite, was overcome by a new fit of sneezing, which prevented him from pointing out to Victor that the Roman candles he'd found in Pierre Andrésy's shop could have been made out of defective playing cards.

Cyprien Plagnol's mother proved to be his spitting image, a

stout brunette in a royal-blue tea-gown, whom he addressed considerately.

'Maman dearest, our callers are keen to find out about a young man employed at the printing works before we bought the lease.'

'Heavens! Look at the state of you, Cyprien! You're covered in dirt! Sit down, gentlemen,' she ordered, crumpling elephant-like into a wing chair.

'You'll have a glass of anisette,' she proposed. 'Anyone would think we were in Marseilles with this heat.'

Victor declined the offer.

'And what about the tow-haired young chap?'

'I don't mind if I do,' Joseph replied, ignoring Victor's disapproving look.

'Maman dearest, where have you put the old register with the moleskin cover?'

'At the back of the desk with all the other papers from the notary. How does he manage to get his clothes so filthy? I realise we're all stewing in this hot weather, but I'm no washerwoman! Well, young man, do you like it?'

Joseph sipped at his anisette. The alcohol was taking effect. His vision was obscured by a purple haze and the furniture was beginning to sway. He thought he'd better put down his glass before the dresser turned into a rhinoceros. Cyprien Plagnol came back carrying the register and handed it to Victor.

'You're in luck, this should have been thrown away, but we kept it thinking it might come in handy; there are still a hundred or so blank pages left.'

'Who owned the printing works?' asked Victor.

'The original owner had recently sold the lease to a Monsieur Martin, and he was the one we dealt with when we bought it in September 1871,' Madame Plagnol recollected.

'Monsieur Martin? Damn!' Victor cursed, opening the cover. He read:

A good book is the precious lifeblood of a master spirit
(Milton)

YEARS *1869–1870*
Employees

He turned the page.

January 1870

Bruno	*Typographer*
Clouange	*Binder*
Grandjean	*Apprentice engraver*
Grinchard	*Layout man*
Leglantier	*Proofreader*
Meunier	*Engraver*
Mathieu	*Stereotyper*
Tardieu	*Typesetter*
Theneuil	*Master Printer*

Victor held his breath; one of the keys to this mystery was hidden in these names.

The next few pages gave details of the various jobs done by the printer's. The same names appeared at the beginning of each month until September 1870, when there were four missing: Bruno, Clouange, Meunier and Tardieu – no doubt called up to fight for their country. The printing works continued operating with a reduced staff. In October, Grinchard and Mathieu's names had also disappeared. Only Grandjean, Leglantier and Theneuil remained.

'Good grief, Boss, do you see, Grandjean, Leglantier and Theneuil all worked together!'

The hubbub on Rue de Buci roused them from the apathy their astonishing discovery had plunged them into. Victor finally managed to swallow the lump in his throat.

'Boss, we're getting close, I can feel it! We can prove that the three men were connected. They were the only ones left up to the siege of Paris in December. Grandjean and Leglantier are dead, and Paul Theneuil has vanished into thin air . . . Well, what's the matter?'

Victor was staring open-mouthed at a florist's display on the other side of the street. The words of a ditty flashed through his mind . . . she *loves me, she loves me not* . . . Tasha's hat! Tasha, their first meeting, her auburn hair which she wore in a bun and the little hat decorated with daisies.

He grabbed Joseph's wrist.

'Quickly, we must go back to Passage des Thermopyles.'

'Why?'

'I have a hunch.'

Marthe Theneuil had left the printing works to attend to her haberdashery. She was upset when Victor and Joseph burst in unexpectedly and regretted having confided details about her personal life to them. Victor's excitement caught her unprepared.

'Madame Theneuil, was the flower your husband signed his love letters with a daisy?'

'What a nerve, what right have you . . .'

'It is of the utmost importance.'

'Yes. I hate the name my parents gave me. I wished I'd been named after a flower, so Paul used to call me Daisy.'

'Did you ever give him a watch?'

She looked at him incredulously.

'How did you know? Oh dear God! Something awful has happened!'

Joseph lied with ease.

'We don't know, Madame; on the contrary this may well be an encouraging sign.'

'Paul likes to be punctual,' she murmured. 'A few years ago I bought him a fob watch.'

'Did you have it inscribed?'

'Yes. Oh, I beg you, tell me the truth, I want to know . . . He's dead, isn't he?'

'No, Madame. What was the inscription?'

'*To Paul from his Marthe* in the middle of a daisy.'

'Thank you, Madame. Rest assured, you will soon receive word,' Victor said as he hurried outside.

'Are you going to tell me what this is all about?' Joseph growled once they were out of earshot of the haberdashery.

'The watch that was found next to Pierre Andrésy's corpse, the one Inspector Lecacheur asked me and Monsieur Mori to identify, belongs to Paul Theneuil! *To P— from his —e*! To Paul, not to Pierre! To Paul from his Marthe, do you see?'

'So that means—'

Joseph was unable to finish his sentence. In front of the Square de Montrouge a newspaper vendor cried out, 'Read all about it in *Le Passe-partout*! Special edition! Police inspector murdered in his own bed!'

Printed in bold capitals on the front page of the daily paper was the name Gustave Corcol.

CHAPTER THIRTEEN

Evening of the same day

T HEY were both keen to get to the newspaper first. Exasperated, Victor pushed Joseph over to a bench and sat down next to him beneath the crook of a bronze peasant girl from the Auvergne.

'I'll read aloud and that way we'll avoid tearing it:

'The body of Inspector Corcol was discovered yesterday evening at his home in Rue Jean-Cottin by his colleague, Monsieur Raoul Pérot, assistant chief of police at La Chapelle, who was alerted by his unusual absence. The door was unlocked, and Monsieur Pérot entered the apartment. Inspector Corcol lay naked under a sheet, with several stab wounds to his upper body and a bloodstained message on his stomach:

'Remember, the month of May, how lovely, how gay, the month of May. God on high! Your saints are food for tigers and leopards.'

'Boss! The leopard!'

'There's more, Joseph:

'The murder must have taken place the previous night. The downstairs neighbour, a stockbroker's widow, heard some curious noises during the night, but didn't dare go up for fear of disturbing Monsieur Corcol, who, by all accounts, was not an easy man. The police are linking his murder to that of Monsieur Léopold Grandjean, who met a similar fate on 21 June, and that of Monsieur Edmond Leglantier, who died from gas poisoning on 17 July, because of the messages referring to a leopard left at each of the crime scenes. Monsieur le Duc de Frioul, a suspect in the Leglantier affair, has been cleared of all suspicion. As for the actor Jacques Bottelier, who was to play Ravaillac in *Heart Pierced by an Arrow*, he will be charged with unlawfully wounding a fellow thespian with the intention of stealing his role as the Duc d'Épernon.

'I'll spare you the exclusive interview with Inspector Lecacheur,' Victor concluded, folding up the newspaper.

'The leopard and Sacrovir are one and the same!' exclaimed Joseph. 'You were right not to trust Daglan – he's the culprit.'

Victor flicked through a notebook he'd taken from his pocket.

'You yourself told me that the Gallic chieftain distinguished himself at Autun. That's where Mariette Trinquet said her Sacrovir hailed from. Daglan is Italian.'

'So he says. Oh, he's a cunning devil! He plays the victim but he's pulling the strings.'

'It doesn't make sense, Joseph. He wasn't obliged to contact me. And what is Paul Theneuil's part in all this? What was his half-melted watch doing at Pierre Andrésy's?'

'Daglan might have pinched it after bumping him off. Then when he set fire to the bookbinder's shop he dropped it by accident.'

'Why would Daglan set fire to Andrésy's shop?'

'To steal the Persian manuscript.'

Victor stood up, frowning, and began circling the statue.

'It doesn't hang together. You're forgetting the Ambrex shares.'

'I'm damn well not forgetting them! This is how I see the sequence of events. Our four accomplices set up their fraudulent scheme. Each man has a speciality: Daglan steals the cigar holders; Grandjean, the painter, comes up with an eye-catching design for the shares which will attract the buyers; Theneuil prints them; and Leglantier, the smooth talker with the social contacts, sells them.'

'And what about Corcol?'

'He's the man in charge. They chose him because they knew he was crooked. A *flic* in their pocket is an asset. But before they can start they need money. Corcol has an idea, he knows something about the value of books, and he knows that Pierre Andrésy restores rare works which can easily be sold to unscrupulous book dealers. He steals the manuscript and now they're ready to bring the cigar holders and the shares into play. Leglantier extorts a fortune out of the mugs who buy the shares. Only they haven't taken Daglan into account. He wants to keep the spoils for himself. He kills Theneuil, sets fire to Andrésy's shop where he drops the famous watch then gets rid of Grandjean and Leglantier and, thanks to the messages implicating the leopard, pretends he's the victim of a conspiracy in order to convince you of his innocence. There, don't you like my little story?'

'What about Corcol? What does your famous intuition tell you about that?'

'Daglan gets rid of him, no more witnesses.'

'Bravo, Joseph, I applaud you with both hands!'

'Well, I'm only putting forward theories. Isn't life a series of inexplicable events?' Very nice, Joseph old chap, a perfect epilogue for *Thule's Golden Chalice*. 'What are your objections, Boss?'

'It's the idea of the money which bothers me. What did they need it for? They had no accomplices to pay off because, as you so brilliantly pointed out, they each had their own speciality. Besides, do you think Daglan and Grandjean would have been foolish enough to sign their names on the Ambrex shares as directors? And how do you know Theneuil is dead?'

'The watch, you yourself . . .'

'The watch may be a red herring. It wouldn't be the first time a criminal left a false clue.'

'All right, what if Theneuil is still alive and he and Daglan are in this together?' Joseph suggested.

'Let's not get carried away. We must . . .'

Victor stood aside to make way for two stout ladies carrying folding stools, who installed themselves a few yards further on.

'We must keep in mind two riddles, which aren't necessarily related. One surrounds Pierre Andrésy and the other the Ambrex shares affair, which I refuse to believe he was mixed up in.'

'Not wishing to contradict you, Boss, your two mysteries have one thing in common: Gustave Corcol,' said Joseph, drawing level with Victor.

Irritated by a flock of pigeons gathered round the two stout ladies' feet, they turned off towards the town hall.

'I've another idea, Boss. Corcol dreams up the shares swindle and decides to abscond with the proceeds. He murders Theneuil then publishes the death notice in order to point the finger at Daglan. He kills Andrésy, steals the Persian manuscript, and sets the shop on fire after planting Paul Theneuil's watch as evidence. Then he eliminates Grandjean and Leglantier and is planning to get rid of Daglan when Daglan strikes first. Are you listening to me, Boss?'

'Yes . . . yes . . . Wait a minute! That song . . .'

'What song?'

They walked along Avenue du Maine where a cluster of cabs was attempting to overtake the lumbering trams. Victor suddenly grabbed Joseph's arm.

'The month of May! The Commune! Josette Fatou told you she'd heard Grandjean's murderer singing "The Cherry Season". Well, the song's author dedicated it to a woman called Louise, a stretcher-bearer from Rue de la Fontaine-au-Roi, on Sunday 28 May 1871.'[66]

'I'm amazed by the things you know!'

'Be quiet a moment! Corcol assured me that Pierre Andrésy's brother was dead . . . But what if he's still alive? What if he is Sacrovir? Or maybe it's Daglan. He must have been about twenty then.'

'Could it be Theneuil, Boss? His wife made a point of saying how youthful he looked. We have his photograph – all we have to do is show it to Mariette Trinquet and—'

'If you weren't a man, Joseph, I'd kiss you! Hurry over to Rue Guisarde and find out. I'll go back to Rue Fontaine and telephone our friend Raoul Pérot.'

*

Josette Fatou walked back to her house, hugging the walls, clutching the bag of potatoes she'd gone to buy after parking her cart. These past few days, her anxiety had swelled up inside her like a balloon until she felt she was suffocating. Powerless to resist the pressure, she waited meekly for the worst to happen.

She did not have to wait long.

Just as she reached the gate, a gloved hand closed round her wrist and a voice breathed, 'Make up a bundle of clothes and follow me, quickly!'

The balloon burst, deflated in one go. What was the point of struggling? He would find her wherever she went. She might as well give in.

'Why?' she had the strength to ask.

'Because it's the only solution. I'll stay here. Hurry.'

'Where are we going?'

For a moment she felt as if it wasn't she who had spoken.

She stared up at him, open-mouthed. His words had frightened her and yet she could scarcely feel his presence.

She walked cautiously down the corridor, the ground swaying beneath her feet. She felt terribly afraid and yet strangely removed.

As she climbed the stairs, she understood that death had been moving towards her since the day she was born. Sometimes slowly, sometimes fast, always unpredictable. It was up to each of us to make friends with death. And if hers took on the appearance of desire would that not give it a certain beauty? Weren't love and death related? *Love*. She wondered why he'd behaved so tenderly towards her after he broke into her lodgings. In her semi-conscious state she had yielded not to the demands of the stranger, but to an instinct deep in her own body whose impulses she had always suppressed. She was sure of one thing: this man provided the answer to all her questions. Very well, she would go with him, and if death conquered love then so be it. She had waited years for this meeting, for this awakening of her senses, cursing men and dreaming of a gentle lover. What a shame that her Prince Charming should also turn out to be her killer.

Wrapped in his greatcoat, his hat pulled down over his brow, Frédéric Daglan stared into the darkness of the doorway. There was a scrunch of gravel; a harridan in clogs crossed the courtyard. A chicken clucked and a dog chained beside a hut whined expectantly.

'Shut your trap!' the harridan cried as she walked away, but not before shooting a malevolent glance at the man standing under the lamp-post.

Suddenly, Frédéric Daglan began to feel flustered. His plan was an absurd fantasy; the flower girl would barricade herself in her apartment and rouse the neighbours. He'd been afraid she might cry out and put up a struggle. He'd been prepared to use all his powers of persuasion to convince her to go with him. Her submissiveness had thrown him – she was like a person who suffered from vertigo and was fatally attracted to heights. Had it been a ruse? Had she already escaped through a back door? No, she was back, carrying a carpet bag on her arm. She'd combed her hair and changed into a cheap dress that showed off her figure.

He remembered her small hard breasts cupped in his hand

the night she'd fainted in fright when she saw him. He had seldom desired a woman so intensely. But he was suspicious of the fact that she'd gone along with his decision so easily. He must tread carefully.

He led her in silence to Rue du Faubourg-Saint-Antoine, where a cab was waiting beside the pavement. Josette drank in the sunny façades of the buildings, forcing herself to hold on to the image before the cab door clicked shut.

A man slipped nervously into the bookshop. Kenji, who was busy selling an illustrated edition of *Orlando Furioso*[67] in three volumes, noticed the visitor's unassuming manner out of the corner of his eye.

'How may I help you?'

'Are you Monsieur Legris's associate? We've met before. I'm a watchmaker on Rue Monsieur-le-Prince. I'm here on a rather delicate matter. About ten days ago, I entrusted Monsieur Legris with a fob watch belonging to Monsieur Andrésy. He was to give it to you. Only, this morning a man claiming to be his cousin came in asking for it. Without thinking, I told him I no longer had it. I hope I haven't made a mistake.'

How typical of Victor to be so secretive, thought Kenji.

'No matter,' he replied, 'I'll bring you the watch as soon as we close for lunch. Just now I'm alone and . . .'

He gestured discreetly towards a customer at the back of the shop.

'Oh, there's no hurry. The cousin said he'd return late afternoon.'

'I believe I've met this cousin,' Kenji went on, 'a tall, slender young man with a beard. Somewhat eccentric.'

'It's difficult to say exactly,' replied the watchmaker. 'He was bundled up in a greatcoat. Can you imagine, in this heat! He wore a hat pulled down over his eyes, dark glasses and a beard à la Victor Hugo . . . A real eccentric. Well, I must be going, until later, then, and my apologies for any inconvenience.'

Kenji saw the watchmaker out. They were saying goodbye when the man snapped his fingers.

'I've just remembered something. While he was browsing through various trinkets I noticed a long scar on the palm of his left hand, does that mean anything to you?'

'No.'

Puzzled, Kenji walked upstairs to his apartment.

'Iris, dear, are you busy? I have to go out, and those rogues Victor and Joseph are playing truant. Could you . . . Would you . . .'

'Play shopkeeper? Yes, Papa. Honestly, for somebody who hasn't much interest in books, I'm practically a prisoner in a reading room!'

'My omnibus is rather good, don't you think, Kochka?'

In the background of the painting, the yellow vehicle belonging to the General Transport Company stood at the foot of a hill while an old man hitched a spare horse to a team of two bays. Perched on his seat in a coachman's uniform and a silver-ribboned stovepipe hat made of boiled leather, the driver surveyed the same scene as the viewer of the painting. Still in sketch form, a family of acrobats stood in a line waiting to perform a series of daredevil feats. The couple and their six children were all in tights, side by side with their hands on their hips, poised for Tasha to bring them to life.

Kochka mewed and rubbed a paw behind her ear.

'Bad cat, you'll make it rain! That's an idea, what if I make it rain on my acrobats? No, too depressing.'

She began whistling the third movement of Vincent d'Indy's *Symphonie Cévenole*,[68] which she'd heard at a concert Victor had taken her to recently. She reflected which colours to use. Black was forbidden except for the coachman's hat. She recalled what Odilon Redon had said: 'You must respect black; use it sparingly.' Others' words came back to her, above all those of Degas: 'Light has an orange tint; the shadows of flesh are red; half-tones are green, and beware of white!' She chewed her thumbnail while Kochka rubbed against her ankles, then suddenly she decided to follow her intuition, to be her own mistress as Victor had always advocated. She set down her palette, prey to one of those fits of restlessness that frequently upset her concentration.

Flitting from one end of the studio to the other, she replaced the top on a flask of oil she used to dilute her colours and put it next to a bottle of siccative oil and a tube of cadmium lemon.

'When I paint I am like Poussin, who fled chaos, except I'm stuck with a cat that keeps chasing after a piece of string,' she reflected as she tickled Kochka's whiskers with a piece of frayed cord. As the animal leapt about excitedly, it knocked over a boot and a pile of books lying on the floor, and began chewing a slipper. Tasha grabbed an apple in passing, and paused at the table where she'd spread out a few sketches for a chapter of the *Odyssey*. Circe was watching with glee as Ulysses' crew was transformed before her eyes into a herd of pigs. Tasha still hadn't resolved the problems posed by the composition and she felt guilty. She was behind, and the publisher was getting impatient. Even so, she turned away from the sorceress, tossed the uneaten apple onto the bed and returned to her painting, her thoughts refreshed.

Just then, Kochka miaowed to be let out.

'Do you need to do your business, darling? Follow me.'

They crossed the courtyard to the locked apartment. Kochka had her little ways and ran straight over to her box filled with old newspapers in the kitchen where she began scrabbling furiously. Tasha went back to the studio, leaving the door ajar. After reflecting for a moment, she thinned a mixture of cobalt and Indian yellow on her palette as she hummed Vincent d'Indy's air. She was about to add a drop of oil when Kochka reappeared, tail puffed out, hackles up, ears flattened.

'What is it, little one? A nasty old tom? The butcher's moggy or the Marquis de Carabas?'

Kochka hissed and scurried to the back of the alcove. Curious, Tasha went outside. All she saw were some flies performing their aerial ballet above the fountain. She narrowed her eyes and watched them dart back and forth in the sun's last rays, caressing the acacia leaves as she entered the apartment. Since the theft of one of his cameras, Victor had been scrupulous about closing the shutters in order to avoid another break-in. Without bothering to light the lamp, Tasha walked around the room, cursing Euphrosine's mania for leaving the bedside table next to the water-closet door after she'd finished dusting.

The pale refection of her face rippled in the mirror. A strange mysterious girl with flowing red hair, like the creatures in Gustave Moreau's paintings. She moistened her forefinger and tamed an unruly lock. Mysterious, her? Nonsense. She was a woman who aspired to independence, creativity and love; she was neither the sphinx nor the succubus so dear to male artists, whether symbolists or realists.

A muffled sound like the rustle of fabric drew her towards the darkened bedroom. A dancing candle flame traced eerie shapes in the gloom.

'Victor? Is that you?'

She bumped into someone. She choked back a scream. An icy cold spread through her stomach, gripping her heart, a hand closed over her mouth.

'Be quiet,' a man's voice ordered.

He had one arm round her shoulders and with his full weight was trying to force her to the ground. She felt herself fall, and fought back, lashing out with her fists. She managed to escape his clutches and almost reached the door, but he caught her, twisted her wrist and, despite her resistance, dragged her back to the bedroom. A sharp pain ripped through her skull; the blow to her temple sent her plummeting to the bottom of a black pit.

Just as he entered the courtyard, Victor heard what sounded like a woman's scream coming from the apartment. Imagining Tasha in distress, he broke into a run.

'Tasha! Tasha, where are you?'

A click. Followed by a command: 'Don't move, Legris. Walk over here slowly, your hands above your head.'

Victor moved forward. The stranger tripped him up and he fell onto the bed, where Tasha lay motionless. Her torn blouse revealed the silky roundness of her breast. His head was spinning, his limbs felt heavy.

'Damn you!'

'Calm down, Monsieur Legris, you're not in any danger. Get up slowly.'

Victor could see the gun pointing at him. The man was enveloped in a greatcoat. A top hat and dark glasses made it impossible to identify him.

'She only has a small bump, Legris. I didn't come here looking for a fight. I need that watch. Do you know why?'

Victor shook his head.

'We're wasting time, Legris, I know you've got it.'

That voice, those clothes . . .

'You had me fooled, Daglan.'

'Give me the watch, quickly! Don't try anything, my gun is pointing at her.'

Victor walked over to the wardrobe.

'No tricks, Legris, put your left hand behind your back.'

'I need both hands to open the lid.'

'The box of photographs! I should have known. Turn round. One false move and I'll shoot her.'

'Put your gun down on the pillow or I'll shoot you,' said a deep voice.

The stranger moved towards Victor, urged on by the pistol

Kenji was pressing between his shoulder blades. Suddenly he swung round.

'Kenji! You? . . . Perhaps it's just as well. I've done what I had to do, I leave in peace.'

Everything happened with the strange unreality of a dream. The man placed the barrel of his gun against his chest and pulled the trigger. Victor had the impression of being suspended in mid-air for what seemed like an unbelievably long time, and then the man fell to the floor.

Kenji dropped his gun; he was shaking.

'I didn't mean that to happen,' he said to Victor. 'Go and see to Tasha.'

He went to open the shutters then knelt down beside the dying man, gently removing his top hat and glasses.

'Why, Pierre, why?'

Pierre Andrésy smiled feebly. He managed to speak with great difficulty.

'Fourastié . . . He knows why . . . Fourastié, Rue Baillet . . . Kenji . . . Is every man's fate predetermined?'

'I believe that we are the authors of our own lives. We write the play, and the performance goes on until the end.'

CHAPTER FOURTEEN

Friday 28 July

'You have to be philosophical in life and not worry about things; one day you come within an inch of disaster, the next everything is fine. You're right, Papa, you're right,' Joseph said to himself, crossing Pont Neuf at a brisk pace.

Admittedly, nothing had come of his second visit to Mariette Trinquet, since she hadn't identified Paul Theneuil as the famous Sacrovir, and so he'd missed his big chance to crack the case. But when, in the early evening, Monsieur Legris had telephoned to inform him of the tragedy, and had gone on to say that both he and Monsieur Mori were counting on the unfailing collaboration of their assistant, he'd felt reassured.

It had been getting on for midnight when Victor, after finally being released by the police, had turned up at Rue Visconti, much to Euphrosine's annoyance, looking peaky, his eyes hollow. Joseph had taken him off to his study.

'Monsieur Mori and I have had a most unpleasant time, Joseph. Inspector Lecacheur grilled us for hours. We pretended we knew nothing and were simply looking for the missing Persian manuscript. We didn't mention the watch.'

'Did he believe you?'

'No. And I'm sure he isn't finished with us yet.'

'Does he know about the leopard?'

'The leopard? What leopard? Do you know anything about a leopard?'

'No, Boss, I avoid all contact with felines. Is Mademoiselle Tasha feeling any better?'

'It's severely tried her nerves, but she's recovering from the ordeal. I'm afraid there'll be a backlash when I go home.'

'Who are you more afraid of, Mademoiselle Tasha or Inspector Lecacheur? Only joking, Boss, only joking. What was that you said on the telephone about my unfailing collaboration?'

'Before he died, Pierre Andrésy whispered: "Fourastié . . . he knows why . . . Fourastié, Rue Baillet . . ." He's a cobbler, he . . .'

'Has a shop in Rue Baillet, near the Louvre,' Joseph cut in, polishing his nails on his jacket lapel.

'How the devil . . . ?'

'Mariette Trinquet told us his name, Boss. You've got a memory like a sieve.'

'Stop showing off, Joseph, and listen. Kenji has been doing his own investigating. Fourastié is the one who sold the Persian manuscript to the bookseller, Adolphe Esquirol. Tomorrow morning . . .'

Victor looked at his watch then corrected himself.

'This morning, open the shop and ask Iris to stand in for you . . .'

'She won't like it.'

'She's the future wife of a bookseller, isn't she?'

Joseph turned pink with pleasure.

'Go straight to Rue Baillet. I don't need to draw you a map, do I?'

'No, Boss. I leave the Elzévir bookshop with a package under my arm, a delivery. l shake off Lecacheur's henchmen and head for Rue Baillet. Then what?'

'Fourastié holds the key to this affair. I'm counting on you to get it out of him. You're good at that.'

'What about you?'

'I'm going home to get some sleep. Monsieur Mori and I have been summoned back to the police station.'

Joseph turned off Rue de l'Arbre-Sec into Rue Baillet. He was sweating. The leather notebook Iris had given him the year before was sticking to the lining of his jacket pocket. He reached the cobbler's. There was a notice nailed to the shop front:

We repair every type of shoe and boot

A sign hanging on the doorknob said:

Temporarily closed

Joseph knocked several times. When there was no reply, he stepped back, looked up at the building and, at the risk of rousing the whole neighbourhood, yelled, 'Fourastié! . . . Fourastié! . . . Fourastié! . . . Come down. Fourastié! Pierre sent me. I'm his cousin from Autun!'

The sun was dazzling and he lifted his hand to shield his eyes. On the second floor a curtain twitched.

Joseph flashed his most charming smile at the beautiful

brunette who was standing in the doorway to her tobacconist's kiosk, drawn by his cries.

'Well,' she exclaimed, 'what a way to behave! I thought he'd gone to Belval-sous-Châtillon to see his daughter. Although it seemed a bit strange him leaving his birds . . .'

A face appeared behind the glass in the door. Joseph pressed his mouth to the keyhole.

'Monsieur Fourastié, my name's Joseph Pignot, I'm an associate of Kenji Mori, the bookseller. He came here himself, but the shop was closed. Monsieur Mori is a friend of Pierre Andrésy's.'

'What do you want from me?' asked a steely voice.

'I've come to tell you that he killed himself . . . I must speak to you. Please, it's important!'

'Important for whom?'

'For both of us.'

Fourastié unlocked the door and opened it a crack.

'Come in, quickly.'

Fourastié was a plump man with a drooping moustache, grey hair and broken veins on his cheeks. Joseph avoided looking into his cross-eyes. The cobbler led him through the shop into a workshop crammed with shoes. He moved slowly, without a sound. Joseph noticed a rush of warm air, the pungent smell of the place and the awful din. Birdseed was flying everywhere. Along the partition wall was an aviary divided into tiny cages where pale-yellow canaries, sparrows, hummingbirds, a parrot, Japanese warblers and whistling blackbirds were hopping around and flapping their wings. Fourastié pointed to a stool.

'Meet my family. Take a seat. Would you like a drink?'

'No thank you.'

'Then I'll drink alone.'

Fourastié poured himself a glass of red wine, drained it in one gulp then pulled a chair out from the other side of a greasy table.

'So, Monsieur Mori killed himself?'

'No. Pierre Andrésy.'

Fourastié turned pale. His hand shook as he reached into a drawer and took out a folded letter. He stared at it in silence.

'When did it happen?' he asked.

'Early yesterday evening.'

'Poor Pierre!'

Joseph felt a mixture of anger and exasperation.

'Your poor Pierre nearly killed my boss and his fiancée! He murdered four men!'

'I know. It's a terrible business, Monsieur, a terrible business. I'd do better to keep my mouth shut.'

Joseph tried to find the right thing to say.

'I . . . Believe me, Monsieur Fourastié . . . The last thing I want is to cause you any problems. The police will never know about this conversation . . . Only, my bosses insisted that I take notes.'

'That won't be necessary,' murmured Fourastié, handing him the letter. 'This is addressed to Monsieur Mori, it explains everything.'

'I want to hear the story from your own lips.'

'Can't you leave me alone? Let the dead bury the dead.'

'Listen, Monsieur Fourastié, I was very fond of Pierre Andrésy. I want to know the truth.'

'You're tough, aren't you? Go on, be my guest. Turn the place upside down – maybe you'll find the truth hiding under the mattress! Oh, and assuming there's a "hereafter" I'm sure Pierre would heartily approve; he didn't leave any unfinished business.'

More like he started a funeral business! Joseph thought, catching the beady eye of a red-crested cockatoo gently trying to soothe its yearning for a distant Malaysia as it swung on its perch.

Fourastié cleared his throat. 'Take notes if you like. I first saw Pierre again two years ago, in 1891, on the banks of the Seine. I was fishing for bleak, it's my hobby. He was rifling through the booksellers' boxes for rare bindings. We hadn't seen each other for twenty years. We reminisced about our youth, about the war. He'd refused to take part in the slaughter and had escaped to England. After the surrender, I joined the Commune. I was arrested on 25 May in Rue de Tournon. A captain interrogated me, and the provost marshal, without glancing up from his papers, gave the order: "Take him to the queue." In less than five minutes I was sentenced to be shot. I ended up in a tiny courtyard outside the Senate building. It was full of people – men, women and children – surrounded by policemen and soldiers in red uniforms . . . No, no, I can't go on, it's too much!'

He drained the last drops of his wine and studied Joseph's sympathetic expression.

'The police know nothing about you, Monsieur Fourastié, you have my word of honour.'

'If you only knew how little I care! We could hear the

crackle of rifles. I knew I was going to die, that none of us would come out alive. I'd almost resigned myself when I noticed a fellow with a tricolour armband. I knew him. We lived on the same street. He was a plain-clothes policeman . . .'

As he spoke, Fourastié turned towards a photograph standing on a shelf next to a conch shell.

'My daughter – she's all I've got left in the world. She's married, lives in Marne.'

'She's lovely. Now please get to the point. I want to know about Pierre Andrésy.'

'This is important for you to know, Monsieur. The fellow with the armband called out: "You, come with me!" I followed him. As I passed close to a queue of condemned men and women, I recognised Pierre's wife, his fourteen-year-old kid and his younger brother, Sacrovir. I turned round. I thought of my little girl, all alone at home . . .'

'Sacrovir?'

'That was Pierre's brother Mathieu's nickname. He was a member of a workers' group modelled on the Carbonari.[69] He'd become involved through a friend. Pierre was violently opposed to it. He said that type of movement could only spell trouble, especially when you ran a printing works. He and his brother fell out and Mathieu stormed out of the house just as war was being declared and went to live in Rue Guisarde.'

'A printing works? In Rue Mazarine? Was Pierre Andrésy the owner?'

'Yes. It was a thriving business. When he left for England, his wife took over.'

'Was Mathieu's friend's name Frédéric Daglan?'

'I don't know . . . Pierre said he was an idler, a good-for-nothing, an anarchist of sorts who believed in stealing back from society – in short a thief.'

'The leopard!'

Fourastié looked surprised. For a few seconds he remained motionless, succumbing to the effects of the alcohol.

'The *flic* took me aside, rubbed his finger and thumb together to mean money, and said, laughing: "As you're a neighbour we're going to make a deal. If you can pay I'll arrange for you to be sent to Versailles; hard labour is always better than the grim reaper."'

'And the name of this *flic*?'

'That's my business,' Fourastié cut in suddenly, his chin quivering as he bit his lip.

'Don't upset yourself, Monsieur Fourastié, don't upset yourself like that . . . Come on, you can tell me!'

Choked with emotion, Fourastié remained silent, but he shook his head. Joseph persevered.

'Was it Gustave Corcol? . . . He's dead. He was found murdered the day before yesterday.'

Fourastié tried to smile, but only managed a whimper.

'Yes, Gustave Corcol, nicknamed the Spaniel, a real swine! I can't help it, when I remember . . . It'll pass, it'll pass.'

His voice grew calmer.

'Corcol ruled over the Latin Quarter. When the Versailles Army besieged Paris, his zeal was second to none. He escorted the officers who carried out the raids. They'd surround a whole block of houses and search every building from top to bottom. The smallest incriminating object and everybody went before the provost marshal. After a summary ruling, suspects who weren't proven to have taken part in the Commune were sent to Versailles, while the rest were thrown into the cellars of the Senate to rot until the cellars were full. And then they made space . . .'

'Made space?'

'They shot people in batches, in the Luxembourg Gardens, by the pond . . . It was a miracle that I escaped with my life. I could pay. Corcol saved my skin in return for money. During the raids, he lined his pockets thanks to the denunciations. You can't imagine the number of anonymous letters, sackloads. Even the military authorities were shocked by such baseness, and they weren't exactly driven by compassion. People denounced their neighbours, their bosses, their creditors, their rivals in love. Ah, Monsieur, weakness is universal, but this!'

'Not so fast, Monsieur Fourastié,' begged Joseph, sticking out his tongue as he scribbled.

'Imagine what a shock it was to see Andrésy again twenty years after this tragedy. I thought he was dead. He told me he'd lost everyone he loved. Neighbours had described to him how during the siege his family had sought refuge with a cousin near the Sorbonne. The building had been reduced to a pile of rubble. Do you know, Monsieur, nearly fifteen thousand shells fell on Paris?'

'My mother and I lived in a cellar while my father was fighting at Buzenval. I was under the impression that Pierre Andrésy returned to France before the Prussians surrounded Paris.'

'I've no idea. In any event, the printing works had changed hands . . . Are you sure you're not thirsty? I am.'

Fourastié stood up, opened a second bottle, poured himself a drink and paced up and down the workshop holding his glass.

'Pierre was convinced that his family had perished during the shelling. I thought I was doing the right thing telling him the truth, so I described what I'd seen, his family being shot, the deportations, the humiliations. I thought it would help him to get over it. What I should have done was confess my own cowardice. What a fool! If only I'd known . . . I gave him the name of their executioner: Gustave Corcol. He stood before me, dazed, like a man driven to distraction, without speaking, and then he put his head on his arm and sobbed. He blamed himself for having abandoned his family!'

'Is that what sparked his desire for revenge?'

Fourastié sat down again, wearily pushing the glass and bottle to one side so that he could lean his elbows on the table. Then he hid his face in his hands. Long minutes went by during which he relived his disappointed hopes, his failed attempts at happiness. Suddenly, he looked up at Joseph, with an expression of utter despair.

'Vengeance is worse than a burn for which there is no salve. Andrésy went away with a crazed look in his eyes – like an animal going to the slaughter. I heard nothing more from him until late summer '92. One day, he asked me to put him up. He confided his plan to me, and I swore to keep silent because I felt responsible.'

Fourastié stared at the bottle, his eyes red, his face tense.

'Pierre had finally traced Corcol to La Chapelle police station. He'd studied his habits, found out where he ate, where he lived, which bars he went to. He began going to his local bar and gradually the two men became friendly. He made up a story about a brother who was in Hôpital Lariboisière dying from a chest wound he'd received in May 1871 while routing a group of National Guardsmen who were manning the barricade in Rue de Rennes. He showed him a scar on his hand and told him it was a war wound he'd got at Reichshoffen. What a joke! He'd cut himself by accident once on a trimming guillotine. He didn't bother to conceal his name, his address or his profession. There was no way Corcol would remember a family arrested and shot in 1871. Pierre sang the praises of Thiers and the repression, harshly criticising the Communards. Corcol was completely taken in.'

'I can understand why he might want to punish the *flic*, but the others?'

'During their conversations at the bar, Corcol confessed that although he detested the Communards, he despised their informers even more. There were three in particular who worked at a printing shop in Rue Mazarine. They were responsible for the arrest of at least thirty people, including their boss's family. He didn't know their names, but Pierre worked out who they were by a process of elimination.'

'Grandjean, Leglantier, Theneuil and Daglan. The swine!' Joseph cried.

'Daglan? No, Monsieur, there were only three. I don't know who Daglan is.'

'But why did they denounce them?'

'Self-interest. Once the family had been wiped out, they obtained the deeds to the printing works from the authorities.

They immediately sold it and shared the proceeds and everyone went their own way.'

For a while now, Fourastié had been eyeing up the bottle.

'Oh, to hell with abstinence!'

He downed two glasses one after the other.

'How did Pierre Andrésy manage to get into Théâtre de l'Échiquier?'

'He mingled with the joiners. He knocked Leglantier unconscious, opened the gas tap, typed the message then raised the alarm . . . When Monsieur Mori came here, Pierre started worrying. He . . . Oh, it's my fault, it's all my fault . . .'

He slumped in his seat then resumed his account in a slurred voice, his lips moist, his eyes unfocused.

'They sent me to the penal colony in New Caledonia. Nine years without my little girl. That's where I developed my love of birds and learnt to be a cobbler . . . The past always catches up with you in the end . . .'

All of a sudden, Fourastié sat up straight.

'That's enough, lad. I've given you Pierre's letter, now push off – I need to be alone.'

His mind brimming with questions, Joseph wandered down the quiet avenues of Jardin des Tuileries. He sat on a bench. Around him were well-dressed couples, smiling children, goats harnessed to carts, well-tended lawns, a peaceful existence. Far removed from war, massacres, shattered lives. Joseph felt thirsty. He pulled the letter addressed to Kenji out of his pocket . . .

*

Dusk was already casting shadows into the study at Rue Visconti where Joseph was busy imparting what he'd learnt from Fourastié, with no regard for the purplish shadows under Victor's eyes or Kenji's yawns.

'. . . There were three informers: the master printer, Paul Theneuil; the apprentice engraver, Léopold Grandjean; and the proofreader, Edmond Leglantier – a talentless rhymester who boasted of having been applauded by the Empress Eugénie. It took Pierre Andrésy time to find them after twenty years. Meanwhile, Corcol had confided in him his need for money; Andrésy lent him small amounts on several occasions and put to him an idea for the perfect swindle: selling shares in a fictitious company making synthetic amber that looked like the real thing. Corcol swallowed it hook, line and sinker. All he had to do was to produce some authentic-looking shares. Corcol would take charge of the operation. Andrésy provided him with the addresses of his three ex-employees. The enamellist came up with the design, the printer printed them, and the theatre manager sold the worthless pieces of paper. Naturally each man received a substantial payment. Monsieur Andrésy explains it all in his letter. You may congratulate me, Monsieur Legris, on the theory I put forward last night, which was almost flawless. What a brilliant strategem! Andrésy gave half the profits to Leglantier and half to Corcol, each man believing himself to be his only associate.'

Joseph paused, raising his hand in a theatrical pose. He imagined treading the boards – at Théâtre du Gymnase, for instance – upstaging Coquelin Cadet by playing opposite Sarah

Bernhardt. But which role would he play? The vaivode Otto von Munk or Sublieutenant Wilkinson?'

'Get on with the story!' thundered Kenji.

'Pierre Andrésy's plan was worthy of Machiavelli. Leglantier failed to make the connection between Grandjean the apprentice engraver and the name on the Ambrex share certificates.'

'Wait a minute! These two knew each other and yet Leglantier didn't realise?'

'Apparently, since he went ahead. He was desperate for money and, in any case, his back was covered – his name wasn't mentioned anywhere.'

'Did Corcol also suffer from amnesia? He was an inspector, after all,' Kenji retorted sarcastically.

'It was a long time ago. I already told you, in '71 Corcol would pick up the lists of people to be arrested from the police station in the fifth arrondissement. He was snowed under. People were being shot left, right and centre; he had no idea who the informers were.'

'How did he know they worked at a printer's?'

Kenji, hands in pockets, wrinkled his nose and closed one eye, as if to say: you won't get anything past me.

Joseph, frustrated, turned to Victor.

'They told the police in order to avoid being picked up. Anyone with grubby clothes or hands was being systematically arrested. As for Daglan, he had nothing to do with it,' he declared emphatically.

'Yes, tell us more about Daglan,' ordered Kenji.

'Pierre Andrésy blamed him particularly for having led

his younger brother Mathieu astray. If it hadn't been for Daglan's influence, Mathieu would never have become Sacrovir. He would have kept away from the Communards and his family would have come through the slaughter. Do you see?' he said sharply to Kenji.

'Wipe that surly expression off your face and carry on with your saga.'

'They needed cigar holders made of real amber in order to dupe the investors. Monsieur Andrésy gave Corcol the name of an enterprising burglar – an urban Robin Hood known as the leopard of Batignolles.'

'Victor, please translate this gibberish for me,' Kenji said, 'my nerves are beginning to fray.'

'Once the Ambrex shares had been sold, Pierre Andrésy wreaked his revenge. He killed Grandjean, then he killed Paul Theneuil, dressed the corpse in his own clothes and placed it in his shop before setting fire to the premises. A dead man can act freely without fear of hindrance. He killed Leglantier then he killed Corcol. His revenge was almost complete.'

'What about my Persian manuscript, clever clogs?' Kenji asked Joseph.

'Seeing as he was officially dead, Monsieur Andrésy needed liquid assets. He asked his friend Fourastié to sell a few rare editions belonging to his customers.'

'And I thought so highly of him,' muttered Kenji.

'He thought highly of you, too, or he wouldn't have turned his gun on himself – he would simply have shot you.'

'How did Pierre Andrésy come across his brother's watch?'

'It's all explained in the letter. Mathieu, to be on the safe side, had hidden his green Communard membership card and his fob watch under a floorboard in his room in Rue Guisarde. The *flics* must have been in a hurry and they just swiped the few belongings he owned. When Pierre returned to France in October 1871, he asked the new tenants if he could take a look around. They were good honest folk and they gave him back the watch. They had torn up the card.'

'And what part did the cousin play?'

'There is no cousin. He was an invention. In case Pierre needed to reappear for any reason.'

'Which is precisely what happened,' said Kenji. 'Pierre suddenly remembered that he'd taken his brother's watch to be mended. Posing as the cousin, he went to Rue Monsieur-le-Prince to try to get it back, but it was too late, the watchmaker had already given it to you, Victor. When the watchmaker came to the shop yesterday, he told me that the cousin had a scar on his left hand. I knew that Pierre Andrésy had cut himself on a guillotine six or seven years ago. It couldn't have been a coincidence. I fetched one of my antique pistols and rushed over to Rue Fontaine. But why did Pierre think up such a complicated plot? The cigar holders, the shares . . . Why didn't he just kill them one after the other and disappear?'

'He wanted them to feel fear, to remember their heinous crime before dying. In order to achieve this he needed to cook up a scheme that would involve all five men without arousing their suspicions and would tarnish their good name. Daglan was the last on his list, and he would be the scapegoat. The messages left on the victims, the death notice, the letter addressed to

Theneuil's book-keeper, Monsieur Leuze, all prove this. Unfortunately, Pierre made a mistake by failing to take Paul Theneuil's watch out of his waistcoat. It never occurred to him that we would go nosing about in his affairs.'

'In one sense, you two prevented him from carrying out the grand finale of his revenge,' Kenji concluded.

'How is that?'

'By denying him the satisfaction of seeing Daglan's head roll. The reason he wanted to retrieve the watch at any cost was not to avoid punishment, but to implicate the person he considered most to blame. I can't listen to any more. I'm exhausted. I'm going home to bed. Joseph, give me that letter, and in future please refrain from opening correspondence addressed to me. As for you, Victor, I'm still waiting for Pierre's watch, which you forgot to give me. Good night.'

'Well, I'm damned, Boss!' exclaimed Joseph when Kenji had gone. 'He's got a nerve! He's just as much to blame for Andrésy's failure!'

'Have you two quite finished!' bellowed Euphrosine. 'I get up at the crack of dawn. I've got work to do. For blooming heaven's sake, it's worse than being in a henhouse! Ah, the cross I have to bear!'

Joseph tiptoed over to close the door, and put his finger to his lips.

'Not a word, Boss. If Maman ever found out . . .'

Victor waved a rolled-up newspaper.

'Too late, it's in all the newspapers. *Le Passe-partout* has printed a special edition detailing the police's initial discoveries. Both my and Monsieur Mori's names are mentioned. This time there was no getting round Inspector Lecacheur. I'm worried that the publicity will be bad for business.'

'Cheer up, Boss, our customers will come flocking. I'll take the opportunity to fill the shop window with detective novels . . . I'm curious to know how Daglan will react.'

'He sent me another coded message. I deliberately avoided mentioning it in front of Monsieur Mori.'

'Did you manage to decipher it?'

'I'm not a complete idiot, Joseph. I applied your method. Daglan is leaving the country.'

'Monsieur Andrésy's letter exonerates him: it clearly states that he had nothing to do with the murders.'

'With his criminal past he thinks it's advisable to make himself scarce. I like the fellow, I hope he succeeds.'

EPILOGUE

WHY did people say that the sea was blue? Ruffled haphazardly by the wind, it resembled those fields of cinders at the city's edges. At best it might deign to take on a greenish tinge if the clouds freed the sun from its shroud. Leaning against the rail at the stern of the boat, Josette Fatou watched the ship's wake edged with foam and, beyond, the French coastline fading into the distance.

'Serves you right, serves you right,' a seagull squawked above her head.

It was sheer madness to have fallen into this stranger's arms, submitting to his will to the point of leaving everything behind in order to follow him! But the die was cast, there was no going back. She felt sick with panic, and then she glimpsed the figure outlined against the sky, turned towards her, and her fears dissolved, floating away on the sea spray.

'Just our luck, the weather's turning today of all days – a taster of that wretched drizzle which is so good for the English lawn. What are you thinking about?'

'About lawns scattered with daisies, which I will pick and sell in the streets.'

'You won't need to work again. I'm going to fill our pockets by relieving the English of their pocketbooks. London's a pickpocket's paradise – at least they don't have an Alphonse Bertillon.'[70]

'I prefer to make my own living.'

'You're right, it takes thousands of paupers to make a rich man, the sheep must die to feed the wolf. As you please, my pretty one, I'm sure the flower sellers at Covent Garden will happily move over and make a nice place for you.'

He pulled her to him. She tried to move back, but where could she go? He loosened his hold, brushed her salty lips with his.

'My little wild one, that's how I like you, unkempt and indomitable. Your scratches and moans show me that I still haven't tamed you.'

'You always get what you want, don't you?'

'I try at any rate. You won't be able to change that about me.'

He grinned, as if to say he knew that she was flirting with him, and tried to take her in his arms again, but she pushed him away.

'At first I took you for a criminal, now I know you're just a petty thief.'

As she said the words, she felt her cheeks flush. It's true, she thought, he wouldn't hurt a fly. If I'm certain of anything, I'm certain of that.

'A petty thief is a fair description,' he said. 'I thought I was offering you seventh heaven. You seem disappointed. Perhaps you'd have preferred the smell of blood on me?'

His voice betrayed a hint of playfulness, and to her great surprise Josette caught a glimpse of another happier, more cheerful, carefree world.

She shrugged.

'What will our future be?'

'The future is a butterfly, which, once captured, perishes. Damn and blast it, how society bores me! Shopkeepers filling the hourglass of time with their hoard of grain, weaklings hiding pathetically from death behind a pile of possessions . . . Cast aside your fears and take a deep breath of freedom; I promise you, we'll have a good time!'

Her lover's impetuosity, so fervent despite his age and his old man's disguise, overcame her fears: exile, destitution, the idea that sooner or later she would be abandoned by this man whom she knew was fickle. Then a sudden cloud darkened her horizon.

'What will become of me the day they throw you in prison?'

'You'll wait for me or you'll find someone else.'

'Are you even capable of love?'

'Ah, love! A mirage that vanishes as soon as we think we've attained it. I don't talk about love, I make love. It was different before, when I was young. I had faith; I swallowed whole the vows of fidelity that go with the words *for ever*. The result? A broken heart, because my lovers and I were powerless to keep such promises. Love? A catch-all phrase, my little one. Love of God, of the fatherland, of good food, of freedom! The promise of a better tomorrow and an end to social injustice! The slaughter of '71 brought me down to earth with a crash. I saw my friends die in the name of freedom, their hearts full of love! I promised myself two things then: never to settle down, and to practise individual reclamation, not driven by the desire for a more just society but as a means of escape. You see how the defender of the poor has ceded the stage to the petty thief.'

'Wanted by the police and forced to flee the country.'

'You know perfectly well I had nothing to do with those murders. I don't know why somebody wanted to pin them on me, but I trust my friend Legris to find out.'

'And yet he's one of those bourgeois types you're so suspicious of.'

'Bourgeois? Only on the surface. Beneath his veneer of respectability Victor Legris has more in common with me than he imagines.'

'How long will you and I have things in common, Frédéric?'

'*Chi lo sa?*'[71]

He took her hand.

'Our lives have crossed at this moment in time,' he whispered. 'Come, I want you.'

Frédéric put a hand in his pocket and closed it around Joseph's lost gardenia.

Victor kissed Euphrosine's fleshy hand. She simpered, swelling with pride, as pleased about the lace flounces and pistachio-green satin ribbons weighing her down as she was about her wide-brimmed Italian straw hat.

'To think that finally I'm going to see the sea! I can't believe it! How kind of you, Monsieur Legris, to offer us this holiday at Houlgate!'

'Monsieur Mori is the one you must thank – it was his idea.'

She began waddling over towards Kenji, but the shrill whistle of a shunting train stopped her in her tracks. When she came back to her senses, it was to count the number of packages and bags strewn across the platform. She'd brought a whole array of stuff with her: plates, goblets, flasks of eau de Cologne, lemon balm, shawls, cushions, rugs, and of course the food hamper. Suddenly she gave a start. Somebody had stolen the basket where she'd put the potted meat and cheese! Oh, thank goodness! There it was, behind one of Mademoiselle Iris's three suitcases – my future daughter-in-law, she thought, enchanted by the slender figure, which she was already picturing heavy with child. I'm so looking forward to being a grandmother – even if I am still Mademoiselle Courlac!

'These farewells at train stations are becoming a habit, aren't they?' remarked Victor.

'I'm only leaving you for three weeks. And you're the one who insisted on me going,' retorted Tasha.

Her face strained after the recent attack she had suffered, she'd managed to control her anger and shock at Victor's behaviour and its repercussions; this man whom she loved to the point of accepting his chronic jealousy was also a shameless liar; despite his promises, he'd been working on a case all along, and had it not been for Kenji's intervention . . . But how could she bear a grudge against the man who had showered her with gifts and covered her with kisses in order to earn her forgiveness, against the man she was going to marry? She'd agreed to go away. This holiday would enable her to finish the illustrations of Homer's works and would give her a rest from Victor's possessiveness. Kenji had assured them that the villa was big enough for them to get away from each other – including those who would gladly spend more time together than was proper, he had added, casting a stern glance at his assistant and his daughter.

Iris, radiant in the dove-grey crêpe dress she had persuaded her father to buy her, was making a mental list of all the bathing costumes she'd bought at the Grands Magasins du Louvre. The one in white ribbed cotton, waisted, with a flounced skirt descending from the hip was sure to create a stir . . .

Completely oblivious to the sartorial time bomb packed in his sweetheart's suitcase, Joseph was listening obediently to his boss's parting instructions.

'Make sure she doesn't let go of the cord – she's as light as a feather and before she knows it she'll be dragged out to sea. No swimming for at least four hours after meals, because the risk of fainting is . . .'

A plaintive miaow rang out. All eyes fell on a basket that was giving little jolts. Tasha picked it up and tried to comfort the unhappy occupant.

'Poor little Kochka, it'll be all right. Only a four-hour journey and then you'll be able to scamper about . . .'

'Won't you keep her inside? She'll run off,' Victor commented, a hint of anticipation in his voice.

'You'd better keep her locked up in case she does her business all over the carpets. Once an alley cat always an alley cat!' declared Euphrosine.

'What are you insinuating? Kochka is perfectly house-trained,' retorted Tasha.

Unwilling to offer his opinion on feline hygiene, Kenji was about to resume his list of instructions when he realised that Joseph and Iris had slipped away, and were buying a newspaper from a vendor near to where Victor was smoking a cigarette. He found himself face to face with Djina and stepped back slightly. She suppressed a smile. He's afraid of me . . .

'It's strange, this desire to send me away. I understand you wanting to spare Tasha and Iris the inconvenience of a lot of publicity, and that you would place them under Joseph's wing. I approve of your generosity towards Madame Pignot. But I'm surprised at your insistence that I should join them.'

'Your pupils are away, you have no more classes, and a short break would do you good.'

'It's kind of you to be concerned about my health.'

'I imagined that you and Tasha would be happy to spend time together,' he muttered.

'You will think me ungrateful, but, not being familiar with your generosity, I assumed that you wanted me out of the way because my company displeases you.'

He turned bright red and felt ridiculous; he was tongue-tied. Surprised that this man who was always in control should lose his composure, she felt a flash of joy, as though she'd just won a victory. The steam engine hissed. Like a cock rounding up his hens, Joseph shepherded the four women into the compartment and with Victor and Kenji's help heaved the baggage up after them.

'What a lot of luggage! Anyone would think we were off to China!' he cried out to his bosses, waving his hat from the window. 'Don't worry, I'll look after them!'

Kenji blew a kiss to his daughter and cast a long, anxious glance at Djina. Victor stared at Tasha, half squashed by Euphrosine.

'Jesus, Mary and Joseph, it certainly spits out enough steam – what if it blows up?'

A guard closed the doors and the whistle screeched. The train jolted into life and made a loud grating sound as it moved towards Pont de l'Europe before being swallowed up by the Batignolles tunnel.

In the stuffy cab racing along Rue de Rome, Victor tried hard to force out the image of his ex-lover, Odette de Valois, who had also left Paris for Houlgate four years before.

'What are your plans this evening?' Kenji asked.

'To go back to Rue Fontaine and sleep, provided the gentlemen from the police department and the press will allow me. How about you?'

'I'm going to take the ashes, which are not Pierre Andrésy's, to Paul Theneuil's widow. Then I think I'll go out, just to take my mind off things.'

'Ah! I see . . .'

'What do you see?'

'One of your many fervent admirers,' murmured Victor, not daring to name Eudoxie.

'You're wrong. I'm going out with a man.'

'A man?' echoed Victor, raising his eyebrows.

'Wipe that startled expression off your face. My sexual preferences haven't undergone the radical change you are insinuating. I'm simply inviting a very dear friend, who is like a son to me, to a show, because, although he prefers burying himself in a corner, I'm determined to cheer him up.'

'You don't mean . . .'

'Yes, you, Victor. I thought we'd go to the Folies-Bergère. The sight of all those pretty women will lift our spirits.'

'Is that the wise man or the old roué speaking?'

Kenji wore his cat-like expression, one eye half closed, the other twinkling. He pretended to yawn and fall asleep, oblivious to the jolting of the cab. Touched, Victor made as if to thank him then thought better of it and leant back in his seat, forcing himself to study the fountains in Place de la Concorde. The criminal case that had come to an end dissolved into droplets of water and was borne away on the breeze.

'Jesus, Mary and Joseph, all those gory murders . . . What a violent world we live in. And to think you were mixed up in all that!' remarked Euphrosine, closing *Le Passe-partout*.

In order to create a distraction and clear the atmosphere, heavy with disapproval, Joseph declared, 'There are doctors who recommend even more dangerous activities – such as sport, for instance. Football alone has accounted for seventy-one deaths in England in the space of eighteen months!'

'Don't change the subject. Helping Monsieur Legris and Monsieur Mori in their foolishness is more dangerous than any sport. You expose yourself to terrible dangers protecting the innocent! Can't you just write nice romantic stories that make humble folk cry? Don't you agree, Madame Iris?'

'Yes! Why, only yesterday Joseph took *Thule's Golden Chalice* to Antonin Clusel, who promised him it will be coming out in October. He even gave him an advance.'

'Is that true, pet? Why didn't you tell me before!'

'We were saving the news till now.'

'So, 1893 will be a good year after all. Monsieur Victor and Mademoiselle Tasha's marriage, your marriage, and a novel! This deserves a toast! Come to think of it, I'm feeling a bit peckish – it must be the speed.'

While Tasha and Djina congratulated Jojo and Iris, Euphrosine began unpacking the provisions. The compartment was soon filled with the smell of garlic sausage. The red wine flowed into the goblets and they drank a toast.

Joseph, dying to give away details of the case that had gone unreported in the press, stifled the urge with one of his mother's wedge-like sandwiches. After he'd swallowed the last mouthful, he began giving a summary of his next novel. It would be entitled *The Devil's Bouquet* and would relate the criminal exploits of a theatre manager who murdered young actresses with bunches of poisoned flowers.

Djina was miles away. The scenery rolled by, like a landscape on a canvas, unreal. She was recalling Kenji's delicious awkwardness. She would savour the memory of it over the next three weeks. Euphrosine's shrill voice interrupted her reverie.

'By the way, pet, with respect, ladies, once you've become Monsieur Legris's brother-in-law and Monsieur Mori's son-in-law I trust you'll stop calling them "Boss". As for me, I'll be hiring a cleaning lady, that's for sure!'

NOTES

[1] 'Le Temps des cerises' ('The Cherry Season'): lyrics by Jean-Baptiste Clément, music by Antoine Renard. The song was composed between 1866 and 1868 and published by Egrot, Paris.

[2] The site where the new Sorbonne would be built between 1885 and 1901.

[3] Jean-Baptiste Clément: 'The Captain "Backs to the wall"', 1872.

[4] Known as Grotius.

[5] Pseudonym of two French novelists: Charles Causse (1862–1905) and Charles Vincent (1851–1920).

[6] Built around Paris between 1841 and 1845. A project of Adolphe Thiers.

[7] Now Porte de Pantin.

[8] Play by Anicet Bourgeois and Ferdinand Dugué.

[9] Play by Auguste Maquet.

[10] Théophile Gautier (1811–1872): 'First Smile of Spring'.

[11] A line from *The Barber of Seville* by Beaumarchais.

[12] 'Behold the man.' The words uttered by Pontius Pilate to refer to Jesus.

[13] In 1870, French cannons fired at a range of 1,600 metres at the very most, compared to Prussian artillery which could reach up to 7 kilometres.

[14] Politician (1830–1915).

[15] Annual celebration organised by students of the École des Beaux-Arts.

[16] Francis I.

[17] See *The Marais Assassin*, Gallic Books.

[18] 'Quite right.'

[19] Chronophotography, developed and practised by – among others – Étienne-Jules Marey (1830–1904). His chronophotographic camera was patented on 28 June 1893.

[20] He would publish *The Gods Are Athirst* in 1912.

[21] 1 May–30 October 1893.

[22] American artiste, born in Fullersburg, near Chicago (1862–1928).

[23] French painter (1861–1917), famous for his portraits of society people.

[24] The exhibition that took place 15–30 March at 11, Rue le Peletier.

[25] Monsieur Lepine replaced Monsieur Loze as Chief of Police on 11 July 1893.

[26] *Les Cuirassiers de Reichshoffen*, lyrics by Henri Nazet and Gaston Villemer, music by Francisque Chassaigne, 1871.

[27] *An Old Man of Letters* by Monsieur du Campfranc.

[28] This expression dates from 30 September 1836. A century earlier, the *London Post* had published *Robinson Crusoe* by Daniel Defoe, in serialised form from 7 October 1719 to 17 October 1721.

[29] Renamed Rue du Pré in 1920.

[30] The electric tachyscope was marketed by the German firm, Siemens.

[31] Invented by Émile Reynaud (1844–1918) in 1876, it created the illusion of moving images (using drawings). It was patented on 14 January 1889.

[32] See *The Père-Lachaise Mystery*, Gallic Books.

[33] By Jules Barbey d'Aurevilly (1808–1889).

[34] By William Bunasch, music by Louis Varney.

[35] *Poetic Meditations*: 'Le Lac'.

[36] Georges Moinaux, known as Georges Courteline (1858–1929).

[37] Poet, playwright and novelist (1848–1909).

[38] The protagonist of *Lost Illusions* by Honoré de Balzac.

[39] Published in serialised form in 1846.

[40] Novel by Paul Féval (1817–1887).

[41] See *The Marais Assassin*, Gallic Books.

[42] Editor of the magazine *La Plume*.

[43] Successful author of, among other works, *Family Life* and *Madame la Boule*.

[44] A well-known writer whose collection *The Horns of the Fawn* was praised by Verlaine.

[45] Nickname for Prison de la Santé.

[46] Invention of Monsieur Marinovitch and Monsieur Szvarvady, which involved placing microphones in the main Paris theatres and connecting them to the central telephone exchange in Rue Louis-le-Grand.

[47] Rue Duphot.

[48] Published in 1878.

[49] Defender of Paris in 1814 – this statue by Guillaume was erected in 1863.

[50] What would later become the department store Dufayel.

[51] Two films were added to the series subsequently: *Dream at the Fire's Edge* and *Around the Cabin*. The projections took place between October 1892 and March 1900 and attracted 500,000 viewers.

[52] See *The Montmartre Investigation*, Gallic Books.

[53] 'Yes, of course' in Russian.

[54] Paris, Nepveu, 1823.

[55] One of many nicknames given to Emperor Napoleon III.

[56] French author (1846–1907). The book appeared in 1881.

[57] Published in 1872.

[58] Mikhail Alexandrovich Bakunin, Russian revolutionary and anarchist, 1814–1876.

[59] French geographer and theoretician of anarchism, 1830–1905.

[60] French anarchist, 1854–1939.

[61] His real name was Alphonse Victor Charles Gallaud (1864–1930). Contributors to his paper included such well-known people as Georges Darien, Félix Fénéon and Tristan Bernard.

[62] French humorist (1855–1905). Alphonse Allais gave up studying to be a pharmacist in order to become a writer.

[63] 1801–1887.

[64] Born in Recanati, in Ancona in 1798, died in Naples in 1837.

[65] A card game.

[66] This dedication is printed at the beginning of 'The Cherry Season' in *Songs*, a collection published in 1885 (Imprimerie Robert et Cie, Paris).

[67] By Ludovico Ariosto (1474–1533).

[68] French musician (1851–1931). In 1886, he composed this work for piano and orchestra (also known as *Symphony on a French Mountain Air*).

[69] 'Charcoal burners' so called because at first they used to meet in the woods. The name of a secret political society formed in Italy at the beginning of the nineteenth century.

[70] Pioneer of biometric research.

[71] Who knows? (in Italian).